The Sunstone Slipper

Shattered Glass
Book 1

The Sunstone Slipper

Jacqueline C. Lewis

The Sunstone Slipper
ISBN 978-1-947005-08-2
Copyright © 2018 by Jacqueline C. Lewis
Published by Blue Water Books
Cover design by Shaela Odd

To Brian

for Cedars of Lebanon, chocolate-covered strawberries, and
always believing that this day would come.

Chapter 1

I run faster and faster, fleeing from their judgments.

Did you eat the whole supper table last night, Charlotte? Suck it in, so she can pull those laces tighter.

Each step takes me farther from the palace and their constant criticism.

Smile bigger. Less teeth. Sweeter, like your sister. I know you're not happy with this, but it's time to accept it and move on.

Why can't Mother understand why this is so hard for me? I'm not ready for Papa to be replaced. And why does Lacey have to lord it over me every time my deficiencies show?

I run until I am out of breath and my favorite lavender dressing gown is brown with dust from the road, then I slow to a stop as I approach the Wall which surrounds our kingdom. I cannot go any farther. I haven't touched the Wall since Papa died examining the mines. Not even once.

Will feeling the rough stone under my hands—the protection he worked so hard to gain—finally take the pain away?

The Wall is crumbling here, more than it should for its age. So many stones are missing that it only reaches my waist, when it should be well above my head. It was once so beautiful, but now its edges are jagged and raw. Bits of rock litter the ground beneath my feet, even though I'm still a few steps away.

This is the exact spot Papa took me and my best friend, Kade, to when he first taught us about the sunstone and moonstone in the Wall and how the two work together to repel magic from our kingdom. The Wall was only seven years old then, nearly the same age as I was. My hands could not get enough that day. I touched every stone, counting each one, and begged Papa to explain in further detail how the pattern worked. The Wall seemed so big then—just barely taller than my father—and so strong. Invincible.

I wish I was old enough to remember the day it was finally completed. The day the Moon Queen was cursed, forced to leave the Autumn kingdom of Lunain to live in the Underground as a goblin; and the Snow

Queen and her malicious magic were expelled from our kingdom. The people cheered in the streets and danced through the night, finally unafraid. The Shard War was over. We were safe. I've touched the Wall a million times, imagining the triumphant celebration of that day, but ever since Papa—

I just couldn't.

"Do it," I whisper. "You're being ridiculous."

Pushing past all reluctance, I force my feet to move through the stones and dirt, remembering too late that I forgot to wear patent overshoes to cover my new silk slippers. I can already hear Mother's scolding in my head.

You've ruined them, Charlotte. They're absolutely ruined. What are you supposed to wear to the wedding now? You're seventeen years old, for Spring's sake, why can't you be more responsible? Why can't you be more ladylike? Why can't you be more like Lacey?

I can promise my mother a hundred times that I will try harder, but my efforts are never enough to satisfy her expectations. I will never be like my sister, and truly, I am glad of it.

Papa was glad of it, too. I was his shadow, learning everything I could from him. I was never interested in embroidery or fashion, but the way magical stones work together for the good of our kingdom has always fascinated me.

As the creator of the Wall's magic-blocking pattern, he became the official Overseer of the Wall soon after I was born. Once it was complete and successfully keeping the Snow Queen outside the borders of Floraison, we moved to the palace, where he could meet frequently with the king without leaving his family behind. He loved bringing me to the Wall with him, even when I was little.

Papa loved me for who I am, not who he wanted me to be.

I stand face to face with the crumbling wall. The sun peeks from just above the mountains, and it's hard to make out the difference between the two stones with the glare in my eyes. I can't feel any warmth from the sunstones or see any light radiating from the moonstones. I suppose this proves they are working together, cancelling out their usual magical properties, even though the Wall is in the sad process of being slowly torn apart by goblins.

They pick and tear at it when they come out each night. Papa told me if they came out during the day, they would burn in the sun, but they want the Wall torn down, so they pick at it when they can, so long as our guards don't catch them. Papa said the goblins have sharp claws and long teeth, that they are stronger than any man, and they are angry. But I know the secret to keep them away, just as all the children of Floraison do, and I know not to linger outside after dark, even if it would be terribly exciting to see them lurking in the shadows.

I follow the Wall to where it appears sturdy and tall—nearly six feet—and take a slow, deep breath, reaching my hands to the highest point. Memories of my father come rushing at me, flooding my mind as I pull myself up.

That's exactly the thing. Who knew my little girl would grow to be so clever?

Stones tumble and crack against the rubble below.

I wouldn't be surprised if the king started coming to you for advice, instead of me. You wouldn't want to replace your dear papa, now, would you?

Any moment I might lose my footing and fall, crashing to the ground with the stones, but I don't stop. I pull myself high, then flop onto my back, making sure I am centered atop the thick Wall.

My cheeks are wet with tears, but I am done crying now. Like Mother says: there's no use to it. I close my eyes, letting the sun warm and calm me as I remember all those afternoons spent at my father's side.

"You do realize, Mademoiselle, that climbing the Wall will earn you at least two days in the stocks?"

The voice surprises me, but I don't bother to sit up. He's no threat to me.

"Please don't say you followed me out here to tell

me about some imaginary law you just invented." It's a pathetic attempt at a joke, especially since I know how far it is from the truth. He followed, because he knew I would need him. Had he been watching for me through a palace window, or did he assign a few servants to notice my whereabouts? Did he know I would become so fed up with Mother and Lacey and the entire morning that I would run away from them all?

I shift a bit and look at Kade standing beside me. He is tall enough the crown of his head is just barely above the Wall, and he is inspecting me with those brown eyes that can see my thoughts even before I, myself, can think them.

"You should be proud of yourself," he says. "How many times have you stared at this thing during the past six months?"

I don't say anything. My heart aches just thinking about the emptiness I've felt since Papa's death—an emptiness even Kade hasn't been able to fill.

He gives me a sad smile, then his eyes brighten, as if he has just thought of something extremely clever.

"And what, in all the mines of the realm, are you wearing? Aren't you supposed to be at the palace, *getting dressed*? Unless you're attempting to start a new fashion by wearing your dressing gown to the wedding."

"Of course not. Don't be ridiculous."

"Says the girl laying on the Wall in nearly her underthings." He stretches to his tiptoes with a mischievous grin to whisper in my ear, "Charlotte, what if someone were to see you?" Then he raises his eyebrows and nods his head, knowingly.

I push him away, but he barely stumbles. "It's only you," I say.

"*Only me?* Well, it's nice to know how important I am."

"Ka-ade!" I stretch his name out, exasperated. I'm in no mood for his teasing.

"Think of your mother, then. It's a pretty big day for her."

"I know. I know. I should be grateful she's getting married. Perhaps now she'll leave Lacey and me alone and stop pressuring us to find," I contort my voice, adding all the authority my mother exudes, "a suitable match."

"Well, you could always marry me. Certainly, she'd be pleased with that."

I smile. Probably the first real one of the morning. "Honestly, I wonder if even that would make her happy with me. She always finds something to complain about. I know she loves me—I do—but so many times, because I'm not genteel enough or as refined as Lacey, it just feels like I can't measure up."

Kade reaches to gently wipe the leftover tears from

my face, smearing dusty mud across my cheek.

"I'm coming up." He grips the top stones and hoists himself up, scrambling a bit to get a footing with his thick boots. He is swinging a leg to the top of the Wall when a voice calls out from the distance.

"You! Children! Get down from there!" A Wall guard runs toward us.

Kade snickers at the use of the word *children*. He is already taller than most men. Without fully reaching the top, he hops back down again and reaches his arms to help me jump. I land softly. He gives me a quick hug before letting go, and for a moment, all is right with the world.

I pull my dressing gown tighter around me, suddenly embarrassed. Mother is right to worry about my impropriety. Why can I never slow down enough to think things through?

"No need to worry," Kade tells the guard, walking toward him. "We're surveying the damage to the Wall, for my father."

It takes a moment for the guard to recognize Kade, then he throws himself to his knees. "My apologies, Prince Kaderic. Didn't realize who you were. Thought you might be a couple of children—playing. I was concerned for your safety."

"Thank you. Of course." Kade motions for the guard to stand. "No harm done, and as you can see, we are just fine. And," he turns to me, "Lady Charlotte is in a desperate hurry to get back to the palace."

Kade chuckles at my pained expression. "Your mother is frantic," he whispers to me. "They're expected to arrive any minute."

I glare at him, but still head toward the palace. To my surprise, he starts walking in the opposite direction.

"Wait! Aren't you coming with me?"

Kade turns toward me and gives a deep, dramatic bow. Then he looks up, still bent halfway over, with a hand in the air.

"Absolutely not," he says with a smile. "You're a brave girl. You can meet your new stepfather and stepsister all on your own."

Chapter 2

I stare at the girl as her carriage rattles up the drive. She is not *beautiful* as Mother told me she would be; she is radiant. Her golden hair catches the light from the afternoon sun, shining with a brilliance that cannot be outdone by even the finest wig thatcher in the kingdom. The look of excitement on her face when she first sees her new home spreads joy to the rest of the assembly. It makes my already knotted stomach tighten and twist.

I never asked for another sister. One is plenty enough for me.

I take a small step back, and the shadow from the palace covers my face. I'm tempted to keep stepping backward until I can disappear into the foliage. No one would notice I had left, anyway.

The carriage pulls in front of us, sending up clouds of dust behind it. I cough. I'm not used to the dust. It hasn't rained all week, and *now* they decide to show up.

If they would have arrived just a few days ago, as they were supposed to, the ground would still be moist and soft from the usual rains, and I wouldn't be breathing in the infernal dirt that's circling in the air. They are obviously oblivious to the strain this is putting on us, especially with us preparing to get them situated after their arrival and hosting a wedding all in one day.

He steps out first and Mother glides up to meet him. Her new husband—well, almost. My father's replacement. They kiss each other's cheeks and I look away for a moment to blink the wet from my eyes. Mother will scold me for making mud on my face so soon after scrubbing it clean.

Bastien, my soon-to-be stepfather, is short and trim. Or perhaps he appears short from the way he stands hunched over, leaning on his cane like an old man. I suppose he could be considered handsome if you were almost forty years old and trying to maintain your position in society. He smiles at my mother and takes her hand as they move away from the carriage. His steps are quick, and he almost shuffles through the dust. Mother warned us of his war wounds and his embarrassment of the hobbling shuffle they cause, so I try not to stare.

Next is the girl. Brielle. Mother tells me she is not much younger than I am, and we will be great friends. I don't think I can be friends with someone who lowers herself to the ground so gingerly after sitting in a carriage all morning. You would think she had walked the entire way herself the way she reaches down to rub her feet before slipping them into the patents a servant sets down for her. The servant laces the ribbons over her shoes to hold them in, with Brielle wincing in pain the entire time. She recovers quickly, though, so it must not be too bad.

My mother moves forward again. She kisses Brielle on the forehead.

"Welcome. I'm so glad you can finally meet your new sisters, and they are so excited to meet you."

Oh yes, we are so excited. I force myself to smile.

"Come Lacey, Charlotte. Now our family is complete again."

We'll never be complete. Not without Papa.

Mother motions for us to step forward, and I fight the urge to run in the opposite direction. Running away wouldn't erase reality. I must meet my stepsister, eventually. I might as well get it over with.

Taking a deep breath, I move toward my mother and give a curtsy in Brielle's direction. She is even prettier up close. Truly, I hadn't thought it possible. Her skin is creamy and smooth—not a single freckle marring its loveliness, and her dark green eyes remind me of the beauty of the forest trees, mysteriously mesmerizing. She is taller than me in her patent overshoes. Lacey eyes her suspiciously, for she is even more beautiful than Lacey could ever hope to be. I look at the two of them, with their golden hair and long, thick lashes. With my hair the same color as the dust rising from the ground, I will never be able to compete. I guess that makes me the goblin of the bunch—the ugliest stepsister of them all.

I don't care.

I shouldn't care.

I *wouldn't* care, if only Mother didn't put so much emphasis on it. Being beautiful is only good for being something nice for other people to look at, but Mother says that she who is the most beautiful can marry whomever she pleases. She can rise in her social standing. She can be provided for and want for nothing all her life.

I don't know what Mother is so worried about, though. My father's previous position, and I suppose now my stepfather's position, puts us second only to the royal family. We cannot rise any further in society unless one of us married Kade, although the chances of that are quite slim. Lacey and I would offer no political advantage to Floraison. Even Brielle, being from the neighboring kingdom of Lunain, would make a better political match for our prince, though she is not of noble blood.

At least, I don't think she is. I haven't bothered to learn much about Lunain's noble class, for I want nothing to do with them. Why would I want to align myself with those who invaded our kingdom, who incited the Shard War, then lost pitifully to our superior intellect? Yet now I find myself related to one of them.

I am about to curtsy, again, and make a quick retreat

when Mother orders Lacey and me to show Brielle to her rooms. I want to say, "No. Absolutely not," like Kade said to me, but I've been taught better, and I am not a prince who can do as he pleases.

"A few pins are slipping from my hair." Lacey is all sweetness and smiles. "I do beg your pardon, Sister, but I would like to look my best for the wedding." In a few hours. It's going to take that long to fix a couple of pins?

Is she apologizing to me? Or Brielle? I see Mother nodding her head, so I take a chance.

"Yes, I feel like such a mess, with this dust and all. Might I be excused as well, Mother?"

She shakes her head and snaps her fingers at servants, pointing to luggage and crates and baskets.

"Really, Charlotte, don't you want your new sister to feel welcome in her new home? We must get Brielle settled comfortably and as quickly as possible. We weren't expecting them to arrive so late, and we don't have much time until the wedding."

I know, but it's not my fault they were late.

"Yes. Of course. What was I thinking?" I take Brielle's arm and turn toward the door. I suppose I should ask her if there is anything she would like to retrieve from the carriage before we go in, but I keep silent. The carriage horses seem a bit nervous from all the commotion, and I want to keep my distance. I don't much care for horses.

There is a flurry of activity between the carriage and

our private door to the palace. Bastien walks a little way ahead of us, hobbling through the chaos. I would try to maneuver around him, but Brielle is even slower than he is. I can't tell exactly what is happening under her skirts, but from the way she almost jounces across the ground, she must be taking quick, tiny steps. Is that how all the young women walk in Lunain? However fashionable it might be, it's dreadfully slow and inconvenient.

We stop at the entrance to our suite to rid Brielle of her patent overshoes. There is no available servant nearby, so she holds out a foot, leaning against the doorframe for support. She doesn't say a word but purses her lips and simply looks at me. Lovely.

The shoes I uncover after undoing the laces are made from the softest kid leather I have ever felt and lined with soft fur for extra padding. They are laced nearly to her ankles and adorned with perfectly painted flowers that give the appearance of an entire miniature garden. Perhaps this is why she is walking so slow? She might not want them to get dirty in the dust. I gasp at the slipper's beauty, but she doesn't give me much chance to admire them further.

She steps from the patents, hiding her beautiful shoes under her skirts, and starts mincing slowly through the corridor. Her eyes are wide, looking from the ceiling to the floor, then back again and down the other side. She bends down, examining the wall beneath a scrolled table. At this rate, we will miss the wedding and all of next week before Brielle can even see her new bedroom.

"Are you all right?" I ask.

She turns and stands up quickly, nearly bumping her head on the table. "Yes, just fine, thank you."

All right. Let's keep walking, then. I move forward.

"But what about the goblins?" she asks. "Might they jump out and catch me?"

I stop. She can't be serious.

"You're afraid of goblins," I say, trying to hide my amusement. Goblins are a nuisance, that's guaranteed, but I've never met someone over the age of six who was truly frightened of them. As long as one keeps their distance and doesn't stray outside after the sun has gone down, there is nothing to worry about.

She blushes.

"No, of course not. I've just—with the Wall losing its power and everything. Can't the goblins get into the city a lot easier?"

"What do you mean? The Wall has been protecting us for as long as I can remember. My father built it."

She gives me one of her radiant grins. "And now my father has come to make it better. It really is a disaster."

"My father gave his life protecting us with the Wall." I clench my skirts in my hands, working the fabric between my fingers. "They thought they found a new lode of moonstone, and he was inspecting it when there was a cave-in and—"

"And that is why my father and I were forced to leave our home to come and patch things up."

Her voice is like steel, and she is no longer smiling.

I take a slow, deep breath. I just need to get her to her room and be done with it, but I can't help wanting to goad her, even just a little.

"The Wall doesn't protect us from goblins," I correct her ignorance. "It can only keep magic out of the city. Goblins aren't any more magical than you or I." They have been known to get in the palace, though. After all, they have tunnels underneath the whole city, probably under the whole kingdom. Kade and I spent half our childhood searching the palace for goblin holes and hollering silly songs into their depths.

"I've only seen a few, but never up close, and I've lived in the palace most my life. They only come out at night, and they actually bother the royal family more than anyone else. I think they're angry with the king." Her eyes are wide. "It's harmless pranks, only. And your room isn't anywhere near the royal wing of the palace. I don't think there are any secret tunnels in it . . . nothing to be concerned about. Really. I've only seen a couple." I put a hand in the crook of her elbow and pat her shoulder with the other, pushing us farther down the hallway. She is trembling. Maybe I've said too much? Oh, bother.

"Let me teach you something my father told me," I say. "He used to spend all his waking hours either at the mines or the Wall. It's an easy trick. Truly, I don't know why you haven't learned this before. Goblins hate rhyming. They hate verse. I don't know why. It hurts their ears, I guess. I'll teach you a song Papa taught to me when we were visiting the mines. If you ever see a goblin in the palace—if any of them try to bother you—you can sing it and that nasty goblin will leave you alone."

I never went inside the mines—Papa said they were too dangerous—but I would help him inspect the moonstone pulled from the caves. When it grew dark, we would sing the mining songs to keep the goblins from bothering us. Papa would hold my hand and I would pretend to fear the goblin shadows following us home. We would sing louder and louder through the verses so by the time we reached our family's suite in the palace, we were laughing and yelling at the top of our lungs and Mother would scold us for disturbing such a peaceful spring evening.

We reach her room and I struggle for a moment to decide which mining song is my favorite. After taking a deep breath to prepare a bawdy voice to imitate the miners, I start to sing:

'Tis sorrowful to leave you, dear, before the crack of dawn.
Your eyes I'll miss.
No lips to kiss,
But I won't be gone for long.
I'll heave, I'll hit the moonstone, pure, before the day is gone.
I'll break the stone
In tunnels, lone

With my hammer, pure and strong.

Brielle sinks to the bed and covers her ears.

"Is that a mining song? Oh, it sounds just awful! Please never sing that song again!" She laughs at me, and I feel my cheeks burn. There are more verses, but she obviously doesn't want to hear them.

"I'm just a few doors down, and Lacey is across the corridor." My voice is crisp and curt. "Some nights we dine with the king and queen and Kade—I mean, Prince Kaderic, but with the wedding and celebrations this afternoon . . ." Mother said to try. I need to try. "I'm so pleased to get to know you better. Perhaps we will become better acquainted at the ball this evening."

Brielle moves about the room, most likely looking for goblin holes. Ignoring me. I wish I had been allowed to get ready for the wedding with Lacey. I would even help pin her hair and listen to her go on and on about her possible suitors if it excused me from this. I need to get out. I give a short smile and a curtsy, then turn to leave.

"Charlotte," Brielle says before I can reach the door. "Thank you for your help. Even though you're a dreadful singer, I'm sure you've successfully kept the goblins away."

Chapter 3

The palace has been my home for as long as I can remember, and the Cathedral of Our Queen has always been my favorite place in it. The rooms, the corridors, every hall and closet became memorized in my heart a long time ago. I don't remember the first time I saw the throne room or the ballroom, but I do remember coming to the Cathedral of Our Queen for my first season celebration.

When Mother was young, the season celebrations were fanciful, magical times that marked the change of seasons, but also paid homage to the season queens. Apparently, they lasted for days—singing, dancing, feasting, and of course, praying and raising voices high in the Cathedral. Mother says that sometimes they even travelled to Lunain for the Autumn Festival or Solair at the beginning of summer, but she never went north to Neimonte in the winter. Even then, it was best to keep plenty of distance between yourself and the Snow Queen.

I can't think of a single person who has ever spoken badly about the season celebrations of old. They were, indeed, wonderful and happy times, but after the Rain Queen—our beloved goddess of spring—died when the Mirror of Hope shattered, everything changed.

On the day I was finally old enough to worship in the Cathedral, we came to pray for the safety of the season queens and sing the songs of the season, just as we used to—except by then we were also singing with hope that the Rain Queen would return, reborn. It was a solemn occasion, devoid of any dances or feasts or anything that might actually mark it as a real celebration. Mother kept pushing my head back down during the prayers, forcing my reverence, but she couldn't force me to keep my eyes closed or stop me from taking peeks at the grandeur around me. I was amazed at the colors shining through the crystal windows and the gold fairies and flowers covering the walls around us, but most of all, I was entranced by the priestess leading the ceremony: The Hand of the Queen.

She stood before us then as she does now, as she does in all our ceremonies, wearing her emerald robes and the moon-shaped pendant around her neck. It sparkles in the sunlight, which there is an abundance of today. She is already holding the Rose Scepter in one hand, her arm stretched wide. The other three scepters are in their places on either side of her. The Sun

Scepter, a full circle with pointed beams, sits next to the empty slot where the spring's Rose Scepter belongs. Autumn and Winter, a crescent moon on one and a snowflake on the other, sit in their posts on the other side of the altar. The scepters are carved from glowing moonstone and decorated with hints of gold, ice quartz, and sunstone. I love the way they shine, each in their own way, as the Hand lifts them above her head or wide beside her while she speaks.

The pews are filled with nobility I both do and do not recognize. It's easy to see the few who came from Lunain to congratulate Bastien in his new life, for they are set apart from everyone else, toward the back. I'm unsure if it was by choice or if they were politely pushed to sit there. Our relations with Lunain haven't been easy since the Shard War. The Moon Queen—the autumn fairy—played merely a supporting role to the Snow Queen during the fight, but even then, she and the people of Lunain were against us. Trying to take over our kingdom. At the close of the war, the Moon Queen and her followers were banished to the Underground to become goblins, but the people left behind in Lunain were left alone, for they were not directly involved in the nasty politics of war. We are not fighting, but we are not at peace, either.

Will bringing Bastien from Lunain to repair the Wall also repair our relations with our neighboring kingdom? Why would the king suggest him? And does my mother love him at all, or is she just doing what she's told to do for the sake of her daughters? She seems to like him, at least, and she has been so lonely these past months since losing my father. I watch her as she stands in front of the priestess and beside her soon-to-be husband. Inside the hollow of the crescent altar at the front of the room, she glows nearly as bright as the moonstone around her. If she seems so joyful, why is it so hard for me to feel joy for her, too?

The Hand of the Queen begins the ceremony by comparing the early years of marriage to the spring. New love. A new life together. Bringing two people— and in our case, two families—together to become one, willing to grow together just as the flowers do in spring. The priestess sets the Rose Scepter in its stand and picks up the Sun Scepter. She talks about the joys of summer, advises Bastien and Mother to find joy in each other and their daughters.

When she picks up the Harvest Scepter, she deviates completely from the usual speech made during the ceremonies of the young. Bastien and my mother are already in their autumn years of life, having daughters nearly grown. They've made it through spring and summer with separate lives, and now they will prepare to send their daughters into the world together. The priestess cautions them to spend quality time now, during the early time of their marriage, building their relationship so they will still have love and companionship when we are gone.

Seeing the Hand of the Queen pick up the Snow

Scepter fills my heart with sorrow. It always does. I don't like hearing about the time in our lives when we will become old and forgetful, when we must slow down and eventually say goodbye to our husband or wife as one passes on to the next world. It is especially painful today, thinking of how Mother was forced to say her farewells to Papa all too soon. I suppose I should think of Bastien as well, for I've heard he lost his wife when Brielle was just a baby.

We sing the Solstice Hymn, repeating the priestess's ideas. As soon as the song is over, Mother and Bastien will say their vows and pledge their lives to each other, and then everything will be final. No going back.

I peek at Brielle standing to my right. She's not even looking at our parents. I follow her gaze across the room to see—she's staring at Kade! A smile plays on her rosy lips, dimples pressed into her soft cheeks. Our parents are getting married right in front of us, and all she can do is ogle the prince!

I sing louder to distract her, purposefully off key, but she pays no heed to me. I've already earned a few warning glares from my mother during the verse of Spring, but I've not yet had a single glance from Brielle. He is not yours. Pretending to lose my balance a bit, I bump my arm into hers. Her eyes wince with pain, and she shoots me a warning glance.

"So sorry," I whisper, then get right back to my awful singing.

"But of course," she replies, and she's right back to

staring at Kade. I can just imagine the plans she's making in her head, but I will not allow it. Her father might be taking my mother from me, and the two of them have already taken the privacy from our home, but I'll sip soup with the Snow Queen before I let Brielle steal my best friend.

Chapter 4

Even though the ball is held in honor of my mother and Bastien, King Gervais and Queen Sorrel still preside. They sit at the end of the ballroom on great golden thrones, deciding which couples will open the celebration. It has always been my favorite part of a ball, because I can enjoy watching the graceful movements without fear of being asked to dance, myself. It is always Queen Sorrel's favorite dancers who are asked, and I have not been overly stupendous in my lessons. Lacey has been asked a couple of times, but even she has much to learn before she earns the queen's praise.

I stand near the dais, with Lacey and Brielle, watching a couple dance through the candlelight. The lady is pleasantly plump and much shorter than her partner, but she is light on her feet, and her cheeks are rosy. There is such a sweet smile on her lips that we hardly notice their difference in height. The man has performed a few impressive jumps during the song, but it feels as though we are all enchanted by her glowing happiness, and I cannot take my eyes from her.

Pinching my cheeks, I try to smile as sweetly as the dancer. I look down at the floor and go up on my toes, practicing an *elevé*, then glance up through my lashes as I've seen Lacey do on occasion when talking with a duke or a lord.

Brielle turns toward me, her eyebrows drawn together.

"What are you doing? You look ridiculous." She uses a whisper that is not quite a whisper.

"Nothing. I just—um, my stomach is a little . . ." I give her a pained expression to hopefully sum up the rest.

"You will leave if you're about to get sick, won't you? It would embarrass my father greatly if you were to . . . *you know* . . . in the ballroom."

Of course, she doesn't mention how much it might actually embarrass *me*, but I suppose my feelings are not as important to her as her father's.

"Of course," I say with a smile. "I'm feeling better already."

She gives me a lovely smile, and I flinch. She is still taller than me, even without patents on her feet. I look back to the couple dancing, focusing on the happy lady. Being tall isn't so much grander than a happy attitude. I suppose I need to work on improving my disposition, even when times are hard.

Kade strides toward us, moving quickly in front of the crowd. I love watching everyone's heads lower as he passes. A colorful wave in a river of people. What I love more, though, is watching him nod to everyone, acknowledging their reverence to his station. He loves Floraison and its people, and it shows in everything he does.

I curtsy with the others as he nears us. Kade tucks himself beside us with a pained expression.

"Mother has asked me to lead the last minuet."

I play with the lace descending from my sleeve but look up at him with a smile. "And you don't want to."

"Of course not."

"I've never heard of anyone dying from dancing, Kade."

"One can't be too careful." He gives a smug grin. "After all, I am my father's only heir. What would happen to the kingdom if I didn't survive the minuet?"

I laugh, but I won't give credence to his question by answering.

"Will you do it, then?"

I stare at him, blankly.

"Will you dance with me?"

My cheeks grow hot, and I look down at the lace I am picking at. The music swirls around me, and suddenly I am all too aware of Lacey and Brielle and everyone else in the room.

"In front of everybody? I can wait for one of the

group dances. I do so love a courante."

It is his turn to laugh at me.

Lacey starts to say, "If you're looking for a partner—"

"No one ever died from dancing," Kade reminds me with a smirk. Lacey lets out a puff of air when she realizes Kade has ignored her offer, then stomps away.

I look again at the couple before us. Yes, Kade is tall and elegant like the man, but I will never be as lovely as that fine woman, and according to Brielle, I must look *ridiculous* when I dance. Kade is my friend, though, and he did come to me for help.

"I will do it for you, but only because your mother has put you in the predicament of finding a partner so belatedly."

He gives another grin.

"She is not forcing me to find my own partner. It is the only way I agreed to it."

The dancers in front of the dais move closer together, arms outstretched to join hands. The song has gone on for a while now, so it must be nearly over. I rub my hands together, trying to smooth the sweat from them.

Kade steps away from the crowd and reaches his hand out for me to take. The music stops, and everyone applauds while the dancers show reverence to the king and queen and to each other before leaving the floor. I step forward to take Kade's hand, but something is hindering my movement. My skirt is caught on—I don't know what—and it pulls me backward, knocking me off balance. I hear a rip as I fall to the floor, landing on my hands and knees. My face burns with shame, and I scramble to get up, accepting Kade's assistance.

"Oh, no! Your skirt!" Brielle cries. "Whatever happened? You've torn it!"

I look down, twisting around to see my backside. Sure enough, there is a hole in the skirt, and what once was a beautiful ruffle is now a dragging heap of fabric.

Brielle pulls her pretty eyebrows together with concern. "You mustn't present yourself to the king and queen in such a state, Charlotte."

I look to Kade, to the other dancers who are already lining up in the center of the ballroom, then back to Kade again.

"It's no bother," he says. "Come on."

I shake my head, shrinking back into the crowd. "No. She's right. I can't."

"Charlotte, we need to go."

Kade is still holding his hand out to me, torn skirt and all, but I don't take it. I shake my head again, holding my lips tight.

Brielle steps forward, then gives a slight curtsy. "I'll go with you, if you'll have me, Your Highness." She takes Kade's hand and pulls him toward the other dancers, floating like a fairy, to the head of the line.

I back up farther until I am almost against the wall. A tear sneaks down my cheek as I watch the two of them dance. They weave between the other couples, raising and lowering on their toes to the gentle beat of the music. That should have been me. I was the one Kade asked to dance, and she took it from me. The worst part, though—even above my torn dress and sore knees—is that she doesn't even seem to be enjoying herself.

Chapter 5

I scramble to keep up.

"Come on," Kade says. "You're slower than a stone this morning." He sits atop a large boulder as I try to maneuver around it, following him up the mountain.

"I have to fix my hat again." I keep walking while tying the ribbons of my straw bergére under my chin. My foot slips in the fresh mud, and I reach out to the rock beside me, accidentally ripping the half-tied hat from my head. My attempt to catch myself is futile; I am stuck on my knees in the mud, and my elbow is scraped from the rock's rough surface. I pull the hat in place again and struggle with the ribbons as Kade comes to my side to help me up.

"Just leave it." He pulls me to my feet.

"Mother says I need to cover my face when I'm outside, or I'll never be able to get rid of these blasted freckles."

He looks at me with mock disapproval and clucks his tongue.

"Such language, Charlotte. My goodness!" His hands move under my chin, softly brushing my neck as he ties the ribbons. Everything feels wobbly for a moment, and I look up, briefly, to catch a glimpse of Kade's smiling eyes. "I like your freckles," he says, then adjusts the pack on his shoulder and turns back around.

I steady myself against the cold rock and make sure my feet are firmly planted before following him again. I would ask whose idea it was to take a climb up the mountain in the first place, but there's no reason to voice my frustration out loud, because the blame falls upon me. After visiting with Brielle and my stepfather all evening, I knew I would need to get out this morning. If I had stayed home, I'm sure it wouldn't be long until Mother asked me to entertain, but now perhaps Lacey will get stuck with that job.

"You know, there's really no need to rush," I holler up to Kade. "I feel no urgency to get back home."

He stops and waits for me to catch up again. We're almost to the trees, where the ground isn't as slippery. The fallen pine needles will be much easier to walk on than the mud we're in now.

"I'm sure it's not as bad as you say. They've only been here a week. Give yourself time to get to know them. You make this girl out to be the Snow Queen herself."

I shiver. It's rare for people to mention the Snow

Queen, but Kade has never been particularly afraid. He was just a toddler during the Shard War. There was no way he could understand what my mother went through, fearing that her baby girls would be the next to disappear at the hands of the Snow Queen. She has told me countless times of her fears, and how the Snow Queen's search for the new Rain Queen was the reason we moved to our château outside the border.

"Brielle's not *that* bad," I say. "I just—well, it's not fair, and they're so rude. They barely speak during meals, no matter how hard Lacey or I try to ask them questions about their interests or their lives before coming to live with us. All we hear is, 'Oh, we loved the country in Lunain. The country was so lovely and country-like.' I understand they lived in the country. Wonderful. But that's all they can talk about."

"Oh, hmm, Char," Kade begins sarcastically. "It's not like they had to pack up their entire life and move to an entirely foreign place, or anything." He stops and sits on a toppled-over tree.

"Please don't take her side," I say. I'm not finished getting it all out. If I can't complain to Kade, who else is there, truly, to talk to? Mother has squashed my concerns since the moment she announced her marriage.

I pace back and forth on the pine needles. "And Brielle said the Wall isn't working anymore, like she even knows what she's talking about. And she's afraid of goblins sneaking around the palace. One would think she's never seen goblins before—they're everywhere! How can someone live anywhere near here without ever seeing a goblin? Has she been living in the ground all these years? Oh, wait! She couldn't have— that's where goblins live!"

"I think a lot of people are afraid of goblins, actually. Not everyone was raised by your father."

"Yes, well, they should have been." I sit beside him on the tree, not caring how the sap will ruin my already muddy dress. I slump forward as far as my stays will allow. Mother would be furious.

I look up at the sky and let out some air. Gray clouds have gathered, promising to continue the rain from last night. A few streaks of sunlight shine down across the clouds, landing gloriously on the tops of the trees.

"Well, are you ready to see it?" Kade opens his pack and reaches inside.

"Yes," I say, allowing some excitement to creep into my sour mood. I don't need to ask what *it* is. *It* is his newest invention. He's been talking about it for weeks, maybe even longer.

This one is different from all the others so far, because I haven't seen it yet. Usually, I am by his side, watching him plan and develop his crazy ideas, but lately I've had to help ready our suite for Bastien and Brielle's arrival, and Kade told me he's nervous about this one. It's more complex than anything he's ever done, apparently, and he's wanted to keep it secret until he knows it works.

"Yes," I say, again. "Absolutely."

I love to see his new gadgets. I helped him discover how to create the stone cubes he uses to power them all, back when Papa was teaching the two of us about sunstones and moonstones and aventurine and all the other rocks and minerals that sustain our world. It was Kade's idea to try putting them all together, just as my father had combined moonstone and sunstone into the Wall to repel the Snow Queen's magic from our kingdom. Kade was the first to form the square tiles of stone into a cube to see what they would do, but I'm the best at carving the designs into the tiles. He still tries new ideas, inlaying different rocks into the designs, but always comes to me when he has something especially intricate to carve. Maybe I'm better at it because my fingers are smaller or because I've practiced embroidery for so many goblin-cursed hours for my mother.

Kade pulls out a small wooden dog—no, a cat— but it doesn't have a head, and there are far too many legs . . . I have no idea what it is.

I move to kneel on the wet ground, reaching to take the contraption he offers to me. I turn it over, marveling at the cogs and wheels that fit perfectly together on the underside of its belly. I've never understood the way he knows how to fit them all together. He reaches to straighten one of the wheely thingies, and his fingers brush against mine, lingering for a moment before turning back to his pack.

"What is it?" Its body is about the size of my fist, perhaps a little larger. It has long legs stretching out from the center, which are hinged at the joints and about halfway down to allow movement.

Kade takes the contraption from me, then sets it gently on the ground. He fishes around in his bag for a cube. None of his gadgets work without one; it is the cube that gives them life. Once he's found it, he fits it into a square hole on top of the round body.

"And there's the head," I say, finally seeing the vision of what he's made. "A spider?"

"A very large spider. You should see how it moves."

I back up, giving him some space to work. He pushes the cube in a little farther, and the mechanical spider stiffens. The carved designs on the cube glow softly.

"Spider, jump!" He commands, and the spider pushes off the ground with its jointed wooden legs and jumps into the air. I jump back, too, as the spider nearly reaches my face, giving a surprised shriek.

"Yes, that was quite funny," I say as Kade leans back in laughter. "Now we know it can frighten unsuspecting ladies. What else can it do?"

"Spider, turn around."

The spider turns in one complete circle, then stops.

"It obeys your voice." I've never seen anything like it. "That's amazing! Can it really understand you?"

"To a degree," he says. "Watch this. Spider, run."

The spider runs toward Kade, still sitting on the log. He lifts his feet out of the way, and there is nowhere for the spider to go, but right up the log. It makes it halfway up the rough bark, but it is unable to form any grip with its legs, and falls to the ground. Then it stretches its legs in all directions, rights itself, and moves in the other direction.

I'm on my feet now, watching it move.

"Spider, stop," Kade commands, but the spider doesn't stop. It runs away from us, toward the trail we just came from. It hits another tree, climbs up just a bit, then falls on its back. I stare, fascinated, as the legs bend in multiple ways to right itself again. Kade grabs his pack and runs toward the spider, but just as he lunges toward it, the thing scuttles away down the trail. It scurries back and forth, running into things and over things and all around. Kade and I chase it, and I believe we could catch the thing if only it would continue running in one straight direction. Even with the two of us scampering after it, we cannot catch it.

"Spider, stop!" Kade yells, over and over again.

The spider climbs up a smaller rock, and I am almost able to snatch it before it falls, but one of its legs hits a ridge, and it bounces in the other direction.

"Stop, spider, stop!" We're both yelling now, but the spider isn't listening. Even if we can't grab it, we might at least be able to knock the cube from its body. That would stop it for sure, but it is so fast, and its movements so erratic, I don't think we could accomplish even that.

I slip in the mud. Yes, the same mud I slipped in on the way up. But instead of pitying myself over the fall, I use it to slide as far as I can. Kade and the mechanical spider are farther ahead of me, and I watch as Kade darts left and right, trying to catch the crazy thing. I thought he said it had been tested. He said it worked fine. He's never had an invention go berserk like this before.

I hit dry earth again and run down the mountainside to catch up, moving faster than I ever could on flat ground. Kade stops at the bottom of the mountain, next to the small river that runs alongside the palace gardens. The spider is nowhere to be seen. Kade must still be searching, too.

I'm moving too fast. I can't slow down. I've hit soft, wet ground again, and it's hard to keep my footing. I try to slow, try to grip the ground beneath me, but my foot hits a rock, and I find myself flying forward. I wave my arms, grabbing through the air around me, but there are no trees, no branches this far down the mountain. Instead, my fingers grab the sleeve of Kade's shirt and my face slams into his back as I knock both of us into the river.

Cold water splashes over me, and I continue waving my arms. It takes a moment to right myself in the water, but as soon as I do, I push my feet against the rocky bottom to stand.

"Blast, that's cold!" I yell, wiping wet hair from my eyes. Kade helps to steady me, then his eyes catch on something behind me.

"There you are!" He exclaims, and I turn to see him reaching into a stand of bulrushes. He looks to me as he pulls the spider from the reeds. "It got stuck in the mud. I hope it still works."

I laugh. "It never worked to begin with."

"Charlotte, get out of the water this instant! You look like a drowned goblin."

My shoulders stiffen, and I whip around. There, on the bank, stands my mother with Bastien, Lacey, and Brielle. She glares at me. Whether it's from my unladylike tumble down the mountain or my unladylike curse upon falling into the water, I don't know. Probably both. It's just easier to let words like that slip when I'm with Kade.

"You're out early," Lacey calls with a pleased smile. She loves to see me in trouble.

"As are you." Kade moves toward the bank, confidently. "Good morning!"

If only Mother was allowed to scold him for falling into the river. My boots slip on the slick rocks as I make my way to the group.

"What is that contraption?" Brielle asks as we near them. "It came down the mountain so quickly."

Kade inspects the spider for damage as he walks. The cube is no longer attached, and I worry for a moment it might be lost, but then I see it folded in

Kade's palm. He grips it tightly with his pinky and ring finger while poking at the spider's underside with his other hand. He looks up, realizing she's talking to him.

Mother curtsies in his direction and says, "Your Highness, you remember my newest daughter, Brielle. You were introduced at the ball last week, I believe."

"Of course." He bows, dripping water all over the grass around him. "It's a pleasure to see you again, and surely you have no interest in this undisciplined contraption. It's turned out to be a complete failure."

"I don't believe that for one second," Brielle says. "It looks amazing."

I step closer to them. "Prince Kaderic has hundreds of these inventions. I help test them all the time."

Brielle leans toward him to get a closer look at the workings of the spider. A thick golden curl of hair touches his arm and he jumps. Perhaps, not realizing what is touching him, he moves to brush it away, then startles.

"Your hair is wet!"

"Just a splash from when you fell in the water." She looks up with sweet, innocent eyes. "I'm afraid I was too close to the river at the time." Kade sets the spider in her hands and pats his side where his bag normally hangs when we're out exploring.

"I have just the thing." He wades back into the water, then swims quickly to the other side where his pack lies on the bank. He holds it high above his head with one arm to keep it dry on his way back. In his excitement, he seems to have forgotten he could have run a short distance to the bridge, instead of swimming back and forth. I shake my head with a smile as he emerges, once again, from the water, already fishing around in his pack. "This is something I made just a while ago. I haven't been able to get much use out of it yet. Char, come take a look."

Now I see why he is so excited about her wet hair. I've only seen this invention once, when Kade put the finishing touches on it a couple months ago, but he hasn't had any reason to use it, as far as I know. It is a brush with a sunstone frame that collapses in on itself to be stored easily in his leather bag, along with a few other of his smaller inventions. He pushes the bristles open now, attaches the cube to the end of the handle, and Brielle gasps in surprise.

Without any command given, a fan rotates within the warm sunstone frame and the brush blows air from its bristles. Brielle laughs as Kade lifts the wet curl from her shoulder to comb it dry.

I watch, dripping and shivering in the morning air.

"There," Kade says. "Would you like to see more? I could give you a tour of my workshop as soon as I've changed into dry clothes."

Brielle claps her hands enthusiastically. "What a wonderful idea!"

Lacey steps beside me. "Yes, it is! Might we all go?"

Kade is flustered for a moment, as if he has forgotten we are all here. Mother and Bastien decline and turn to walk back to the palace, he leaning heavily on his cane. Bastien must need to leave soon. The Wall certainly won't rebuild itself. Lacey moves to stand beside Kade, talking about how fascinating his inventions are. She's never cared much about them before.

I don't know where to go or what to do. I am soaked to the bone with river water. I can still feel it rolling down my face. The dark clouds overhead threaten to pour rain on us all, and all I can do is stand with my arms folded around my middle, shivering.

The three of them start to walk away, but Kade turns to look at me.

"Are you coming, Charlotte?"

I shake my head, not saying anything for a moment, then let out a small, "No," and wipe a clingy wet curl from my face. "I should change into dry clothes," I say a little louder. "I'll meet you three later."

Chapter 6

I watch them leave. Brielle walks with her strange, fancy shuffle. Lacey leans a little too close to Kade, bumping his shoulder more often than, I'm sure, is necessary. And Kade gestures wildly with his arms, most likely telling them about all the wonders that await to be seen in his workplace. He doesn't seem to be affected at all by his soaked clothes. I suppose princes are impervious to wet and cold?

The first drop of rain thumps against my cheek, then another lands on top of my head. There is no need to hurry inside. What more could a little bit of rain do to my already ruined state?

Not wanting to follow the happy group, I cross the garden to a servants' entrance. My feet are soggy in my boots and I am quite aware of the trail of water I am leaving through the corridor. I don't bother to wipe up after myself or try to keep the drips under control, though. Pretty soon, it should be wet all around the palace grounds, and I won't be the only person tracking in muddy footprints.

Moonstone is built into the walls here and there to give light, but these back corridors are different than the brightly painted walls I am used to. I continue forward for a bit, but then stop, confused. It's strange; I truly have no idea where I am, but how could I have become lost?

I keep walking, getting colder with each step. I've never been afraid of goblins before, but here in the dark, all alone, I pray none decide to make an appearance. I start to hum, just in case.

A couple more turns, and soon there is nowhere for me to go, but through a tall wooden door. It is unlike any I've ever seen in the palace—plain and dark. Why have I never seen this door before? Surely, Kade and I would have come across it during all our years together, exploring the palace.

I pull on the latch, and it opens easily, revealing a circular staircase enclosed by stone walls. I've never seen this stairway before, either. Where could it possibly lead?

Cold air drifts down through the tower, carrying an icy chill with a hint of pine. It makes me think of the forested hills beside the palace. Kade's mother only decorates the palace with flowers from the garden. Perhaps this staircase leads outside, and I might be able to find a more suitable entrance to return to our suite to change.

I shiver as I climb round and round, up the staircase. If only I had a small sunstone to warm my hands. The thought seems like heaven itself.

At last I turn around the bend in the wall and see a room which opens onto a large balcony. No more steps. My wet legs feel like ice, and I wiggle my frozen toes to bring life back to them. My arms are wrapped around my body as tight as I can hold them, but still, I am cold. I need to find the way to my room, so I can change out of this blasted wet dress.

Wet dress. Not blasted. Just wet.

A woman stands at the edge of the balcony, her back to me. She is surrounded by a flock of pigeons, and they coo and bob their heads, walking all around the railing. A servant, perhaps? Her hair is long and straight. It almost sparkles, despite the darkness. There must be a roof of some sort, because she is dry even though she stands so close to the rain.

No. Not just rain.

Snow.

Snow?

I am sorry to bother her, but she must know the way back to the main palace. I'm surprised I've gotten lost in the first place. My head spins with confusion.

"Excuse me," I say, and I suddenly find myself amidst a flutter of wings and feathers. The pigeons crisscross above us, moving about the room and out the large balcony window.

"You've disturbed the poultry," the woman says when the noise has died down.

"I am sorry. Truly, I am, but I've lost my way." I am about to ask for directions when she turns to face me. Her silver hair is brushed back from her face. She has a cunning look in her knowing eyes.

"Come to me, my dear." She reaches out a delicate hand. I take a small step forward. My legs are stiff. "Do you know who I am?"

I shake my head, afraid to say who I think she might be. I don't even want to admit it to myself, but one thing is certain: she is no palace servant.

Even my mind feels cold now. So cold and slow. Snowflakes drift around me, blowing in from the balcony.

"What are you doing here?" the woman asks. She lifts an arm, and the snow swirls higher. "How did you get here?"

"Here?" The cold has seeped to my bones, and it feels as though I will never be warm. My words come slow through chattering teeth. "I was going to my room to change." I motion toward the wet fabric that's slowly freezing around my legs. "I've gotten lost, though I don't...know...how."

The woman steps toward me and takes my chin in her hand. Ice shoots through me, freezing me in place, and now I am sure—I am absolutely sure that this woman standing before me, touching me with her icy fingers, is the Snow Queen.

My thoughts try to keep up, but I am in too much of a shock and far too cold to fully process this information.

"And what shall I do to you? Hmm? Where shall I send you?"

I am too cold to respond, but how could I answer such a question, anyway? I am in the palace. I am home. She is the one who needs to leave. The Wall should be keeping her out.

"Send her home, Tyra. She is not the one you're looking for," a woman's voice calls from behind me. The voice is calm and sweet, with just a hint of warning. I want to look, to see who she is, but I cannot move.

"Then how did she get here?"

Why does she keep asking that?

Footsteps sound on the stones as the woman behind me moves forward to join the other. She stands, confidently in front of me, examining me with drawn eyebrows. Her golden hair cascades around her face in waves the color of sunshine. Warmth flows from her body, melting my limbs ever so slightly.

"She is nothing," she says. "Send her home."

"But I can use—"

A blast of warm air hits me hard, softening my icy body and knocking me off my feet onto the hard, unforgiving stone.

"She is of no use to you." Her voice turns harder. "Send her home."

"I did not bring her here. How could I possibly

know where she lives?"

"I'm in no mood for games, Tyra."

"Aren't you the least bit curious how she came to be here?" The Snow Queen looks closer at my face, then glares at the warm woman. I can hardly believe what I am seeing, that I am in the presence of not one, but two season queens. "Or do you already know? Just who are you protecting, Lissette?"

The Sun Queen ignores her question and turns to me. "Take the stairs behind you, and you will find yourself at home."

But how can that be? I wandered so long before finding the stairway, and I hadn't even been close to my family's suite. And apparently, I'm not even in the palace, for why else would the Snow Queen keep asking how I came to be here?

As if she can read my mind, the woman says, "I've created a door for you. You will find your way."

So many questions swirl through my mind, like the snow drifting around me, but unlike the snowflakes I can easily catch in my hand, these thoughts are so quick I cannot hold any of them before another flies by.

My legs are stiff, and I am afraid I won't be able to stand, but I've got to move. I've got to get away from the Snow Queen and her icy stare, for who knows how long the Sun Queen can keep her at bay? After pushing myself up, I take one last look at all that white through the balcony. It sparkles and gleams in the sunlight, covering the ground in a soft, cold blanket. I've never seen such a sight, and I can't help but stare at its beauty.

"Go!" The woman commands, and I turn to stumble back down the stairs, my limbs still stiff and clumsy from the cold. I find myself in front of the great wooden door at the bottom in just a matter of moments. Was all that time I spent wandering the corridors before just my imagination? Or my weariness from climbing? I push on the door and step through the opening.

Just as the woman told me, I find myself in the hall, outside our family's suite. The door slams behind me, and I whip around, catching one last glimpse before it disappears, leaving smooth stone in its place. Just as this wall has always been.

"Charlotte, there you are!"

I jump at the sound of Mother's voice, letting out a sudden shriek. I am shaking from the cold still taking up residence in my bones and the shock of my experience, and I find that all I can do is stare at the blank wall…that I walked through only moments ago.

"Goodness, Lottie, you're freezing. Why haven't you changed yet? Let us draw up a hot bath for you, and you can have a good soak before supper."

I follow her to our rooms and stand shivering as she removes my wet clothes while the maids fill the tub with hot, steaming water. I want to say, "Mother, I've seen the season queens," but the words don't come. It's not like the queens visit their kingdoms anymore. As far as I know, no one in Floraison has seen any of them since the war. And now I've seen two. Together, discussing me and the possibility that I might be…the new Rain Queen?

Impossible. The Sun Queen said as much, but then the Snow Queen hinted that she knew—that the Sun Queen knew how I had come to be wherever I had been, and might that possibly mean she knows who the Rain Queen actually is?

How wonderful it would be to have the new Rain Queen take her rightful place and unite the season queens again. Whoever she ends up being—for it is certainly not me—I'm sure she will make everything better for all the kingdoms.

And I can't wait to see it happen.

Chapter 7

Supper is just as unbearable as it has been since they came, but for entirely different reasons. Instead of being unable to get her to speak, we cannot get Brielle to stop talking. She is absolutely fascinated with Kade's inventions, and she tells her father about this one and that one and—oh, there's one that's particularly special, because Kade worked on it while he was sick with a fever, and it turned out lopsided and crooked while still working tremendously well. Just hearing her talk about it so intimately makes the food in my stomach churn. I know that gadget, too, and it *is* special. Kade's fever lasted for days, and I wasn't allowed to see him for even a moment. They thought the sickness would spread. They thought Kade would die.

She is still talking. I can't remember when she last took a bite of the mutton cutlets in her bowl.

"The shelves are overflowing with his inventions.

I've never met any person like him. I think he's right that half of them are useless, but not because they're not clever as he says, but because they're so silly and fun. He has one that just rolls around the room. It looks a little bit like a real person doing turn-abouts, and with each roll, when the square hits the floor, a tiny horn sounds. It rolls and honks about the room. Oh, it's such a sight!"

Brielle laughs, and I cannot keep myself from smiling. When Kade was working on that little gadget, he accidentally locked one of the gears in place, and it would not stop honking for two days. He was so elated when he finally pulled it loose. Brielle is right that it serves no real purpose, but I loved seeing the joy and satisfaction on Kade's face when the extra noise stopped, and it was properly doing its honk and roll.

"He showed me the inside of the spider's body, and even took out a few of the gears to show me how it works. Father, it was so amazing. While he was pointing everything out, we noticed the cam was stuck by a loose lever in the housing, so we took them both out and fit them together again and added an extra gear to absorb the alternate energy from the pinion rack. Once it was complete, he said it worked better than ever before. Now it won't get stuck on one mode like he said it did this morning."

Wait.

Cam, pinion rack, absorbing alternate energy. She understands how all those contraptions work?

I set my fork next to my plate, and the serving girl standing behind me assumes I am finished and takes them both away, replacing it with a clean dish. How is it Brielle can spend one morning in Kade's workshop and—all of a sudden—know about all those gears and cogs and what-nots, when I've been watching him fool around with those gadgets almost my entire life and still have trouble identifying which part is which? I have no idea what any of those bits and pieces actually do, and Brielle helped Kade repair the run-away spider after just a few minutes.

"Does that not make you happy?" she asks, looking in my direction.

I think of missing out on a workshop tour that, it seems, was the highlight of Brielle's existence. (Maybe she *has* been living underground all her life.) And I think of being sopping wet and wandering the palace, miserably getting lost and—if I hadn't fallen in the river with Kade, I wouldn't have found the Snow Queen. That would have been a good thing, certainly, but I also wouldn't have met the Sun Queen, either, and now I know that the Rain Queen is returning. If the Sun Queen knows who she is, then all will be better soon. Should I tell everyone? Would they believe me?

"When I was young like you three ladies," Mother interrupts my thoughts, "we used to swim in the river when it was hot out. My best friend and I would sneak to a hidden spot in the woods, strip down to our underthings," with this she blushes, "and dip ourselves in the cool water. I thought my parents were oblivious to the whole thing, but now that I'm older, I can guess they were turning a blind eye to two young girls who were just trying to escape the heat. I daresay we weren't the only children swimming in the river, even though the thought of it now gives me the shivers—all the fish and other slimy things and snakes."

"Snakes!" Lacey presses a hand to her neck. "Mother, you used to swim with snakes?"

"Yes, I suppose I did." She grins, and Bastien chuckles at Lacey's surprise.

"There are snakes all about the kingdom," he says. "Little ones, yes, but they're there all the same."

Something my mother said tickles the back of my brain. I am thinking about her and her friend, swimming in the river. Why does it bother me they would do that? It's not that I care much about propriety. Otherwise I wouldn't be stomping about the mud with the prince in the early morning hours. I replay the conversation in my mind, trying to pinpoint what it is Mother said to unsettle me. *We used to swim in the river when it was hot out . . .*

She would swim in the river when it was hot! It never gets hot in Floraison.

"Mother," I say. "How often did it get hot when you were young?"

"Every summer. Like clockwork."

I wonder what that would be like—to be truly hot from the sun. We've never had a real summer that I've ever known. The months circulate just the same as they always have, but there is no change to the weather. We have mild sunshine with a bit of rain most days. Even when it is sunny out, it has never been what anyone would describe as hot. And we've certainly never had snow, which I've found can be stunning in both good ways and bad.

"How old were you when the seasons stopped?" I ask. I scoop a small spoonful of the velvety white chicken blanquette sauce, taking care to keep the triple tiered sleeves of my formal dress out of it.

Mother wipes her mouth delicately with her serviette.

"Not too much older than you girls, actually, but I was already a young mother. You were just a baby when we heard of the Rain Queen's death, Charlotte, and Lacey was not much bigger. That is when Floraison became stuck in the season of Spring. The other kingdoms are unchanging as well—Is that not right, Bastien? Each in their own season?"

"Yes, exactly," he says. "I was in Solair a lot then. There was a loud noise, and almost immediately it began to rain. It rained for days, hardly letting up. It was as if the Sun Queen herself was crying for the loss of her best friend, and the world had to cry right along with her. There was nothing could console her in those days."

"You talk as if these fairy queens are real people," Lacey delicately spears a cut of chicken with her fork. I freeze, a shiver dancing through my body. They are most definitely real. "I thought they were just excuses for Lunain to invade our kingdom."

Bastien bristles at that, almost coughing into his soup.

"Don't you believe in them?" Brielle asks.

Lacey sits back in her chair and raises her eyebrows, considering. Mother answers first.

"They are certainly real enough. They are fairies, yes, but real all the same."

"Are they tiny?" Lacey asks. "Like the fairies in story books?"

"Normal size, just like us," Mother says. "I saw the spring fairy once when I was a little girl, before she died. She was the most beautiful woman I've ever seen. What about you, Bastien? Have you ever seen one of the season fairies?"

The color rises on his cheeks. Is he embarrassed to talk about fairies, as if we are at some little girl's tea party? But we are not discussing imaginary creatures of children's imaginations. Mother has seen one of the season queen, which means what happened to me this afternoon is all too true. They exist, so I cannot think back and wonder if I am crazy.

Bastien clears his throat, still seeming a little uncomfortable, and I find myself leaning forward to hear his answer.

"Yes," he finally says. "The Sun Queen, when Brielle and I lived in Solair. I've heard many things about the Snow Queen, but I've never seen her in person. And I've seen the autumn fairy, before she became the Goblin Queen, of course." So he's seen two as well!

"You mean the Goblin Queen was once a fairy?"

It is Lacey again. Doesn't she know anything? I ask her if she does and get a sharp look from Mother in return.

"It's no harm to ask questions," she says.

Brielle sets down her glass and turns to her father. "Did the Moon Queen turn into a goblin during the Shard War? Or was it after, when the goblins were sent to the Underground?"

Bastien coughs into his serviette. "I don't much like to talk about the Shard War."

"Of course," Mother says, too quickly, before anyone can push the question further. "Maybe it's time we turn the conversation. If everyone is finished eating, perhaps we can have you ladies play us some music to complete the evening."

Bastien tries to excuse himself, claiming exhaustion, but Mother presses him to join us. The servants standing by help us from our chairs, and we make our way to the salon. How many others saw the season queens before the war? Did they walk among us, like normal people, back then? Will they, once again, when the Rain Queen returns?

Before I can enter the salon, Mother gives a surprised gasp.

"Prince Kaderic," she says. "We didn't expect to see you this evening."

I look quickly to the mirror hanging on the corridor wall. Surrounded by thick golden scrolls, it is nearly as large as I am, making it easy to check the folds of the silk train attached to my shoulders. My hair is loosely pulled back, with the curls tucked around each other at the nape of my neck. I sweep one loose strand back from my forehead, hoping it will stay. My freckles are scattered defiantly across my cheeks, daring me to hate them. I find that I can't.

I enter the salon last and find everyone greeting Kade. Everyone except Bastien, who is already leaning back in a chair and closing his eyes. My father never seemed so drained in the evenings, even when he traveled to the farthest reaches of our kingdom to inspect the Wall.

"I thought you would be tired of us after we spent all morning pestering you with questions in your workshop," Lacey exclaims. She places a hand delicately on Kade's arm, standing between him and Brielle. He smiles at both Lacey and Brielle, then catches my gaze and winks at me as I approach.

He's still in his court dress as we are, most likely just having come from dinner with his parents. He seems just as comfortable in his garnet colored suitcoat and velvet breeches as he was in the plain clothes he wore this morning, exploring the mountainside with me.

"I was just wandering around the palace," he says,

"and thought I would stop in for a visit. One of your servants informed me I could expect to hear the loveliest music if I made it to your salon." He wipes a hand across his face, disturbing the wavy dark curls on his forehead. "I must say, it was a difficult trek, but I made it in one piece."

"Oh, you're too funny!" Lacey giggles, leaning her head on his shoulder. He glances down at her, a puzzled look on his face.

"Word travels fast through the help, I suppose," Mother says. "Which of our daughters would you be pleased to hear from first?"

Kade takes a step back, patting Lacey's arm as he slides it from his own. He looks around the room and spies a pile of sheet music, then picks it up from the bench. Brielle takes a small step forward as he asks, "Are these yours?"

She nods, a dainty smile on her lips.

"I do believe, then, that Brielle will be the first to soothe our troubled minds with her melodious . . ." he puts one hand to his chest and holds the other in a dramatic pose, then after a moment's hesitation, pulls a confused smirk. ". . . melodious melodies," he finishes. "I'm sorry. I cannot do any better. Words are not my friends tonight."

"Oh, no, Prince Kaderic, I couldn't," Brielle says. "Surely, let the other ladies go first." She looks suddenly nervous and unsure. I don't want to be first, anyway, so I try to reassure her.

"You have a lovely voice, Brielle. I stood beside you at the wedding, remember?" And I can't help but say, "Surely, you can do better than a common mining tune," then after giving her my sweetest fake smile, "Please, go first."

Kade hands the sheet music to Brielle, then takes a chair beside Bastien.

Lacey takes the seat on the other side of Kade. Mother sits on the opposite side of the room, leaning back on the grand chaise. There is nowhere else for me to go—but to the window behind my mother. I sit on the sill and look out to the gardens while Brielle gets situated at the harpsichord. Carefully manicured hedges and flowers border the walkways below with the shadowy rise of the mountain towering over our beautiful garden. It is so different from the snowy landscape I beheld on the balcony. The Snow Queen is absolutely right. How *did* I get to wherever I was this afternoon?

Brielle's fingers press down on the keys, startling me from my musings, and she begins to sing. She does, indeed, have a lovely voice. Oh, why couldn't her voice have been ugly?

She sings a song I've never heard before, strange and hypnotic. The notes rise and fall and sometimes tumble about each other, but the patterns never repeat themselves. Her words tell a story about a man who lives in the forest, surrounded by trees and lakes and rivers. I can imagine the water rushing past the man as her voice carries across the room.

The music turns sad, and she sings of the heartbroken man who is separated from his love. They will never have a life together, and he doesn't know if he will ever see her again, but he is glad for the sunshine. In it he can see her beauty, her goodness, and feel whole again.

We are all transfixed, staring at Brielle. I don't know how much time has passed from when she stopped singing to when I begin to see the room around me again. I wonder if the others saw the forest surrounding them as I had, or perhaps I am the only one who had gotten lost in the beauty of Brielle's song.

No. Kade is just as entranced as I felt just a moment ago.

He stares at Brielle with a look I've never seen on him before. It is certainly not a look that's been cast in my direction, or even Lacey's.

Curse that girl and her blasted beauty!

I look to my mother, to Bastien, to Lacey. They are all trapped in the spell she has cast. If beauty does indeed rule the world, how will I ever survive with Brielle here?

Mother rushes to Brielle and gives her a hug. "I never guessed you would be so talented, child! Why did you not tell us right away?"

We all clap our hands politely, and Kade shouts a "Hurrah!" before the room begins to calm again. Lacey turns to Kade. She looks at him but addresses me.

"Charlotte, will you play for me?"

I don't want to. I can't follow Brielle. My fingers already feel stiff and uncooperative. They have abandoned me, because they know I can't compete. But at least this way—accompanying Lacey—I might not be forced to sing. My voice would shake with nervousness, and I cannot give Brielle that satisfaction. I have played and sung for my family, and even Kade, hundreds of times, but after my stepsister's performance, it feels like I have a million pigeons flapping around in my stomach.

"Of course," I say, my voice shaky. I take a long breath to calm the pigeons down.

What else can I do? I'm sure if I tried to decline, Mother would force me.

I move from the window to my harp. Solid oak, carved intricately and polished from top to bottom. Our love for it is the only thing, it seems sometimes, Mother and I have in common. She taught both Lacey and I when we were little. Lacey grew bored of it, though, and she was meant to switch to the harpsichord, but never did. I spent much of my childhood complaining of the unfairness of this, only for my grievances to fall on the deaf ears of both my parents. Now, I am glad to know the feel of the strings beneath my fingers, even though I am not as talented as Mother wishes.

The chair is a little too far away, but it needs to be to accommodate my hoops and skirts. I sit, sliding off my slippers to keep my feet flat, then reach for my harp and move it into position. It rests gently on my shoulder, and my fingers glide over the strings, plucking some sharply while only nudging others. It's been a while since I've played, and some of the strings are grossly out of tune. I wince at the sound.

"Clouds above! How have I forgotten?" Kade exclaims, jumping up from his seat.

We are all a bit stunned and confused.

"I made you a tuner," he calls over his shoulder while rushing out the door. "I'll be right back!"

For a moment, we all look at each other, not really knowing what to say. Bastien and Brielle are definitely seeing the true Prince Kaderic, not the stuffy suited boy in all the royal portraits they probably knew him as before moving to the palace. Our Kade will jump up in the middle of an impromptu recital to run down to his workshop, all to retrieve a simple tuner.

I think on that for a moment. He made a tuner. For me.

It's not long before he comes back, panting, but holding out the most beautiful wooden tuner I've ever seen. Flowers and leaves are carved into the wood, sweeping so beautifully from front to back that I gasp with delight.

"You made this?" I've never seen him use so much detail in his carving work.

"It took a long time. Remember when I was sick? I didn't have much else to do." He traces a finger over the wood, brushing my hand and sending a tingle up my arm. "Maybe I'm better at carving wood than I am at stone."

I look down at the tuner again. A tiny bellows is attached to the pipes and what appears to be a tuning key sticking out one end. Kade must see my confusion as to how to work it, because he takes the tuner from me and places it at the top of the harp, right next to the crown. He pushes the energy cube in a bit more, and two feet spring out, grasping the harp's neck.

"Pluck the string where it's sitting," he says.

I do, and the bellows fill and release air through the pipe, playing the note of the string I just played. The two sounds are a little off, so the tuning key turns the pin until they match. It moves to the next string, which I pluck, and again it plays the note, turning the pin to match the sounds.

"Brilliant!" Brielle calls, clapping her hands wildly.

Brilliant. It truly is. I have never seen nor heard of anything so remarkable in my life. My heart swells with pride and gratitude. Kade is, indeed, brilliant.

My harp is tuned faster than I've ever done it before, but even so, it must have bored Bastien to sleep, for he leans almost sideways in his chair, snoring. Once the tuner is finished with the last string, it slides back up the neck of the harp, resting in its original position beside the crown. I'll keep it there, always.

Lacey moves to stand on the other side of the harp. I don't need to ask her which song we will perform. I have picked the one she and I are both the best at. It is time to remind everyone Brielle is not the only girl in our family with talents to share.

My fingers move across the strings, and a certain peace settles over my heart. Papa used to love listening to me play in the evenings. I glance at Bastien, who has woken from the noise. He gives a weak smile while adjusting himself in his seat.

I pick up the pace of the music, ready for Lacey to join in. Her voice carries beautifully across the room, singing a happy song that should invite our audience to tap their toes or sway side to side with the melody. Instead she is interrupted just a couple lines into the song by a gruff snort from Bastien. After a brief pause, Lacey joins back in the song, finishing the first verse. Bastien shifts in his chair and shakes his head.

"Enough!" he shouts. "That is quite enough!"

Lacey startles into silence and my fingers freeze at the harp strings. We both look in Bastien's direction, confused.

Mother looks from her husband to Lacey and me, then back to Bastien. Her eyebrows are drawn tight in bewilderment and embarrassment.

"Bastien," she murmurs soothingly. "Did you have a bad dream?"

"What makes you think I was sleeping? I was merely resting my eyes."

I look down at my toes peeking out from beneath my skirts. I don't want to be the one who tells him of his snores. No one says a word.

"It is far past bedtime," is all he can say when we don't answer. "Enough of this music. Brielle . . ." It seems to take him a moment to remember he has two other daughters now. "Ladies, off to your rooms. It is quite late."

Brielle immediately stands and gives a quick curtsy to Kade, who has jumped to his feet as well. Kade gives me a quizzical look, then bows to Brielle as she says, "Good night, Prince Kaderic." She bids the rest of us to sleep well and glides out of the room.

Kade shuffles from one foot to the next and raises his eyebrows.

"Yes, well, it is getting quite late. I agree. I'll be off then, too." He gives two short bows to my mother and Bastien, mumbling, "Madame, Monsieur," then hurries out of the room as fast as respectably possible.

Brielle and Kade might be happy to comply, but I will not be ordered around so willingly. Who is this man who thinks he can take the place of my father? I am almost a grown woman. We will all be married soon, and it will be none of his business when, or even if, we go to bed. It has been years since either Lacey or I were ordered to our rooms by anyone, and it will not be starting now.

"I'm not tired," I say, like the child I am being treated as. I push the harp away from me, standing quickly. "How dare you tell me what to do?"

"Charlotte," Mother warns. "You will show more

respect for your new father."

I open my mouth to speak, but I see my mother shaking her head, her lips in a tight frown, her eyes begging me to be polite. Very well. If that is what she wants. I glare at my mother, then curtsy as deep and dramatically as I can, letting my head tilt gracefully toward the floor.

"Good night, Father," I say sickly sweet. My throat tightens. It feels lumpy and hot, as though a sunstone is lodged inside of it.

My eyes begin to water. I lift myself from the curtsy, my legs burning from the length of it, and turn in Mother's direction.

I cannot trust my trembling lips to speak. Everything feels so upside down and backwards. I want Bastien and Brielle out of my family, but I assume the chances of that are as little as waking up to snow tomorrow morning. I want my father back, but I know that will never happen, either. I only want everything to be as it used to be, but we cannot live in the past.

This is my life now.

I make my way for the door, but before I can take two steps, I realize I have not returned my slippers to my feet. I pause. I should retrieve them, but I don't want Mother or that wretched Bastien to see the tears on my cheeks.

Oh, curse it all!

I leave the slippers and storm out of the room.

Chapter 8

I make my way through the palace, not caring where my angry path takes me, so long as I don't end up in my bedroom. I find myself in the garden, and by the time my feet touch the cobbled path, the tightness in my chest has settled, making it easier to breathe. The smell of roses, forget-me-nots, and lilacs dances through the air. I take it in as if it were life itself. The smell of peace and order.

There are neatly laid rows of bushes and trees all around me, all flowering with the beauty of spring. Music fills my imagination as I stroll, and I pretend the trees at the end of the lane are the king and queen on their dais in the ballroom. The roses, lilies, and jonquils are the attendees, dressed in splendid finery of pinks and greens and yellows. A handsome prince is beside me, and we are opening the most splendid ball the kingdom has ever seen. And I am not the least bit nervous.

Raising a hand in the air beside me and leaving the other close to my hip, I bend my knees outward, sinking low. I slide my left foot up my right ankle and lift to an *élevé*, hoping I look as graceful as I feel among the gorgeous flowers and warm spring air. I take a couple steps, rising and falling in a *demi coupé*, circle my invisible partner while flashing him a dazzling smile, then finish it off with a swift twirl that would never be considered proper in a real ball.

The dust on the cobblestones is most likely clinging to my stockings, but the uneven path feels almost therapeutic to my feet, and it feels so good to be alone. To have a quiet moment to myself so I can forget about stepfathers and season queens, and just dream for a little while.

The sun lowers itself behind the mountains, casting a yellow glow through the air. I gently break a violet off its mother plant cascading from a basket above, then laugh when I realize that strolling through the garden and picking flowers are things I'm sure both Mother and Bastien would approve of. For all the lectures I receive about not measuring up or ignoring the rules completely, it seems as though I am not as rebellious as I'm made out to be, even when I'm angry.

Though my heart is now calm, I am not ready to

return just yet. I twirl the violet between my fingers as I wander farther through the garden, past the crumbling Wall I ran to not long ago, and through the garden's gate. I follow the dirt path, watching the Wall as I walk. It looks strong in places—almost perfect, as if it had been built only yesterday. Parts of it *are* as new as yesterday, I suppose, because we are forced to add more stones on as the goblins break it down. We need to keep the magic out of our kingdom until the Rain Queen returns to protect us again.

Brielle can't be right that the Wall is failing...but then, how can I explain the unexpected staircase or meeting the season queens on a snow-covered balcony while wandering our very own palace?

The clashing sound of metal on metal pulls my attention from the Wall. A group of soldiers are fighting in the shade of the mountain. I am alarmed at the scuffle for only a moment, though, because it becomes obvious rather quickly they are practicing, not truly fighting against each other. They step, dodge, and strike with their swords, then stop to talk or shake out their arms, only to start right back up again.

I should turn around. It's much safer in the garden, but something catches my eye. Rather, someone captures my attention.

He is dressed as the other soldiers—or more accurately, undressed, because he and the other men only wear military issued leather breeches. They have all abandoned their green jackets and linen shirts, which lay in piles near the Wall. He is one of the taller men in the group, and though his shoulders are not quite as broad as some of the others', I can still see his muscles flex with each strike of his sword.

The violet slips from my fingers.

There seems to be a pattern to his steps that doesn't match the rest of the men's. He is faster, lighter, and I find myself staring, watching his movements closely as he weaves around his opponent, dodging every blow. I admit his skill is amazing, but what, in the name of Spring, is he doing out here?

"Kade!" I shout as I near the group, but he doesn't hear me. I cannot tell if the swords they are using are real or not. They might be quite sharp. I hasten my pace to get a closer look. The man Kade is sparring against lunges toward him, his sword raised high. Kade deftly steps aside, then grabs the man's wrist with his free hand, lifting their arms above his head and stepping forward, his sword ready to strike.

They break apart, laughing at something I obviously missed. Kade bounces his shoulders, then shakes his arms, cocking his head to one side, then the other.

"Kade!" I call again, louder. I am close enough for Kade to hear me, and he whips around, panic in his eyes.

"What are you doing?" I start to ask as I near him, but he shushes me and tries to maneuver me away.

"Don't say anything. Go back in, Char. I'll tell you late—"

"Prince Kaderic, is that you?" A man on the opposite side of the group steps toward us, handing his sword to one of the soldiers.

Kade raises his eyebrows at me, staring intently to make sure I realize I am at fault for whatever it is that's happening. The air around me grows cold, and I feel a chill run down my back.

"Yes, General." He turns to face the man. "It is."

"I would lecture you," the general says, "but we've had that talk before. With your father."

"My father is wrong."

"Your father is king. He is never wrong."

Every sword was lowered the moment the general spoke up. Each man stands watching, waiting to see how this plays out. Kade's jaw is set, and he looks toward the palace, turning the hilt of his sword in his hand.

"Who knew?" The general looks around, and several of the men slowly raise their hands. He shakes his head.

Kade steps toward the general.

"How am I supposed to get any better if I don't practice?"

"You get plenty of practice in your private lessons. You don't need to sneak out after dark to practice with us." The general doesn't seem to be angry, as I first assumed him to be, but the exasperation in his voice is proof they have, indeed, had this argument before. Possibly many times.

"Dancing around with a rapier will not prepare me for a battle with goblins. Those lessons are merely ceremonial, and you know it. My father—"

"Your father forbids—" the general interrupts, but Kade doesn't let him finish.

"My father fought alongside his men during the Shard War, and they were successful because of it. He doesn't think I can fight, but I can."

Why does Kade want to fight? He doesn't think it will ever come to that, does he? The Wall is keeping us safe.

The general lets out a puff of air.

"You'll have to take it up with him, then. I could lose my position—or more—if he thought I allowed you to be here without his consent. Now, go on back to the palace, and take your lady friend with you, before either of you gets hurt."

I bristle at the callous title the general gives me. *Lady friend.* Doesn't he know who my father is? Or, who my father was?

Kade hands his short sword to the nearest soldier,

then digs a shirt from a pile and pulls it over his head while walking back to me. He shakes his head in frustration, then looks toward the palace again. He might want to go back inside even less than I do.

"What was that all about?" I take his offered arm, remembering his strong movements just moments ago. I can feel the heat from his exertions through his shirt, warming my both hand and my cheeks.

Kade gestures behind us as we walk away.

"The soldiers practice at night while they're guarding the Wall. I usually wait 'til later to join them, but the music was cut short, and Father already thought I was with your family. I couldn't let the opportunity pass."

I think of him rushing off after Bastien yelled for us girls to go to bed. I didn't blame him, but I assumed he would go to his workshop or head toward bed himself.

"How often do you do this?" I ask, but he doesn't have to answer. I saw how quickly he dodged the soldier's sword, how he pushed the man off balance, how sure he cut each strike through the air. This has obviously been going on for quite some time.

How could I have not known? Why would he not confide in me? Is he so afraid of his father finding out that he would keep this secret from even his closest friend?

"I'm sorry, Kade. I didn't mean to—"

"No, it's not your fault. The general was bound to find out, eventually." He considers a moment, then gives me a grin. "Okay it *was* your fault."

I laugh and apologize again.

"It's time I find a different troop to spar with, anyway. I don't want to get anyone in trouble, if my father *were* to find out. The less the soldiers recognize me, the better."

"You're the crown prince." I reach my hand up and rest it atop his head. "And very tall. Nearly everyone recognizes you."

He laughs and absentmindedly hits his hand on one of the moonstone pillars guiding our way through the fading light. A cold breeze whips past my face—in stark contrast to the heat radiating through Kade's thin shirt. I lean closer to him.

"Kade," I say, starting my question before I have thought it through completely. "Do you really think we'll have to fight the Snow Queen's armies? Or the goblins? The Wall is keeping them Underground. They're not strong enough to come up for more than a few minutes. The curse—"

A sudden *crack!* rings out behind us, and we turn to see what the soldiers might be up to now. A wall of ice—three times higher than the Wall my father built—stands before us. It is as if a wave of water has crashed into the wall, soaring upward, and freezing on impact.

A blast of cold air follows, nearly knocking me over. I've never seen so much ice in my entire life! Yes, the ice traders bring blocks of it down from Neimonte from time to time, but this cold barricade towers over us, nearly blocking the mountains from view. My veins run cold.

"It's the Queen!" a soldier shouts. "Where is she?"

The men scramble about, running along the length of the wall, their swords drawn.

"She must be here!"

The Snow Queen.

She can't be here. When I saw her this afternoon, there was snow. I looked out the balcony, and there was snow, everywhere. And she kept asking how I had come to them. And the magical door. And…Oh, blast. She can't get in through the Wall, can she? Surely, it's strong enough to stop her, or else her ice wall would be on this side, not the other.

Right?

Kade grabs my hand, yelling for me to follow him. I resist. I want to see what happens.

"It's not safe out here!"

He is right. My heart beats not only from excitement, but also fear, remembering the Snow Queen's icy touch. I follow him through the garden to the nearest palace entrance.

Bastien comes bursting through the doorway,

hobbling crookedly down the steps. His eyes widen as he sees the ice, and I can see the panic in them, even in the darkness. He sees me next. I didn't think his eyes could grow any wider, but they do.

"What are you doing out here, girl?" He grabs my arm and pushes me toward the door. "Get inside this instant! I told you to go to bed!"

All the anger that has slowly drained from my body since the interrupted recital comes back, full force.

"You are not my father."

I rush up the stairs, pushing past my mother to get through the doorway.

I can hear her shouting, "Clouds above, Charlotte!" as I race down the hallway, but I ignore her. I run to the nearest window to watch the soldiers try, unsuccessfully, to find the Snow Queen.

Chapter 9

I stay up so late watching all the excitement that I find myself sleeping later than usual the next morning. When the maid comes in to check on me, I request to have breakfast in my bedroom. Hopefully it will speed things up, so I can investigate the ice at the Wall sooner.

I rush to the window to find the ice has partially melted through the night. It glistens with an iridescent radiance in the morning sunshine. How thick is it, and how far along the Wall does it extend? I'm surprised there aren't more people milling around, gawking at its splendor, but perhaps they are too frightened at the possibility of meeting the Snow Queen.

Why would she do such a thing? Was she hoping to break through the Wall, or was it merely a tantrum caused by the frustration of being locked out of our kingdom for fourteen years?

A maid lays out my dress for the morning while a young girl carries in a tray of sugared strawberries and sweet bread and sets it on the table.

The door bursts open, and my mother marches into the room.

"Leave us," she commands, and the servants scatter. Lacey is right behind her, but she doesn't look as if she has anything important to say. She simply sits on the chaise against the wall, waiting for the confrontation.

"Mother," I begin, but she cuts me off before I can get any sort of explanation to form on my lips.

"Really, Charlotte, you are not making this transition easier on any of us." She paces the room, and I push the tray from my lap and swing my legs over the bed. My nightgown slides to just above my knees. Even though we are in the privacy of my own room, showing so much leg is not appropriate for my age. I don't move to fix it.

Mother continues. "I don't know what we would have done if Bastien hadn't come along."

I should have known this would be coming after my behavior last night.

"But, Mother, there is a wall of ice!" I gesture toward the window. If we can get through this quickly, I can soon go down to look.

"That is not what I'm here to talk about."

Of course, it isn't. She is grateful Bastien and Brielle are here, and she expects the rest of us to be, as well.

"Do you honestly think they would have pushed us out of the palace?" I ask. "Surely, we are closer to the king and queen than that."

"Our rooms are for the Head Overseer's family and for the Head Overseer's family only. The Head Overseer must be close to the king, so they can both be aware of the needs of the Wall and the protection it offers." Now it's her turn to gesture to the window. "Last night is a perfect example." But then she's right back to praising her new marriage. "We're lucky King Gervais approached me with this offer. If I hadn't married the new Head Overseer, we very well could have ended up in our mountain château on the edge of society. What kind of marriage offers would we receive for you girls out there? Do you fancy yourself marrying a sheep or a bull?"

If my mother spits out the title *Head Overseer* one more time, I will scream. Does she expect a response to her ridiculous question?

"I would rather marry a sheep than a man like Bastien," I say. "He was a beast last night, and in front of the prince! He was as rude as a goblin. He can't even listen to proper music, and I do not want him bossing me around like he was truly my father. He is not. He will never be!"

I am crying now. I have no idea when the tears began to flow, and I cannot get them to stop. I suck in a huge breath of air, but it turns into more of a snort and a hiccup.

"And ever since he and Brielle showed up, you are acting like it's completely normal and we should love each other as if we were a real family. I hate pretending to like them. I hate that they're here. If you love them so much, then I will just leave. Brielle is a better daughter than Lacey and I combined. Just think of the marriage offer you will get for her! I'm surprised all the gentry aren't already lined up at the door."

I see Mother's face soften.

"Oh, Lottie," she says. "No one can ever replace you as my daughter." She looks to Lacey. "Either of you."

She moves toward me, as if she will put her arms around me, but I slide off the bed and go to the window, crossing my arms.

"We all have our lot in life, and we must be prepared to accept what it brings." The coldness is back in her voice. "You were just as much a beast as Bastien last night, and just the same—in front of the prince. Your stepfather is already at the main entrance to the North Mines. You will prepare yourself at once, without finishing your breakfast, and go to apologize for your behavior. I will ask him about it this evening and his account had better be favorable."

"But the ice!"

"There hasn't been any sighting of the Snow Queen, and you will be within the Wall the whole time. It's perfectly safe."

She doesn't understand. I want to explore the ice, not avoid it.

"But I—"

"This is not optional. I will have a carriage prepared to take you to the mine immediately." She gives a look that clearly signifies the discussion is over. There is no use arguing. Besides, this is the first time, I think, she has referred to Bastien as my 'stepfather.' A small success.

Mother leaves without another word. I am expected to obey.

She knows I will.

Lacey looks a little unsure of herself and her position on the chaise. Perhaps our argument wasn't as exciting as she thought it would be.

"I will help you dress," she says. "That way we don't have to call back the maid." I try to stop her, not trusting this kindness from her, but she ignores me as usual.

She moves to my bed and picks up the dress the maid has chosen. Her eyes squint and she scrunches up her cheeks. It is not that I am clueless to fashions of the day; I simply do not always agree with being as confined as the ladies in court.

Lacey drops the dress to the floor and moves to the wardrobe. She fishes through the gowns and dresses with a practiced hand, pulling random pieces from the top shelf, the back corner. I am surprised at her swiftness and ability. Coming back to the bed, she makes a quick upward nod with her head, and I pull off my nightgown.

"You would be admired more if you simply put a little more effort into your appearance." She lifts the shoulders of a pair of stays over my arms, then pulls the stays close around my body, covering my chemise. She yanks on the laces behind me, and I gasp, taking in air when I should be letting it out.

"A little warning would be appreciated." I grit my teeth as she pulls again. My maids never lace me this tight, even for royal affairs.

"I'm not pleased about any of this, either," she says, and I can tell a lecture is coming. "I am also not whining about it every moment, though. Or sulking in my room all day."

Is that where she thinks I spent yesterday afternoon?

She brings my wide mantua hoops from the other side of the room, and I step into them, tying the ribbon around my waist. I only ever wear these when Mother forces me to put them on for dinner or for a ball or other royal events. Next comes the petticoat, then the over petticoat. The skirt of this petticoat is done in a creamy white color and has flowers embroidered with silk ribbons all about the front. I slip into the blue robe Lacey holds out for me, then she ties it to the stomacher in front. Both the stomacher and the robe are covered in similar flowers as the skirt, but there are jewels sewn into the petals that sparkle, brilliantly, from the light shining through the window.

"I have plans of my own," Lacey continues. "You don't see me throwing fits, just because Brielle might be prettier than me. I would never be able to succeed with that sort of attitude."

She pushes me, not too roughly, to a chair and starts pulling at my hair. It is torture, but I endure it silently, just to keep her from scolding me more. She seems to want to keep talking about herself, though.

"I won't let her get in the way. I just have to assert myself in the right situations, and she will learn her place soon enough. I won't be marrying down, just because some foreigner has crowded her way into the palace."

With everything pinned and tied into place, Lacey brings my stockings and helps to slide them on my feet. I wiggle my toes, stretching the thin material. Last come the shoes. Painted satin, trimmed in white lace.

I stand, feeling stiff, enveloped too tightly by so much fabric. I look in the mirror, standing back a bit to see the full effect. I am still me, with just a touch of Lacey mixed in. I smile. Lacey stands behind me, and I can see her smiling broadly at both of our reflections. Perhaps I am not such a goblin, after all.

"Is this how you always feel?" I ask, amazed.

Lacey adjust a curl that is trying to escape.

"What do you mean? How do you think I feel?"

I hesitate, afraid she will laugh at me. Me, who grew up playing around the mines and carving stones. Me, who cannot sit in respectable society for more than a few minutes without accidentally mentioning a favorite hobby the other ladies look down on with disdain. Me, who couldn't put together an outfit this lovely on my own, even if my life depended on it.

"Beautiful," I say, still staring in the mirror.

Lacey rests her hands on my shoulders and gives a gentle squeeze.

"Well, your freckles are atrocious, but I suppose the rest of you will do." I turn away from the mirror, defenses raised. But then I see the smirk on her face and realize she is teasing me. A rare occurrence, indeed. "You should present yourself to Mother on your way out. She will be so proud."

Chapter 10

It is busy at the North Mine today. Men walk back and forth—as always—carrying barrels of stone out of the mountain, dumping the stones into wheeled carts to be pulled to the shaft house. Accented by the cracking of stones tumbling into the bins, their deep voices blend together in a strong cadence of words—the mining songs used to keep the goblins from venturing out of the Underground tunnels. I hum along with them, feeling at home and thinking of my father.

They must be running low on their supply of moonstone to employ so many men. There are too many for me to count, and I don't recognize any of them from when I used to visit.

I scan the many faces moving about the mine entrance, but I don't see Bastien. Dare I check in the mining tunnels? Papa never let me inside before. The air turns cool as I approach, and I breathe in the rich smell of dirt that is so familiar. A few of the men give me strange glances, but I hold my head high.

How deep do these tunnels wind? Are they digging for stone at the very heart of the mountain? I itch to follow the tunnel before me, forgetting about the delicate fabric of my dress. It couldn't be too terribly dangerous for me to explore, just a little. I need to find Bastien, after all.

"You, girl!" A man shouts. "Get out of the way! You're not supposed to be here." He emerges from the tunnel, carrying a barrel full of stones. The muscles along his arms bulge with the weight of the stone-filled barrel. He is much older and larger than I am, but I am wearing my jeweled stomacher and it gives me confidence I would not normally feel. I stand a little taller, tilting my head back and raising an eyebrow.

"I am looking for my father, the Overseer of the Wall," I say in the most commanding voice I can manage. In my mind, I am Lacey demanding chocolates to be fetched by a servant. The missing *step-* from the word father was omitted before I could realize it, and now it is too late to correct the mistake. "I have every right to be here."

He stares, considering. I raise myself on my toes, just a bit, standing even taller. I am thankful for my stays Lacey tightened so fiercely, because my back is taller and straighter than it's ever been.

"Do you know where he is? The Overseer? I have a very important message from my mother." Important, mostly because delivering it or not determines what sort of scolding I receive upon my return.

"Back in the tunnels is the last place I saw him." The man points a thumb behind his shoulder, and my heart leaps at the thought of actually stepping into the mine to find Bastien. I take a small step in that direction, which is difficult to do while trying to maintain my tip-toed height. "I don't think he'd like you in there."

"I don't see how that is any of your business," I say, then wait for him to move before relaxing my stance.

"I thought his daughter had golden hair," I can hear him mutter as he walks away.

Is it that important what color my hair is? Oh, curse all men and their fascination with golden hair! I have no time for that now. There's a mine to explore. I can't think of another time I might get a chance like this, and I must act quickly before my presence is questioned again.

I take a real step toward the tunnel. Another man with a barrel passes me. He looks confused but doesn't say anything. Once I am fully inside, the light changes dramatically. There is moonstone stuck in places along the walls of the tunnel, casting a faint white glow all around me. I run my fingers along the packed dirt beside me, but only enough to soil the tips.

The tunnel runs fairly straight for quite a few feet, then angles down steeply. I slow my pace to keep from stumbling. Another man passes, and I give a slight nod with my head as he does, as if walking through mining tunnels is not a rare occurrence for me. I imagine I am my father. What did he think of the tunnels? Did he stop and stare when he saw something of interest sticking from the wall, as I do? Did he appreciate the smell of earth and the cold, damp air?

My fingers pass over a moonstone, and my touch causes the light to grow stronger for a moment. That's curious. I've never seen a moonstone do that before.

There is a fork in the tunnel ahead of me. For a small moment, I wonder which path might help me find Bastien, but I don't truly want to find him. Not yet. I look to the left. This path looks straight and well lit. The other angles down even farther into the mountain, and I can only see a short way before it turns sharply.

I take a step to the right, leaning forward a bit so as not to bump my head. I'm forced to crouch even more after just a few steps, and my foot becomes snarled in my skirts for a moment. I clutch them in both hands and hold them high, which makes them feel even wider and more cumbersome. The moonstones are not as close together here, and it is harder to see in front of me.

My heart beats faster, and my hands feel moist. The walls are so close together here. Will I be able to turn around in this dress when I reach the end of the tunnel? Can I even turn around now?

Blast all mantua hoops, and blast all petticoats, and blast all sisters who finally decide to be nice for once by making their younger sisters look pretty!

I consider sitting on the floor of the tunnel to rest, but then I think of the laugh it would be to try to stand again. Maybe I should simply back up? As I stand here, leaning against the wall, my face to the cold rock, I can feel faint vibrations. I turn to press my ear to the rock, and I hear light tapping deeper in the tunnel.

Angling myself and pressing on the sides of my skirts, I push forward. The tapping gets louder as I go, and thankfully, the tunnel stretches taller and wider as well.

The taps sound more like thumps now, clanging on the dirt and rocks. It must be the miners! Perhaps I will find Bastien, after all, and after I make my apologies to satisfy Mother, he can hopefully show me a better way out of the mountain. I understand now why Papa never let me inside the mining tunnels. It is far too easy to get stuck in here.

I follow the tunnel toward the sounds of the picks and shovels. Rounding a corner, I enter a cavern filled with dust floating to the ceiling, moonstone scattered and glowing in the walls, and five or six goblins striking the stones with heavy pickaxes.

Goblins! I have never seen so many goblins at once before, nor have I ever seen them so close. The bodies I have previously associated with lumpy shadows along night-time streets are thinner and stronger than I imagined them to be. They are as tall as any man, and their skin is a dark, splotchy green. Their heads are misshapen with large, pointed ears. They are dressed in old, dirty clothes and have chains connected to their ankles that clank against the stone floor as they work.

I duck quickly back around the corner and flatten myself against the wall. I don't think any of them saw me.

After a few moments of calming myself, my breathing is more under control, and I can hear clearly enough to distinguish voices amidst the noise. I am surprised to find I can understand their words. They still speak our language!

"Ow! Watch it!" one yells. Its voice sounds rough and scratchy, almost like the time some sand became trapped in the gear wheel thing of one of Kade's inventions.

"Yer in my way, not the other way around," another

responds. "You move it!"

Their voices make my mind itch, but I grin, despite the discomfort. To be this close to goblins, to actually see and hear them in the Underground is probably—no, absolutely—the most amazing thing that has ever happened to me. I can't wait to get home and tell Kade!

There is a whistling *thwoosh!* and a *snap!* then a wail unlike anything I've ever heard before. The sharp sound makes it feel as if my head is being torn apart. I bite my lip to keep from calling out.

Another voice—a clearer voice—shouts above the cries. "When I tell you to get to work, that's exactly what I mean! I don't want to hear any arguing or moping or crying!"

The *thwooshing* noise gives a strange rhythm to the chorus. *Thwoosh, snap, thwoosh, snap!* There is so much wailing in their unnatural, grating voices, I must press my hands to my ears to keep my head from exploding. All pleasure from discovering goblins is gone. What, in the name of Spring, is going on in there? What could be hurting them so to cause such agonizing screams? I wish they'd just be quiet, so my head will stop pounding.

Thwoosh, snap! More wails.

My cheeks are hot with tears, and my legs fail me. Is that a human? Beating them? Whipping them? The screams and wails are more than I can take, but I cannot move to save myself. I find myself rocking on the stone floor, shaking my head to escape the pain from their cries.

"That's enough!" the man yells. "Quit your belly achin' and get back to work. The king is visiting' today, and I want him to see some progress. Work has been slower than ever, and with your lousy lot crumbling the Wall every night, we got a lot of catchin' up to do." The crying—on my face and on the other side of the wall— is settling down now, and I wipe my cheeks. "I think we should round up every single one of you goblins and make you put back together all you've broke. You're lucky King Gervais is a more forgiving man than I am. Why, if I was king I'd—"

"You just try catchin' all o' us," a gravelly voice warns. "These tunnels is ours. You might have some of us, but—"

Snap!

No howl follows the noise, only some gurgling grunts that make my skin crawl. Then, a loud thump on the ground.

Oh, heaven help me—he's killed him!

I look left, then right. Is there anywhere I can go? I cannot let this man find me. How do I get out of here? Curse my stupidity! Why did I come here in the first place? Papa was right. He was always right. I'll die down here. I'll never get out. My body will lie forever with that dead goblin, and no one will find it for a million years, and Mother won't even miss me, and Kade will marry some imbecile like Brielle, and I will never, ever see him again!

Stop. I've got to stop. This is ridiculous.

The king is coming. He knows me. He was my father's best friend. For goodness sake, he's *my* best friend's father! He won't let that man hurt me. I'm not going to die. I'll make it home just fine, and everything will be all right.

"Now get back to work!" the man shouts.

The thumping and scratching begins again, and I relax against the wall. The goblins are no longer talking. The man must still be here, keeping watch over them. My head reels, still recovering from those horrible screams, and now I am plagued with questions, which makes my mind spin all the more.

What are goblins doing in the mines? Their punishment for starting the Shard War was their banishment beneath the earth, but were they also made to work as well? Are they our slaves?

Did my father know? Did he see how they are treated? Beaten and killed when they defy their guards? Papa never would have allowed such treatment.

Does the king know? He must! He's coming right now.

The clatter from the pickaxes and shovels picks up.

"Welcome, Your Majesty," the cruel guard says.

I stand. I wish I could see what the king sees right now. I wish I could see his face.

"Not again, Dandre." King Gervais says. "Really, this is getting out of hand. Clean it up, then. Clean up your mess." I can only assume he is talking about the dead goblin.

I peek around the corner to see the guard pick up the body and heft it over his shoulder. The king watches him, with Bastien standing right beside, leaning on his cane.

"We can't afford to lose any more."

It always surprises me how much the king looks like Kade—or, how much Kade looks like his father. Minus the large belly, of course, and Kade's hair isn't graying at the temples or disappearing at the top. Everything else, though—the brown eyes, the dark curls covering his head—perfectly Kade. They even share the same name: Kaderic Gervais Tyrrell Marlon the Third, with Kade being the fourth to bear the name.

King Gervais looks around the cavern, ignoring the goblins all around him. He walks around, his eyebrows drawn together as he contemplates the walls and the piles of rough moonstone in the barrels. I duck back as he turns in my direction, but when I peek back again he is looking at Bastien.

"It's a losing battle," he says. "We're completely out

of Sunstone, and we've nearly run the mines dry. We're not any closer to—"

"Hush, Your Majesty." Bastien looks at the goblins, raising his eyebrows at the king. He hobbles closer to the rock wall and leans against it for support.

"What? They can't understand a word I'm saying. They're merely stupid, ignorant beasts." He gives one a soft kick in the backside. "Could you speak to the Sun Queen? We need more Sunstone, or an entirely different solution altogether."

"You know I haven't spoken to Lisette in years." Lisette! That's the same name the Snow Queen used. So, it truly was the Sun Queen on the balcony with us. "Besides, it wouldn't be safe for Brielle."

The Sun Queen helped us during the Shard War. She was our ally when all around us were enemies. She even saved me from the Snow Queen just yesterday. Why would it be dangerous for Brielle if Bastien sought her out?

"And what of the girl? I'm tired of waiting."

Bastien cringes. "We've gone over this, Your Majesty. We need to give her more time. Lisette said—"

"It's been what—sixteen, seventeen years since the Mirror of Hope shattered? We're running out of time, Bastien. If you're wrong, and we find out too late . . . We need to search. We need to see every girl in the

97

kingdom."

"Yes, Your Majesty, but you have to realize—"

"Realize what? What is there to realize? Don't even try to tell me what to think, Overseer." He says the title as if it's an insult, and Bastien flinches at its use. "We have no season queen for Floraison. We've been effective at blocking the other fairies and their magic out, and we'd be doing even better at it if these hellish goblins," he kicks the goblin again, harder this time, "wouldn't keep sabotaging our work. If we could just—finally—succeed at one *blackdamped thing* before the Wall loses its power, we'll win this thing for sure."

"It's not a war, Your Majesty."

"Of course, it is. Everything's a war."

I pull back behind the corner wall, holding my skirts still so the man can't hear the fabric rustle. They are looking for the promised Rain Queen; that comes as no surprise. Our entire kingdom has been looking for her all these years, just as the Snow Queen was searching for her sixteen years ago. But do they know who she might be? Are they waiting for one specific girl to show her magical powers, or are they just hoping that whoever she is will make herself known?

I can't go to them now. I know that nothing they said is exactly secret—except for the goblin slaves; my father never told me anything about that—but even so, it doesn't seem fitting to interrupt them now. I should have said something sooner.

I just need to leave as fast and as quietly as possible before they are aware of my presence. And hopefully once I am out of these tunnels, the ear-shattering shrieks that echo in my mind will finally die.

Chapter 11

I'm still puzzling at the king's words the next morning while Lacey and I are taking a stroll in the gardens. I can't puzzle out loud, of course, because then I would have to suffer through Lacey's criticisms for my disobedience of going into the mines. I have already been reprimanded by Mother for not finding and apologizing to Bastien. I didn't tell her I went searching for him in the mountain, only to find him amidst a pack of enslaved goblins. I didn't tell her I listened to a murder take place or that I heard the king talk about the Sun Queen and—strangely enough—Brielle. I didn't tell her I was too shaken and confused to make an appearance before the king and my stepfather, and instead spent a lengthy part of my day searching for the way out of the tunnels, only to find myself—as curious as it sounds—emerging from a goblin hole in one of the palace guest rooms.

I *did* tell her I'd had a difficult time finding Bastien, which was true enough, and I didn't want to wait around all day for him. Maybe I wouldn't have received such a scolding if I would have told her the truth? She wants so badly for our new family circumstances to succeed.

"Must you huff so, Lottie?" Lacey asks, giving me the squinty eye. She loves to give the squinty eye, but only around me. "Maybe if you took smaller steps, you could also take smaller breaths," she says. "You sound like a horse at full gallop!"

I think of the way Brielle walks, with those tiny, floating steps. I slow, looking down at the wet path beneath my feet, trying to match my pace with Lacey's. She is also quite out of breath from trying to keep up with me.

"You've never heard a horse at full gallop, dear sister," I say.

"Of course, I have. The coachman sometimes rushes the horses when I've been too long on Market Street and I'm afraid of being late for supper."

"So, you've heard the horses breathing that heavily from your cushy seat in the carriage?"

"Oh, what do you know?" She pushes my arm, knocking me slightly off balance. "You're the one who's terrified of horses. It's a wonder you even ride in a coach at all. You can't possibly know what I'm talking about."

I don't. I admit to myself that I don't like—and might possibly be afraid of—horses, but I certainly don't have to admit it to her.

We are nearing the edge of the garden, and she takes my arm as if we are the best of friends, even though I've already heard numerous times over the last ten minutes how she would really rather be with anyone other than me this morning, but there were no other invitations for her to take advantage of.

"Oh, look!" she shouts, waving frantically with her other arm. "It's Kade!"

I scan the side of the mountain where we usually wander, searching for his tall form among the rocks and trees. I use my free hand to shade my eyes from the sun. Perhaps Mother is correct in her high opinion of bergére hats.

"Not there, stupid! Over there! On the road."

I look in the other direction and see him atop a large brown and white horse. Lacey's arm lowers as her attention turns to another horse and rider coming around the bend in the road.

"He's with Brielle," we say together.

I don't want to, but I wave. After all, family circumstances succeeding and whatnot.

They are upon us far too quickly, it seems.

"Good morning, ladies!" Kade calls from above us. He looks happy and refreshed. Both Lacey and I curtsy and lower our heads for a moment. I catch our movements and wonder at it. I can't think of any time outside of a royal function when we have ever curtsied to Kade. Our Kade!

We nod to Brielle as well and wish her a pleasant morning.

"Prince Kaderic was just taking me for a ride about the kingdom." Her cheeks are flushed, and her smile is radiant. Must she always be so? "I've spent such little time in Floraison. I'm not familiar with the provinces surrounding the palace. They're perfectly quaint and charming, aren't they, Kaderic?"

Charming! Quaint! *Kaderic!*

"I admit I haven't thought about it much, but I suppose you could call them charming," Kade says.

Lacey and I smile. There is no other choice.

Brielle seems to be fighting the urge to give us her version of Lacey's squinty eye.

I feel absolutely stuck.

I want to ask Brielle why she might fear harm from the Sun Queen, what she might possibly have to do with goblins and season queens and prophesies. Why would the king and Bastien bring her up in the mines? She is a nobody from Lunain whose father just happens to have connections in high places. Very high places, it seems.

I want to shout at her to leave my family alone and go back to where she came from. I don't trust her, but I have no real reason other than hearing her name whispered in connection with the season queens in a questionable meeting underneath the mountain.

I have no real reason, so all I can do is smile and pretend as if there are no doubts or suspicions racing through my mind.

Kade jumps from his horse. I wish I knew the beast's name. Of course, I knew Kade could ride, but I never thought he did it for fun. With my silly fear, we've never gone riding together, and I've never quite paid attention to his riding habits. But I am terribly interested in them now.

Brielle watches Kade, and it looks as if she is itching to dismount, but Kade is too interested in an almost-broken buckle on his saddle to notice she might need some assistance. He is most likely dismantling the pieces in his mind to see if he can improve on the design.

"You must have been up very early to be returning at this hour," Lacey says. She is watching Brielle as intensely as Brielle is watching Kade, and Kade the metal buckle.

"Not at all," Kade says. "We haven't been gone all that long. I would have invited the both of you, but I know neither of you are fond of riding." He looks up and notices Brielle squirming in her saddle, then goes to offer his help. Brielle winces as he sets her on the ground, but then gives him a dazzling smile.

"It's no bother," I say. "We are not your keepers." I step to Kade's splotchy brown beast and raise a hand to pet its long nose.

It snorts at me and I nearly stumble out of my wooden patents from jumping back so quickly. Luckily, Kade is still close enough to steady me. My cheeks burn with embarrassment.

"It's okay, Char," he whispers. "Maesy scares the devil out of me, too."

"He does not." I pull away, laughing nervously. I'm standing too close to the horse.

"Oh, Charlotte, you're such a baby!" Lacey takes my place petting the horse's nose. She smiles up at Kade. Yes, Lacey, we all know you're not afraid of the blasted horse.

Brielle has joined them, and once again, I find myself on the outside. If only Maesy wasn't so big and stompy. Summoning all my courage, I take a small step forward. Kade must have heard, because he turns and motions for me to come closer. He takes my trembling hand and lifts it to the horse's nose.

"It's safe, really." He places his other hand on my waist, pulling me closer to both him and the horse.

"Such a beautiful animal!" Lacey looks toward Kade with big, pleading eyes. "Do you think he's too tired to go out for another ride? I would so love to see our kingdom from a new vantage point."

"I'm sure *she'd* be fine," Kade says, "but I promised my mother I would help her this morning. I should be on my way soon."

Lacey gives the horse a quick squinty eye, but by the time she turns her face to look back at Kade, the glare is gone, and her expression reflects only sadness. She's lucky I'm the only one who caught a view of the annoyed look.

"That's too bad. It feels like it's been so long since we've been able to spend any real time together, Kaderic." She places a hand on his arm.

I think of the other morning when she and Brielle spent hours in Kade's workshop and when Kade came to listen to our music. Who knows what the three of them might have done together while I was stuck in the mines yesterday, trying to apologize to Bastien? They could have had a full-fledged masquerade, and I wouldn't know anything about it. No, actually, I'm sure Lacey could never stay silent about a ball. Usually she talks nonstop about them for weeks before they occur and for many days after.

"I have an idea!" Lacey says. "Why don't we have a picnic this afternoon? When you're done helping your mother. Now, don't say no. You've already turned me down once today, Kaderic. You must come. I insist."

The horse snorts again, and Lacey jumps back just as I had, but no one makes a joke of her. Brielle takes the opportunity to inch closer to Kade. They're both ridiculous!

"That's a wonderful idea! Prince Kaderic, you can bring along some of your creations for us to see. I would love to witness more of them in action." Now both Brielle and Lacey are looking at him with big, pleading eyes and I can't help but roll mine.

"I'm afraid of another invention screw-up happening, but a jaunt in the wild sounds wonderful."

Brielle gives a laugh, and there is a merry twinkle in her eye. "But Charlotte, you must promise not to push the prince down any more mountains. We can't afford to lose him from such silly clumsiness. He is much too important to the kingdom." Then she laughs again, as if her teasing is the funniest thing since the snow stopped falling, as if Kade's welfare were truly her concern.

No one is going to hurt Kade—least of all me. It seems to me as if the only one wrongfully pursuing our prince is Brielle, and I don't like it one bit.

Chapter 12

Lacey is a blur as she rushes back and forth between my room and hers. She's trying to find the most suitable picnic dress, and I believe she's going after my wardrobe to lessen the chances of dirtying her own. Yes, this whole escapade was her idea, but Lacey and dirt don't mix well.

Brielle rests by the window in the salon, embroidering.

I'm tired of watching the two of them—the calm and the storm—so I leave our apartments and head in the direction of Kade's workshop. It feels so crowded every time we're all together. It would be so nice to have a few moments to be just the two of us, like it used to be. Or perhaps, if he is not there, I can have a few peaceful minutes to myself.

I knock on the open doorway. Kade sits bent over

a table, studying a contraption of some sort, but he looks up quickly when he hears me enter. Accumulations of half-finished projects, blocks of wood, and lumps of stone clutter the table around him. I can barely see his current project through the mess.

"Is it still as bad as you thought it would be?" he asks, looking back to his work. I know what he means. Bastien. Brielle. Combining our two tiny families.

"I'm not sure yet. I suppose she's not so horrid." I lean on the table, across from him. "You seem to enjoy her company," I tease.

"My father asked me to look out for her. She's a nice girl. I think if you and Lacey gave her more of a chance, you'd find you might like her."

"Oh, I doubt Lacey would. She's almost beside herself with jealousy." I move around the table, peering over his shoulder at the lump of wood he scrapes with the whittling knife. He smells of pine soap and saw dust. "She thinks she loves you. Did you know that?"

He pushes some gears inside the mechanism, twisting them around until he's happy with the fit.

"I've had my guesses, but it's not love. It'll pass."

"She's pinned her hair in eight different styles since we've seen you this morning. She's even resorted to trying on *my* dresses."

A simple "hmm," escapes his lips as he reaches for a power cube that's sitting on the table. One of the tiles in the cube has bits of blue inside, and I reach over to take it from him.

"What is this?" I ask. I've never seen this stone before.

He doesn't mind I've taken the cube from him, but I realize, too late, that I should have asked instead of grabbing. The stone is rough, like it was carved and laid into the tile in a rush, but the sparkling blue looks beautiful against the deep coral rose of the sunstone.

"It's ice quartz. Father gave it to me last night. It's from up North, toward Neimonte. Apparently, there's tons of it up there. Though we don't know what power it has yet."

"Do you have any more? I think if we could chunk it up a bit, then lay it in smooth with another stone, like a mosaic . . ." I set the cube down on the table, then go to where he is pointing to another table across the room, and I find a pile of the ice quartz. The pieces range from being about the size of the width of my finger to a little smaller than my fist. A blue dust covers the wood around the rocks, most likely from when Kade broke some of the pieces already. How late was he up working last night? He just barely received the new stones, and he already has a working tile to test.

There are tools sitting nearby—a small hammer, a crandall, and various chisels. This table is much cleaner than where he is working today, and I don't want to be in his way with the mess I will be making, so I take a seat and get to work.

"You've got that one in a sunstone tile?" I ask, surveying the table for unused tiles. He is too engrossed in his work to answer, and I ignore his silence, because I see a tile of moonstone on one of the counters against the wall. I grab a hunk of sunstone as well and break it in half with the hammer as soon as I'm back at the table. I can feel a surge of heat radiating from the stone as it breaks.

Whacking at the sunstone, I try to get as many tiny pieces as I can without grinding them to dust. The ice quartz comes next, and it is so beautiful I feel guilty for breaking it apart. As soon as I have the right size and number of pieces to work with, I take the moonstone tile and start chiseling a design from the face of it. Swooping lines take shape on the glowing rock, and I dig a little deeper into the stone.

The design becomes clearer, in both my mind and on the tile. The whole process has a soothing effect on me, and I find I am happier than I've been in weeks. It feels like all those times Kade and I sat with my father while he taught us about the stones and what we could do with them.

Kade places a hand on the table beside me, leaning close to watch me work. "I'll never be as good at that as you are." He reaches around me with his other hand to trace his fingers along the lines, clearing the dust away. I turn my head to look at his face, so close to mine, and my stomach does a little dance.

"And I'll never be able to understand those cogs and gears you play with all the time." I look down again, my cheeks suddenly hot.

I blow the rest of the moonstone dust off the tile, and the carved design glows up at me. I want to start placing the sunstone and ice quartz, but we should get going. I'm surprised Lacey hasn't hunted us down and demanded we take her on her picnic yet. The fact she hasn't come looking for us must mean she's still deciding what to wear.

I lean into him, feeling his warmth behind me. Slow down, heart. It's only Kade. I scoot from the bench, needing room to breathe properly, and the only place for me to stand without looking more awkward than I already am, is right in front of Kade.

He gives me a small smile and leans on the table with one hand. "I don't love Lacey, you know."

His comment catches me completely off guard.

"What?"

"Even though you believe it, and she might even believe it, she's not in love with me, either."

"But haven't you seen the way she looks at you lately?"

"Oh, I've seen it. I would have to be blind not to

notice." He chuckles, then clears his throat. "I've been hoping, actually, that—"

"There you two are! Mother says it's finally time to leave."

I spin around to see Lacey at the door, giving me the squinty eye. I glance back to check if Kade has seen it, and I know all her chances—if she ever even had any—at winning his heart are completely over. And truly, I can't say that it makes me sad.

Chapter 13

"Isn't this heavenly?" Lacey sighs. "Nothing to do, no commitments to attend to. It's simply marvelous." We are all sprawled out on blankets, eating bits of meat and cheese as we please, but mostly we are just resting, enjoying the magical feeling of the day. The sunshine warms my skin while a gentle breeze tousles my hair, which came unpinned while we were exploring the edge of the forest. Mother softly hums the Rose Hymn to herself. Kade is asleep on the other side of our blanket, one arm covering his eyes from the sun. Brielle has gathered some flowers and is tying them into a chain.

"What commitments do you ever have?" I tease. "I don't believe attending parties and social teas are valid reasons to give you stress."

"Maybe if you were to come to them yourself

sometime, you would understand just how important it is to be respectable in society and how much pressure that puts on a body, Charlotte." She says my name with venom in her voice.

"Ladies, that's enough." Mother laughs. "This reminds me exactly of when you were children." She sighs. "I miss days like this. Remember all those picnics we used to take in the mountains? We should make time to visit the château soon."

But then we'd have to bring Brielle along with us. I'd prefer to keep those happy memories to myself.

"Too bad your father couldn't join us, Brielle," Mother continues. "The king has him working so hard. That strange ice has almost melted, and it's so important to maintain the structure of the Wall. If only those wretched goblins would simply leave it alone. Don't they see it is a benefit to us all? Them as well as us? What would they think if the Snow Queen waltzed back in and—" She stops, composing herself. "They wouldn't like it, either, I'm sure. That's all I have to say."

Mother looks around, and she seems more troubled than I feel she should be. I think back to how happy she was a moment ago and try to calm her.

"Will you tell us a story, Mother? Of the times when there were still seasons?"

Lacey sits up excitedly.

"Yes, please! Tell us about the Shard War. I was too little to remember any of it. What about you, Brielle? Do you remember?"

My stepsister shakes her head, not even looking up from her flowers. "I was born during the Shard War. I was just a baby for the whole thing."

Like me.

"Oh, Mother, you must tell us, then. You haven't told us stories in *ages*, and this is just the perfect time for it. Charlotte, you must convince her. Please, Mother?"

Lacey's exclamations have woken Kade, and he sits up, rubbing his eyes.

Mother laughs, relaxing again. "I don't need any convincing to tell stories to my little girls—and of course, you too, Your Highness—but if we're to do this properly, we must begin at the very start. This story begins long before the Shard War."

I know what is coming. I love this story.

I move to sit next to Mother and lay my head in her lap. She stokes my hair, and I do feel like a little girl again.

"Long ago there were four beautiful fairies who presided over the lands and seasons as queens. These fairies were not necessarily the best of friends, but they worked together to ensure that all was right in the world. They had power over the elements, and for many centuries, they protected and nurtured the people and the earth together.

"Each year, just as the blossoms were beginning to peek through the snow, all four queens would come together in the tower from which they sprang forth, to gaze in the mirrors that gave them power. Each fairy queen had a mirror that matched the beauty of her season.

"The Fairy of Spring, the Rain Queen, looked to the Mirror of Hope, which showed all the great moments that lay ahead.

"The Fairy of Summer, the Sun Queen, looked to the Mirror of Gladness, which reminded her to live in the moment and enjoy life's blessings.

"The Fairy of Autumn, the Moon Queen, looked to the Mirror of Truth, which reflected all the joys and the sorrows that had come. For it is only after the follies of youth that we begin to see things the way they truly are."

The words flow through my mind, and I think back to a time before all our sadness—when Papa was here, and I was too naïve to think anything bad could ever happen to our family. I look to Lacey and see that she is mouthing the words right along with Mother. She remembers this story, too, and even though it has always been *just a story* to her, she loves it just as much as I do.

"The Fairy of Winter—the Queen of Snow—was a cold and untrusting woman, and she looked to the Mirror of Understanding. But instead of searching the depths of the mirror for goodness and love, she chose to see only the worst in people, and she never saw just how wonderful the world could be. It was quite unfortunate she received the Mirror of Understanding, because of all the fairies, she understood the least of all."

I think of the Snow Queen, of that cunning look in her eyes, cold and calculating. I shiver, remembering her touch.

Mother continues.

"The mirrors were powerful on their own, but their greatest power came when all four fairies stood in the center of the mirror circle, holding hands and learning from the mirrors what the world needed most and what they could do to help all mankind.

"It was one such time—with each fairy queen looking to her mirror—that a face appeared to each of them. They had never seen the face of this old man in their mirrors before, and he spoke as if he were four separate voices. The queens were all frightened—not only of the strange messenger, but also of the prophesy he declared."

I sit up, so I can watch Mother's face as she tells the story. When I was a child, the prophecy would always send chills down my back and make my whole body shiver.

"There would come a time, he said, when the fairy queens would no longer work in harmony with each other. A rift would come between them, and they would be forced to travel down separate paths. He gave no specific details of what would become of each of them, but only gave these words of warning:

"One will steal.

"One will cry.

"One will change.

"One will die."

Mother pauses here, just like she always does, to let it all sink in. Kade slowly tears blades of grass apart, making a tidy little pile next to the blanket. Brielle has dropped her braided flowers and listens, attentively, to Mother's words.

"This cannot be!" Lacey and I shout together, remembering the words that always come next.

"Of course," Mother says. "Patience, ladies. The queens all cried out, 'This cannot be!' and their lamentations were so great they didn't hear all the old man had to say. The Snow Queen, however, leaned in closer to the Mirror of Understanding and heard him tell of a babe that would be born at the shattering of glass, who would someday rise up and make things right again. The queens were so burdened with the news of their fates that they left the tower with heavy hearts, uncertain of their future for the first time.

"Time passed, and the fairy queens all kept to themselves, letting the seasons come and go as they always had, until one day the Snow Queen became greedy. She didn't trust the other fairies and thought they were slacking in their duties to the world. She wanted to take all the mirrors for herself and thought if she could move the mirrors to her grand palace of ice in the north mountains, then she could balance the seasons on her own. None of the fairies had ever thought to move the mirrors before, and she was afraid it would not be possible. She started with the Mirror of Understanding. If she could move her own mirror safely, then she would come back, one at a time, for the others.

"Sure enough, the Mirror of Understanding was cooperative under her touch. It was her mirror, after all. She tucked it away in her sleigh, then flew through the air to her home in the snow. But when she returned for the Mirror of Hope, the spring fairy was waiting for her.

" 'You cannot take my mirror,' the Rain Queen said. 'You're disrupting the seasons already. The Mirror of Understanding is gone. I can feel the magic leaving this tower. You stole it.'

" 'I stole nothing,' the Snow Queen retorted

sharply. 'It is mine, after all.' "

Mother has always done such a wonderful job of making the Snow Queen's voice as nasty as we all imagine it to be, and she does not disappoint us this afternoon. But even she cannot match the cold feelings that creep over you when the Snow Queen truly speaks to you.

" 'And the others?' the Rain Queen asked.

" 'They will be mine soon, as well.'

"It was then that the other two fairies came to the tower—the Moon Queen and the Sun Queen. They feared the changes they felt within themselves when the Mirror of Understanding was removed, and they wanted to stop the Snow Queen from taking the rest of the mirrors, too. They even hoped to convince her to replace her mirror as well.

"The Sun Queen had tears raining down her cheeks, for the time was high summer and she felt the pain of the change the strongest.

"There was a terrible fight between the four fairies, and it was in the midst of it all that they realized they were already fulfilling the old man's prophecy. One will steal. One will cry. They were frightened of what was to come—one will change, one will die—so they left the tower and the three remaining mirrors and vowed to never return again, for fear they would complete the prophecy, killing one of them."

"Many, many years passed before they encountered each other again," I say, continuing the story.

Mother laughs, looking up to the sky with her hand resting gently on my head. It has been so long since I've heard my mother laugh like that, and I think it is the most beautiful sound I've ever heard.

"Oh, that's another story entirely, Lottie, and I've been talking long enough as it is."

"This is when the goblins come in, isn't it Mother?" Lacey asks. "I used to be so scared of the Goblin Queen. I've heard that goblin feet are most sensitive, that they are more fragile than human feet. Is this true?"

Brielle startles at this, and I remember her fear of goblins.

"Just silly stories, dear," Mother says. "But it is no story that goblins exist, so we should definitely start back to the palace now. We don't want to get caught on the road after dark."

Chapter 14

Everything is soft and warm and deliciously cozy. I pull the blanket tighter around me, then relax under the silky weight of it. I don't want to wake up. I have nothing scheduled for this morning. I do realize, though, that if I stay too long in bed, Mother will come to lecture me about using my time wisely to perfect myself and serve others and make friends and all those high and mighty expectations. Only a few more minutes, that's all I need. Then I'll get out of bed. I won't even come close to wasting the morning.

I hear movement in the hallway. Gentle footsteps padding past my door. It must be the servants up to prepare our quarters for the morning.

I roll over on my back and look up through the darkness at the ceiling.

Wait.

Why is it still so dark? What are the servants doing awake at this hour? What, in all the seasons, am *I* doing awake at this hour?

Now that my eyes are open, I cannot close them. I am absolutely stuck awake. I roll over again, curling into a ball. Not any better. It's been only a few seconds since I opened my eyes, and I already miss the warm haze of sleepiness.

Perhaps a warm glass of milk would help? I consider ringing one of the servants, but that might wake everyone. I could ask whichever servant went down the hall just now. Surely, they won't mind.

I sit up, swinging my legs off the bed. The marble floor is cold under my feet. Where are my slippers? I stumble in the dark for a bit, searching the floor. I don't see or feel my slippers, but I do find a shawl discarded near the window. I wrap it around my shoulders and condemn my feet to the chill.

I try to open the door quietly, so as not to wake the others, and once I am in the hallway I wonder which way the servant was headed. The kitchens? The parlor? I look in the direction of the parlor and see the glow of firelight emanating through the open doorway. I must not be the only one having a difficult time sleeping. The floor isn't as cold here, and I find myself loosening my grip on my shawl.

I creep as silently as possible down the hallway. A

voice speaks quietly over the crackling of the fire. I recognize it as Brielle's, but to whom is she speaking? Can no one sleep properly tonight? I peer around the doorway and see her, huddled in front of the massive fireplace. Her golden hair falls over the dark blanket wrapped around her. She whispers into the fire, but I can't quite hear what she is saying, except the word, "mother," said with such reverence and love. But then concern shows in her voice, and she speaks a little louder.

"Please, Mother, come to me. I feel so alone. I need your guidance. You haven't come to me since we moved here, and I miss you."

What is she talking about? Her mother—her stepmother and my real mother—lives right here. Brielle's mother died when Brielle was just a baby. Who could she possibly be talking to, and why is she speaking into the fire? Is she insane? Wouldn't that be wonderful! Locking her away somewhere under the diagnosis of insanity would solve so many of my problems!

The firelight flickers and dies for a moment. Brielle bends over farther, leaning into the fireplace, blowing gently at the coals. With a *whoosh*, the fire starts up again, even brighter than before. Brielle shoots back up and claps her hands.

"Mother!"

A face appears in the flames—the beautiful face of

a woman. But how—? The only possible answer I come to is magic, because it's obviously not a normal, everyday occurrence for people to communicate with each other through fireplaces.

But magic was banished from the kingdom when the Wall was built. That's what my father discovered when I was a baby. Combining sunstones and moonstones together in one giant circle created a barrier that forced magic to stay out of our walls, but now I see it right before my eyes. True magic in our kingdom. In the palace of the king, no less! I think back to the Wall, being torn apart by the goblins each night, and the fact that our men haven't been able to repair it as fast as the goblins can pull it apart. Perhaps Brielle was right when she said the Wall was broken when she arrived a couple weeks ago.

"What is it, child?" the woman asks. "Are you having such a difficult time already?"

"Oh, yes! It's just dreadful here. The prince is the only one I can tolerate for longer than a moment. And the goblins! I am so frightened. Please, let me come stay with you. I know Father needs to stay, but—I just . . . please!" She sniffs.

Why is she crying? It can't be all that bad here. Goodness knows I've tried to make her feel welcome. My mother seems to love her more than she loves me and Lacey combined. She's not allowed to cry! Of all the ridiculous things I've ever seen . . .

"You must be patient, little one. I have so much in store for you."

I wish I could see the woman's face more clearly. Who is this mysterious woman Brielle calls her mother? What was she doing in our fireplace? What is she doing *existing at all* when Bastien is married to my mother?

"But—"

"Hush, child. Do not worry, and go back to bed. Remember: be patient. It is only patience and perseverance that will bring us true rewards. I have been patient all these years, and now I get to see and talk with you. Now go get some rest. I love you."

"I love you, too," Brielle murmurs as the flames die down again. She seems to sink with them, for a moment, then stand, and turns around. I duck back behind the wall.

I don't believe I've ever moved so swiftly down the hallway as I do trying to get back to my bedroom before she can see me. My heart pounds as I catch my breath, leaning against my shut door. Did she see me? Did she hear me? Does she know I saw and heard her?

I listen, but there is no movement in the hallway. Either she has already gone back to her room, or she is on the other side of the door, waiting for me to make a noise so she can catch me awake. My muscles hurt from standing so still, but I won't give her the satisfaction of being the one to catch me. I caught her, after all, and now I might have everything I need to have her and her father sent away.

A magical mother of her own.

If Brielle has a mother—*a living mother!*—how could Bastien have married my mother? He already has a wife. But how can I possibly tell my Mother her new marriage is a sham?

Chapter 15

I spend the entire time getting dressed the next morning debating what to do. I should tell her. I definitely should *not* tell her. I am so nervous that the maid has to remind me, multiple times, to hold still before she successfully hooks my stomacher to my robes.

But Mother is a strong woman. She's lost one husband already, and this one—Bastien—cannot truly be her husband at all. She will most likely have a good laugh about it, then kick him out the door with Brielle right along with him. Yes, that's exactly what will happen. It will be so easy. Could it possibly be that easy?

There is no way it can be that easy.

But I have to try. No matter what happens, surely Mother is entitled to know.

As simple and straightforward as my plan is, I still wait until after Mother has happily eaten her breakfast to approach her. No use taking chances. I find her sitting at her personal desk, studiously copying numbers from various papers into the household ledger. Perhaps I just never noticed the silver hairs wound together with the brown, but she seems to have aged so much during the past months. She is still lovely, though. It is not mere luck Bastien was so agreeable to the marriage. Surely, she'll be able to find someone even better once Bastien is gone.

"Mother, I have something very important to tell you."

She looks up with a quizzical expression, but she seems mostly happy to see me. I don't quite know how to begin.

"Do you—?" I start.

No, that won't work.

She sets her quill down, giving me her full attention. I try again.

"How long have you known Bastien? Do you . . . trust him?"

Mother gives me a gentle smile, but I can see the uncertainty in her eyes, wondering where my questions are leading.

"Of course, I trust him. I would never marry a man in whom I didn't have absolute trust."

My thoughts jump to the time before the wedding, when she left so suddenly to visit Lunain. The king had just announced that Bastien would be the replacement for my father—a man from a different kingdom, even. If she hadn't acted so quickly, he might have been snatched up by someone else, and we would have lost our home at the palace and our place in society. But did their short engagement give her enough time to truly judge his character? His past?

"You barely know anything about him," I say. "Where he grew up, where his true loyalties lie, who he's already married to . . ."

That did not come out as well as I hoped it would.

"Charlotte, what a strange thing to say. What are you talking about?"

I cannot hold back any longer, and all the words start tumbling out, way too fast.

"I was awoken last night, and Brielle was in the parlor. Mother, she was talking to a woman's," I gesture in front of me, wondering how to say it, "*head* in the fireplace and she was saying that the woman was her mother, and Brielle wishes she could live with her, instead of us. I don't know how she was there—in the fireplace—but do you see what this means? If Brielle has a mother of her own, then Bastien already has a wife! You're not really married! I mean, how could you be if Bastien is already married to another woman? He and Brielle don't belong here. They can go live with her, just as Brielle wants, and we can be a family again . . ."

I trail off when I see her expression darken. She must not understand.

"Mother, you're not really married to him. He's not your husband, which means he's not my stepfather, and he and Brielle can go back home to Lunain."

She stands, the ledger held tight in both hands.

"Really, Charlotte, you are seventeen years old—old enough to know better. Are you really . . ."

"No, I—"

"Don't you realize these are real people you're talking about? Bastien. Brielle. Me! You have no idea what has transpired before your time. You come in here, spouting complete foolishness so that *your* life will no longer be inconvenienced? You must not meddle in things you so obviously do not understand."

I shake my head, feeling as though my stomach is heavy as stone. *I* don't understand? She didn't see Brielle using magic to speak with a woman in the fire last night! She is the one who doesn't understand.

"It's not foolishness!" I fear my emotions have been too eager to show themselves lately, and I can't help their escape now. "I saw it last night. Check the fireplace; I'm sure it's full of ashes. The fire was huge! I'm not lying!"

"I'm done, Charlotte."

"Please, Mother! You have to understand!"

"What I understand is that *you* don't like them. You never gave them a chance. I understand you're hurting right now and you're unhappy, but do you know? We're all hurting. I am doing the best I can for this family and this kingdom, and you have been trying to sabotage everything from the moment they stepped foot in this palace. I've told you this before, Charlotte, but you don't seem to understand how desperate our situation was. If I hadn't married Bastien, you wouldn't even be allowed to live here. Have you even tried to figure that out? We need him just as much as he needs us, and I am not going to let you tell me that I've made a mistake when I, for one, am trying my hardest."

Her words sting. I wait for her to take them back, tears building up in my eyes, but she doesn't. She continues to stand there, holding her blasted book and staring at me with cold eyes.

There is nothing I can say. Why, in all the mines of Lunain, did I think that conversation would go well?

I run.

I need to get out, get away, but everywhere I think to go feels too painful. I will not go to the Wall again. Going outside will only remind me of Papa, anyway. Kade's workshop is out of the question. Even if he were to believe what I had seen last night, he might side with Mother in the end and make me feel like a horrid, uncaring goblin.

"It's not fair," I scream, not caring who can hear me. "Not fair!" What am I to do? Where am I to go? I know now that Mother will never understand what I saw in the fireplace last night unless I have solid proof. I will never be rid of Brielle or her father, and I can never go back to the way life was before they came or before Papa died.

I race through the hallway and leave our suite, and the first thing I see once I enter the main corridor is the tall wooden door that brought me from the pigeon-covered balcony earlier this week.

Without thinking, my hand reaches for the door latch, but it will not move. Whether it's jammed or locked, I don't know, but I squeeze and pull and twist with all my might. It doesn't budge. I slam a fist against the door and yell in a most unladylike manner. I want to kick the door and rip at it and tear it down.

I hit the door again, pounding on it with both fists, screaming over and over again in my mind. *Not fair. Not fair. Absolutely not fair!*

To my surprise, the door slowly opens, pulling itself away from my tantrum.

"Charlotte!" I hear my mother approaching. "Charlotte, what are you doing? This is ridiculous!"

I glare at her, hating her for not believing me.

"Stop it this instant!"

I cannot face her right now. I will not apologize for telling her the truth. I will not back down from trying to send Brielle and Bastien away, no matter how much she wants me to pretend everything is right.

Slipping through the doorway as fast as I can, I shut it just as Mother is upon it. Now she is the one banging on the wood and yelling for it to open. Yelling at me to open it. I lean against the door, feeling the vibrations on my back. Mother yells at a servant to run and get the keys, and I hear her ask, "Where did this blasted door come from, anyway?"

I stare into the darkness in front of me, desperation and determination coursing through my body. I have to get away. I need time and quiet to think this all through, but I am also afraid. If I go up those stairs again, will the Snow Queen be there, waiting for me?

Chapter 16

My eyes begin to adjust, and I can see a little way in front of me. A dark tunnel stretches out before me, leading downward. Where are the stairs? Those stairs I came down before—they should be rising in front of me. Where are they? I think back to my adventure, wondering if *I* am the one—not Brielle—who has gone insane.

Never mind. It doesn't matter. My only other options at this point are staying here, hiding from my mother, or going back through the door to receive further criticism. I push ahead.

Mother is now screaming at the servants to bring her daughter back, but it seems none of them can find a key to fit the lock. If she is not careful, the noise may soon bring even the king to quiet her down.

Stone walls surround me as I move farther,

embedded with some moonstone here and there to light my path. I've lost track of how many times I've turned left or right or have followed the tunnel up or down. All the while I am completely dumbfounded by the fact that this tunnel even exists in the palace. How many more secrets does my home contain that I have been completely unaware of?

The air becomes thick and moist, like it does when a thunderstorm is brewing. The walls of the tunnel are rough under my hands. I can hear the *clink! clink!* of metal on rock coming from farther down. I don't think I've been wandering long enough to be in the mines, but time seems to be warped in these tunnels—with no view of the sun's arc across the sky. How long have I been down here? An hour, maybe two?

I let out a grumpy sigh, then turn to track back the way I came, but stop at the sound of voices.

The sound grates my ears. I've heard these rough voices before, or at least, voices like them.

Goblins.

"Hadn't we get a move on? It's awful late already."

"The moon's barely rising. We've got plenty of time."

What? The moon is rising? How can that be, when I just left my mother a short time ago, and it was still quite early in the day? Surely, I haven't been wandering so long.

"I just need a bit more rest after all that hammerin'. These boxes are heavy, you know."

"Of course, I know! I'll be carrying mine just the same as you. Don't you start pretending like you're the only one who does any work around here. I see you loafin' around."

"Oiy, look!" There is silence for a small moment, then a scattering of shuffling feet. "Aventurine!"

"Give it here! Pick it out. Let's take it to the queen."

"I'll take it to the queen! I found it!" More shuffling. A few grunts and hammering on rock. I hear a *thump* *and* wonder who hit whom.

"Quiet, you two. Quit your bickerin'!" A third voice. "We can all take it to her. We can all get the reward."

They hit at the rock again, most likely trying to dislodge the aventurine. I haven't worked much with aventurine before. It is a green stone, pretty abundant in our area, but without magical properties. I can't think of why the Goblin Queen would offer a reward for it.

"Oiy! Stop steppin' on my foot."

"Get over it."

"They hurt this high up. Can't you feel it? Every step I take is like a needle goin' up my leg."

The hammering continues, but so does the conversation.

"Next thing we know you'll be wearing shoes, right

along with those upstairs." Upstairs? Does he mean humans? Are we the ones upstairs? "All to protect your dainty toes."

Do goblins not normally wear shoes? I've only seen them up close the one time, and I didn't think to check.

"The queen wears shoes, you know. She's more human than us, I guess. Not very fair, if you ask me. It's her fault we went to war in the first place and her fault we—"

"Didja know why the queen wears shoes? Huh?"

Silence, except for the axes hitting the stone.

After a moment, I hear a "Got it!" and some scraping and grunting. They must be picking up their boxes.

"Well, come on, stupids. Haven't you ever wondered before? Me, I know why the queen wears shoes. Seen her feet, myself."

"Nuh-uh! You have not!"

What on earth are they talking about? Their voices are getting quieter, moving away from me. I should turn back—apparently, I've been gone all day—but my curiosity wins. I creep along the wall, suddenly desperate to know the conclusion to this silly conversation about feet and shoes and the Goblin Queen. I've met both the Sun Queen and the Snow Queen. What might the Goblin Queen be like?

"I have so! Just last week, as she was comin' by my

tunnel. Had to take a rest, she did, and I saw her massagin' her feet. Wanna know why she wears shoes?"

"For dirt's sake, just tell us already! You're such a knows-it-all, Podge."

"Fine, fine. I'll tell ya."

I keep moving toward their voices, fearful the goblin will whisper his mysterious information and I won't be able to hear it. Then again, I'm beginning to believe goblins don't ever speak quietly, even when they try.

"She hasn't got the mark," he says. "I didn't even see the faintest sign of it."

The mark? What, in the name of Spring, is he talking about?

I hear a round of *nut-uh's* to which Podge swears he's telling the truth. More thumps, some scuffling, then I hear a louder *thump!* and the sound of stone cascading to the ground. One of them must have dropped his box.

"Owwwww!" The roar is so loud that I cover my ears. "That hurt!"

What is going on?

I peek around the corner, hoping to see what they mean about marks and sore feet and whatnot. Two of the goblins are bent over the pile of stone, trying to load them back into the box. The third is holding a foot with both hands and hopping up and down. The hurt goblin flops to the tunnel floor, gently pressing on the bottom of his foot.

Indeed, a mark sits on the top of his foot, just above his toes. I can't see it very clearly from this angle, but it appears to be a moon and a star tattooed atop the green, leathery skin. How strange. Do they all have such marks?

I stretch forward a bit to check the goblins picking up the last few stones littering the ground. One is kneeling down, and I can see—just enough—that he also has the mark on his foot, but on the heel. How did they get them? Is it part of the curse?

I try to scoot back, now that the goblins are done filling the box and most likely ready to move on, but my hand slips on the smooth stone, and I stumble forward. I freeze, hoping none of them will notice me before I can silently back away.

"Oiy!" Too late. "Who are you?"

"I . . . I . . ." I take a step backward, taking in their monstrous forms. Their hair barely covers their heads, they have splotchy green ears and piercing red eyes, the latter of which are looking directly at me. I've heard all my life how ugly they are; they certainly are hideous. Suddenly I cannot blame Brielle for being afraid of them anymore. They are no longer shapeless lumps in faraway shadows, but dreadful beasts. They look as if they might tear me in half with one tug, or rip straight through me with their terrible claws. One look at their sharp fangs sets my heart beating a rapid warning to escape.

"Whatcha think you're doin' here? These is our tunnels. Humans ain't allowed in these parts."

"I-I'm so sorry. I didn't mean to-"

The one closest to me, the one reloading the spilled box, stands, darting his hand out to grab my wrist. He is taller than me, maybe even two heads taller, and he is strong. I can't pull away. Twisting, pulling, I pound on his chest with my free hand. Nothing works. His grip is like iron.

My whole body courses with prickly pins of fear.

I give a big tug with my arm, looking to the ground. Their feet hurt. Isn't that what they said?

With one more strong pull, I stomp down as hard as I can on the goblin's lumpy foot. It makes a crunching sound under my slipper, and the goblin releases my wrist, howling with pain.

I run as hard and as fast as I can back down the tunnel I came through, hoping that I will be able to get back to the strong wooden door before the goblins can reach me. It only takes one look back to make my legs pump faster than ever. All three goblins are following me, climbing the walls, scrambling along the ceiling of the cavern, crisscrossing back and forth and over each other in a fast-paced game.

Where are my wits? I need to use my brain! Sing, Charlotte! Sing!

Born of the sun
Born of the moon
An ever circling round

I am so out of breath that I can barely get the words out, but the goblins must have exceptional hearing. When I turn back for a quick glance, I can see they have slowed and seem to be in pain. Hurrah! It truly does work. I keep singing as loud as I can manage.

Born of ice and wind
And nourished by
The rain upon the ground

My legs feel as if they are going to collapse. My heart beats faster than all the miners' hammers in all of Floraison, combined.

Born of the shadows
Thru the night
With stars, her beauty crowned

There is a change in the tunnel up ahead. It looks like—yes, it is! A blessed opening! I push on, running as fast as I can. I don't know if the goblins will stop once I'm out of the mine. I look back one last time. They are struggling. Stumbling, tripping over their own blocky feet, and covering their ears as they run. My lungs are on fire, and I fear my voice will give out at any moment. Pushing ever harder, I force my tired legs to move.

Moonlight spills into the cavern, lighting my way. Just a few more steps. I can do this. I *must* do this.

Born of the harvest
Bounty pure
Our thankfulness is found

And I am out. The dark sky opens above me. A tall building beckons to me, offering refuge. I keep running toward the shaft house, all the while singing, even though all I want to do is drop to the earth and never move again.

Born of the sun
Born of the moon
Born of the circling round
Born are the queens that give us life
Our hearts securely—Huuuuh!"

Strong arms crush around me, ending my escape. I scream with all the breath left in me.

"Let me go!" I struggle to free myself. "Help! Let go!!"

"Charlotte! You're safe. You're fine. It's me."

I don't need to look at his face. I should have known from the moment he caught me. There's his smell, that wonderful stony, pine smell that is so familiar. I take it in with each gulping breath. Finally, my legs give way, and he eases me slowly to the ground. But he doesn't let go. His arms are still tight around me, pulling me close to him.

"Kade?" I want to ask if the goblins are still there, but I have no air, no strength left in me to say more.

He must understand the reason for my fear from hearing the song, because he looks around and answers with, "They're gone. No goblin would dare come out tonight with so many people about. I believe all the palace staff are out looking for you." He looks at me, smiling and out of breath like I am, then pulls me close again. The moon glows softly overhead, the stars twinkling a happy welcome. I am safe. *I am safe.*

"She's over here!" Kade yells over his shoulder. "I found her!"

Mother runs toward us, her arms outstretched. In that moment I see so many emotions on her face: fear, relief, hope. I forget our argument this morning—all the arguments we've had lately. She is my mother, and she loves me no matter how foolish she might think I am.

Using Kade for balance and strength, I stand on shaky legs. I barely make it two slow steps, and I am enveloped in Mother's arms. She sobs, shaking as she holds me close. She says my name over and over again as she cries. I cry with her, soaking her shoulder with my tears.

"Oh, my sweet Lottie! I've been so terrified!" She finally says. "I went to find Kaderic to see if he had any contraptions that might unlock the door, but when I came back, it was gone. The door—it just disappeared! I was afraid you were gone forever. I'm sorry, so terribly sorry."

I think back to all the strange things I've experienced during the last week. Climbing a staircase I never knew existed. Speaking to a woman I've never seen in the palace before. Watching Brielle converse with her mother through the flames of a fire. And finally, the strange doorway that led me to the mines so far away from the palace.

"Mother," I say, pulling away and looking straight into her eyes. "I believe magic has come back to Floraison. Either the Rain Queen has returned, or . . ." I hesitate. "Or the goblins have succeeded in destroying the Wall."

Mother nods, agreeing with me. She turns and guides me toward a waiting carriage.

"Let's get you home."

Chapter 17

We don't wait for morning to tell King Gervais of our discovery. Mother says it's too important. I don't even know where the day has gone. I was only wandering the tunnels for an hour or two after talking with Mother this morning. At least, I think it was only an hour or two. The darkness outside tells a different story.

It seems the king isn't as concerned as we are. He leaves us waiting outside the council chamber for ages. It feels as though I've sat in this velvet-cushioned chair for longer than I was lost. Perhaps, he already knows that magic has returned to our kingdom.

We hear muffled voices through the walls: King Gervais saying something about the Snow Queen and her icy blast against our Wall. It seems as if they are sending soldiers North, toward Neimonte, to find out what she might be doing. I don't think we are meant to listen, but they are speaking so loudly, and it's hard to ignore any mention of the Queen of Ice.

"Now," Mother clasps her hands together and takes a deep breath. "Let me do all the talking. I can tell him about the door. He'll believe me, I know it. He'll know I am telling the truth." Is she still talking to me? Or is she trying to convince herself?

"What about Brielle and the fire? And the woman up the stairs?" I ask.

"What woman?" She looks puzzled for a moment, then shakes her head. "Never mind that. No. You must be mistaken. I'm sure what you saw was a dream. Brielle is no more magical than you or I. We must keep Brielle from his thoughts."

"But Mother!"

"Hush! I hear someone coming. Don't let them hear you." I can barely hear her last words. The goblins could surely benefit from taking whispering lessons from her.

Sure enough, there are footsteps approaching from behind the closed doors. I stand, clutching the back of the chair to support my weary legs, and when I look up a group of men walk briskly past, and a guard stands before us.

"King Kaderic Gervais Tyrrell Marlon III will see you now."

Really. King Kaderic Gervais Tyrrell Marlon—the

great and powerful—Third. Doesn't he know my father was King Gervais' closest friend? We shouldn't have been kept waiting so long. We shouldn't have to be escorted into the reception hall by some snooty wiseacre guard welcoming us with my father's best friends' title and terribly-long name! You don't see Kaderic walking around announcing himself to us as Prince Kaderic Gervais Tyrrell Marlon Clever and Handsome, the Fourth!

The guard leads us into the council chamber. I've never come in here before. There's never been a reason for me to do so. The room is quite bright, with a large chandelier hanging low over the table, and candle sconces set in the arabesque panels on the walls. King Gervais stands in front of a large window, his back to us, looking out at the dark night.

He turns when he hears us approaching, and Mother and I curtsy. Oh, my legs feel as if they are about to crumble beneath me!

"Ah, you've found her then. Good." He walks toward us, motioning for us to come closer. "I would hate for you to suffer another tragedy so soon after . .." His voice trails off, and he looks just a little embarrassed, but his recovery is quick. He takes Mother's hands in his. "How have you been, Margaret?"

"As well as can be expected," she replies.

For just a moment they are friends again, sharing in their grief over a lost husband, a lost friend. But then King Gervais pulls away and clears his throat.

"Now tell me. What is this all about? Something to do with Charlotte's disappearance?" He is all business again. He lets go of Mother's hands and looks to me. But Mother told me not to speak, to let her tell it, so I let her answer.

"Yes, your Majesty. You see, we had a . . ." I thought she wasn't going to mention our argument. ". . . a disagreement this morning, and Charlotte ran away. A door appeared outside our apartments. A door that's never been there before, you see. Charlotte went through it, and it locked right behind her. Then it simply disappeared."

As if the room is mimicking her story, the handle of a door rattles, and we all turn toward the noise. Bypassing the guards outside, and sparing us the announcement of his rank, station, and full name, Kade enters.

He doesn't wait to see that we are in the room with his father, but our presence doesn't seem to bother him once he notices.

"I'm going with them," he says. "I'll be ready by morning. You can't leave me out of this forever."

The king's face turns red, anger smoldering in his eyes.

"Not now, Kaderic." He steps toward Kade, but his son doesn't back down.

"Yes, now. We will discuss this now. That door Charlotte disappeared through is proof. I can't sit back any longer, and the soldiers are leaving tomorrow. You have to let me help."

"Absolutely not. You will either sit and keep quiet, or I will have you removed from my presence." They are face to face now. Kade has talked of helping the soldiers before, and of course he's been sparring with them without any of us knowing, but I didn't realize he felt so passionate about it, or that he would be willing to travel to Neimonte with them to check on the Snow Queen. I never suspected he would talk to his father this way.

They stare at each other, waging war with their stares, until Kade finally steps back.

"As you say," he mumbles, then drops into a plush brocade chair near a table.

I watch Kade—see the defeat in his eyes, the way he looks at his father, then at the floor. I hadn't noticed—hadn't paid attention—to the discord between them. I suppose I haven't spent very much time with both the king and Kade lately, outside of official events, of course. Perhaps this is the reason I rarely see the two of them together. Is this the end of it? Why has Kade given up so easily? I don't want him to run off to Neimonte with a group of soldiers, but it still pains me to see him shrink like . . .

"Charlotte!" Mother snaps her fingers.

I look up.

"What?"

"The king asked you a question." She looks at me with disapproving eyebrows, and I quickly turn my attention to King Gervais.

"What was behind the door?" He asks for what must be a second time.

"Nothing much, other than a tunnel and the goblins," I answer. I consider telling him about the staircase and the woman I saw the first time, and how everything had changed when I went through the second time, going in rather than going out. But they are already looking at me as though I am crazy, and I wouldn't know quite how to explain it all, anyway. Best to stick with the occurrences of today. "The tunnel was lined with moonstone. It didn't look like any real part of the palace. I wandered around for a bit, not seeing anything or anyone, then found myself in the mines. Then, of course, there were the goblins, and they tried to catch me, but I ran and . . . and Kade found me."

I look to Kade, who sits rigid in that soft, luxurious chair, his hands pressed tightly together in his lap.

"How did you find me so quickly?" I ask.

"Quickly?" It is Mother. "Charlotte, we were

looking for you all day!"

"But when I ran out of the mines I ran directly into Kade, like—"

"Like we knew exactly where to look," he says, standing. It takes him just a couple steps and he is beside me. "I know where you go when you're sad, Char. We had already walked the length of the nearby parts of the Wall multiple times. The next logical step was the mines."

"But I didn't go to the mines. I mean, not on purpose. The tunnel led me there, and it didn't take all day. It felt like only an hour or so for me." Why did the tunnel lead me to the mines?

King Gervais considers for a moment. Does he not believe I am telling the truth?

"Perhaps the Rain Queen has, indeed, returned." He turns away from us, and I hear him mutter, "I shouldn't have let him hide her away."

I look around. Did anyone else hear him? What could he mean?

"The spring fairy?" Mother's voice is shaky and unsure. "Gervais, we can't know for sure. The goblins have been tearing the Wall down. I'm afraid it might not be protecting us from the Snow Queen's magic as well as it used to. There are multiple reasons to explain why magic is returning to the kingdom, and if it's the wrong sort of magic, we have to keep it out."

"It's not," he says. "I know it."

"How, Gervais? It's been seventeen years, and there has been no indication that the new Rain Queen was ever born. We don't even know if that part of the legend is true. We can't put all our hopes on some fairy tale!" Her hands are on her hips now. I recognize that stance. I've just never seen her use it on anyone other than Lacey or me, let alone the king.

"Who's to say it's a fairy tale?" the king asks. "Every bit of it has come to truth. Our beloved Rain Queen is dead, the Moon Queen turned into a goblin. We haven't seen or heard anything about the Sun Queen in ages!" Mother flinches. "And I believe it's safe to bet the Snow Queen is sitting in her ice castle right this moment, planning revenge. Who's to say the babe was never born during the Shard War? By all accounts she should be coming of age now and most likely discovering her powers. This is proof!"

Mother shakes her head. "I don't know. We can't count on the prophecy. I think we should focus more energy into rebuilding the Wall."

"*You think? You* think?" Spit flies from his lips as he speaks. Mother doesn't even flinch. I take a few quiet steps away from them. "Who are you to tell me what to think? You and your husband both—"

"René performed the job you gave him, and he gave his life for it. You're the one who's gone off on silly quests, who's wasted time experimenting to create magic for yourself, only to do what, Gervais? Eventually take control of all the season queens? All the kingdoms? If the new spring fairy does, actually, exist and you happen to find her, what will you do? I don't believe I know who you are anymore."

I've never seen Mother like this.

"You have gone too far, woman!" His face is red again.

"Father!" Kade moves away from me, stepping between our parents. The distraction is just enough to pull the king away from his anger enough to calm down. "Lady Margaret has had a trying day. She's stressed and tired. She doesn't understand what she's saying. We can revisit this in the morning."

King Gervais turns to the window again, motioning for us to leave.

Mother has recovered somewhat, but she is still breathing heavily and glaring at King Gervais' back. I follow Kade's example by going to her and putting my hand in hers.

"Let's go, Mama," I whisper. "We need to get some sleep."

"Yes," she says after a moment, in a sweet voice that sounds exactly the way Lacey does when she is forced to apologize to me. "Please, forgive me, Your Majesty."

With that, she takes my hand and pulls me out of the room, my tired legs struggling to keep up with her brisk pace. She flinches when the doors shut behind us. I have so many questions I want to ask her. What advice did my father give King Gervais? What does she know about his death that she hasn't shared with Lacey and me? Does she really believe there will never be another Rain Queen, or does she know more than she is letting on?

She must see all these questions in my eyes, waiting to burst out of me, because she hushes me before I can even speak.

"No, Charlotte. We will never speak of this again, and I don't want you to tell anyone about it. I did come very close to treason just now. I thought I could help, that I could convince him to . . . never mind. We must wait for the king to forget about it and move on. If we keep making a fuss, we might end up on the wrong end of a cave-in, like your father."

Chapter 18

"I don't know any more than you do, Charlotte. I'm sorry."

We are sitting in Kade's workshop, he at one desk fiddling with one of his creations, and me at another, trying to finish the tile I started before the picnic. I've repeated the argument between my mother and the king multiple times in my head over the past week and more than a few times out loud to Kade, but we've come no closer to answering my questions. I can tell he is done. Talking it to death won't solve anything. Retelling Mother's words, over and over again, hasn't given me any more information about magic, or the Wall, or the new Rain Queen, or my father. It has only left me with more questions.

I sigh. There is nothing I can do about any of it, anyway. If the Wall is broken enough to allow magic into the kingdom, I cannot fix it. If the new spring fairy was, indeed, born during the Shard War, I wouldn't be able to find her to ask if she can bring the seasons back to the four kingdoms. And even if I knew more about Papa's death, there is no way to bring him back, no matter how much my heart aches for it.

I am nearly done carving the grooves for the crushed stone to sit in. I believe it to be the most beautiful pattern I've ever created. Swirls shoot across the moonstone tile, surrounded by small dotted holes that I plan to embed the ice quartz into. I contemplate mixing the sunstone and ice quartz together for the swirls. We've never blended the broken stones into the design before. They've always been kept separate in their own grooves. I wonder what combining them might create?

"Father's started a new crusade this morning," Kade says from across the room.

"Oh?"

"He's planning to hold a ball in a couple weeks. A huge affair. He told us over breakfast. There are going to be jugglers and acrobats and I think, possibly, some fire eaters from Solair."

I look up from my experimental pile of sunstone and ice quartz bits. The prospect of a ball is not too great a worry, and Kade and I might get a chance to make up for our lost dance at the last one. Yes, this is most likely a ploy of the king's to get Kade to stay in Floraison; fill his schedule with royal duties, so he can't run off.

"Fire eaters? Who would possibly want to eat fire? I can't even imagine that."

Kade chuckles.

"It sounds painful," I say.

The mix is turning out wonderfully. There are many pieces small enough for the reds and blues from the different stones to mix together into a vibrant violet color. I get up and cross the room to retrieve the mortar and pestle to crush the stones into a fine dust. Kade is working on his spider now, the one I thought Brielle had already helped him fix. Perhaps he is making it even better. I stop across the table from him, to watch for a moment.

"Why all the extravagance, just for a ball?"

Kade's hands stop, and he sits very still.

"He says it's time for me to settle down. Like I've been parading around the kingdom my whole life, or something."

"I don't understand," I say.

Kade looks up. His eyes are dull—dead even. They drill into mine as if he is searching for something to hold onto. A bit of moonstone amidst all the dust and dirt.

"He's holding the ball to find me a wife."

My blood freezes, sending a shiver to my toes.

"But you're still young," I say, clinging to a small shard of hope. "There's no reason to rush."

"I know."

"I've never heard of your parents pressuring you before. Surely they can give you more time to choose." I set the mortar and pestle on the tabletop. "A few years, even. They shouldn't push you to decide."

Kade stands, pushes his chair in, then leans back on the counter behind him, crossing his arms. This must be weighing heavily on him, and here I've been talking about my problems and concerns all morning. What a wonderful friend I am!

"That's kind of the point, Char. It's not my decision to make. By holding a ball, every eligible girl in the kingdom and from all the surrounding territories will be there. And every member of my father's council will be in attendance as well, watching everything. I really don't think the choice will be mine."

My first instinct is to step closer and put my arms around him, to tell him I'm sorry at the unfairness of it all, but something holds me back. Things feel different now, knowing that in a few short weeks his time will be monopolized by someone else. I had thought we'd have at least a couple more years to enjoy our friendship before we had to worry about adult things, like marriage. How silly of me to not realize how fast we are growing up.

I give a small laugh.

"So, I suppose Lacey doesn't have much chance then? There's no way the council will pick her over every other girl in the kingdom." Or me, either.

He laughs as well.

"Even *I* wouldn't choose her. You know Lacey has never been the sort to win me over." His brow creases, and even though he is looking in my direction, his gaze seems to go completely through me as if I am not here. I stand still, wondering where his thoughts have taken him. His eyes clear, and he takes a step toward me.

"Charlotte," he says. "I . . . "

He seems to be in pain. How can his parents put him in this position? Can't they see he's not ready? Can't they see how they are hurting him? How they are hurting me?

I hold my breath, but he doesn't finish. "What is it?"

He must have gotten lost in his thoughts again, because my voice seems to startle him, even though I tried to speak gently. He shakes his head. "I just wish things could be different."

"Oh," I look down to the floor. "I'm sorry."

Now is the time to reach out to him, to tell him everything will be all right, but I can't. Nothing is right anymore, and now that Kade is going to be taken from me, I don't believe anything will ever be right again.

He flops into his abandoned chair and picks up a tool, staring at it and moving it around with his hands. He is gone again. There is nothing I can say to bring him back, to make him feel better. I pick up the mortar and pestle and move back to my seat. A tear travels slowly down my cheek, and I am glad my back is turned to him. I bite my lip to keep it from quivering. I won't let myself cry.

I can hear him working again. Little thumps and scrapes on the wood. I brush my pile of stone off the table into my hand, then dump it all into the bowl. Taking the pestle in hand, I focus all my energy on grinding those stones to dust. I hammer at the stones to break them apart, then grind the pestle against them, forcing them into smaller and smaller crumbles. I don't let my mind wander to the future. I can't think about Kade marrying without feeling the sting of tears in my eyes, so I force my mind to center on the sound of the stones.

A song comes to mind, and I hum as I work.

Born of the shadows
Thru the night

It's the song I sang to get away from the goblins as I ran through and out of the mining tunnels . . . straight into Kade's arms. Oh, come now, Charlotte, you're being ridiculous!

Why do I always scold myself in my mother's voice?

Born of the harvest

Bounty pure

Not that song! Not that song! I command myself to stop thinking of the words, but they won't leave my mind. Think of something else! I need a distraction.

There's a knock at the open door, and I turn gratefully toward the sound. Brielle stands in the doorway, smiling sweetly. Of course, it had to be her. She asks if we mind if she joins us, and I find myself saying, "Actually, we were just—" at the same time that Kade stands and responds with, "Not at all. Please, come in."

She giggles, stepping through the doorway with small, delicate steps. Her pale blue dress brushes and rustles against the cupboards as she passes. With tiny pink embroidered rosettes covering the skirts and the tiered sleeves, it feels as though summer has come to the drab, gloomy workshop. I look down at my own plain, muslin dress. If anyone were to walk into this workshop, they would probably assume *I* was the poor, foreign girl.

Kade smiles at Brielle as she approaches him. Brielle *is* a great distraction. He must have pushed all worry about the upcoming ball from his mind, but I haven't.

If he was allowed to marry whomever he chose,

would it be someone like her? Is that what he was trying to tell me? I imagine once she is presented at court, she will be overwhelmed with suitors, but if Kade truly had his choice, would she be the one?

"You're working on your spider again!" Brielle is wonderful at pointing out the most obvious thing in the room. I would not have been surprised if she followed with, "Look, there are tables and chairs in here, and so many shelves!"

"Yes," Kade says. "Now that we've got the power drive functioning properly—with many thanks to you," he leans forward slightly, nodding to her, "I'm working on giving the legs a better grip. Angling them different, especially at the midpoint hinges." He picks up the spider and points to the holes where the legs are connected to the body. "See, if we tighten the cogs here, and pull the winding shaft a bit farther to the middle toward the pinion rack..."

It's all gibberish to me now. He's still talking, pointing everything out to her. She makes comments and points as well, but I have no idea how to even follow their conversation.

I turn my attention back to my rocks. The largest bits are about the size of a small spider we would find in the garden, which of course, is much smaller than Kade's mechanical eight-legged beast. The dust has mixed to that beautiful violet, and the larger pieces are shining through in various shades of blues and pinks. I absolutely love it.

"Kade! We need to get this in the tile and see what it does." It takes a moment for me to get their attention. "Kade. Come look."

"What?" he asks.

"I mixed the sunstone and ice quartz together. See how it's turned color? Isn't it beautiful? We should put this in a tile to see what power it has."

He shakes his head. "I don't know, Char. We haven't done anything new since . . ."

I rest my hands on the edge of the table, feeling the cold, hard corner against my palms.

"Since my father died. But I don't see why we can't. I haven't blown up the workshop, yet. Besides, you're the one who wanted to try the ice quartz."

"We don't know what it will do, though." Why is he suddenly so hesitant?

"Which is exactly why I want to get it into a tile, so we can try it out."

I get up from the table to retrieve the gypsum from the cupboard. Brielle leans over the powder, stirring it a little with her finger.

"It is very pretty," she says.

Kade leans against the table, watching me mix the plaster on the other side of the room. Who is he to tell me not to try new things? Honestly, what does he think will happen that could be so bad? We've never had any mishaps before.

"Aren't you at all interested in seeing what will happen?" I bring the bowl of plaster back to the table.

"Might I ask a question?" Brielle stands straight again, wiping her finger off on her dress. "When you put the rocks in your tiles . . . and the cube, it powers machines, but when they put the stones in the Wall, it blocks magic. Why don't they do the same thing? What makes them different?"

That's two questions, actually. I count them, again, in my head. No. Three.

"Oh, that's easy," Kade says. "The stones in the Wall are used as brick, laid in a pattern piece by piece. Charlotte's father discovered the pattern during the Shard War. He was part of a research team my father organized. The team was made up of all the most brilliant men in the kingdom."

I smile.

"He *was* pretty smart," I say. "For the most part, putting the stones together doesn't do anything at all. Except, of course, the moonstone glows and the sunstone gives off heat. But Papa discovered that layering the bricks in a certain way repels the use of magic, which is what started the Wall in the first place. With the tiles, however, when you embed one stone inside the other, it creates an energy we use to power

Kade's machines."

Kade goes to his table to get one of his already completed tiles and brings it back to Brielle, pointing out the details.

"We use one stone for the tile, then embed pieces of the other stone into the grooves. Moonstone on sunstone or the other way around. Charlotte is better at carving the grooves, but I try sometimes." He hands the tile to her. "I carved this one myself."

"It's just gorgeous!" she exclaims, running her finger delicately along the pattern. I've seen him do better. This tile is mostly straight lines and pointed angles. Not very impressive.

Kade takes the tile back from her as she offers it. He cannot take his eyes from her. Her curling blonde hair. Her sparkly blue eyes. Papa used to say my eyes were like the rare diamonds they sometimes found in the mines, illuminated by all the surrounding moonstone. Sparkling. Dazzling. Brilliant. It feels as if they haven't sparkled in ages, and I certainly feel quite dull standing next to Brielle.

I want to go somewhere else—anywhere else, but I remember the bowl of plaster in my hands. It will dry up if I leave before using it. I move to sit but hear shouting down the hall.

We all look to the door. Lacey calls my name three times from down the hall before we see her in the doorway. Tiny bits of hair have come loose from their pins, framing her face in a wild mess. Her eyes are as wide as dinner spoons, and her skin nearly as white as the plaster in my hands. She holds onto the door frame for support, but her message cannot wait for her to catch her breath.

"Charlotte! Mother's in a fright, and I don't know what to do. There was another accident at the mines, and Bastien was caught up in it."

Brielle moves for the door, running faster than I've ever seen her move, and I watch as Lacey's eyes register her presence.

"Where is he?" Brielle asks, trying to push past Lacey. "*Where is he?*"

Lacey has caught hold of Brielle, pinning her with her arms. Both girls fall to the floor, Brielle pushing to free herself, trying to scramble back to her feet. Lacey's face is calm now, and her eyes tell a story of sadness I haven't seen since we first learned about Papa.

"You mustn't see," she says. "It's too late."

Chapter 19

Even though it was too late to save him, they were able to pull Bastien's body from the rocks. Not like Papa's. We never had a proper burial for him—just a memorial service in the Cathedral. This service for my stepfather is starting in the Cathedral, but as soon as all the prayers are said, and songs are sung we will go to the cemetery by the mountain, where we will be able to say our proper goodbyes.

What kind of farewell can I give a man I barely knew—one I have been trying to get rid of since the day I met him? I have wished for this moment so fervently it almost doesn't feel real now that it is here. But I never wanted it to be like this. I didn't wish for Bastien to die. I never wanted him to be gone forever, just gone from us.

The king is speaking, recounting the many acts of

service Bastien had done for our kingdom, including his work in the Shard War. Apparently, he fought for Floraison against Lunain, his own kingdom and people. I had never thought of Bastien's life before he came to the palace, and it seems he was more involved in the affairs of Floraison than I knew.

It's chilly this morning. I don't understand why we couldn't have waited until later in the day to bury my stepfather. I am not used to having to rub my hands together to keep my fingers from freezing. I wish I could hold a small sunstone to warm them. Instead, I bounce my feet a bit, moving my legs in my seat to generate warmth. Mother sits perfectly still beside me. Strong. Calm. A rock.

I peer around Mother to see Lacey moving around even more than I am, hugging herself tightly to keep out the cold. She keeps looking around at the large, empty cathedral. A few self-important nobles sit behind us, hoping to be seen by the king at the Overseer's funeral, but other than that, the pews are barren.

Brielle sits by me, shaking silently with her tears. She doesn't bother to wipe them with her handkerchief, and I stare at her from the corner of my eye as the streaks of wet drip off her face and onto her charcoal-colored dress.

Did I cry at Papa's memorial? Or did the tears come

later? I can't even remember. Everything from that time is a huge, messy bundle of blurry memories. I could feel nothing but sadness for so long, but at least I had Mother and Lacey. Is Brielle afraid to be alone? Where will she go when the burial is over? She must have some relations in Lunain who will take her in if her mysterious mother is unable to.

We all shift in our seats to see the casket carried from the cathedral. I watch it disappear through the side door, then follow Mother as we make our way slowly behind it.

For being such a poorly attended funeral, why does it feel as if we're surrounded by a huge mass of people? They pat us on the shoulders, holding our hands briefly as we pass. Didn't we just do this? Didn't these same people offer their condolences for my own father not too long ago? I never thought I would be in this position again so soon.

A carriage awaits us, and we climb in together. I wish Kade were able to come with us. I didn't even see him at the memorial service. I'm forced to sit by Brielle, because Lacey is faster than I am. I don't know how to comfort her. I know her pain all too well, and I know I cannot take it away. There is nothing I can do.

We sit side by side. Her cheeks are dry now, but her eyes are still puffy. I try to look everywhere else, but at her. Yes, it's silly and more than just a little bit selfish, but seeing her grief brings back my own, and I just can't let that happen right now. I have no comfort to give.

A cold wind hits my face as I step out of the carriage. I wish I would have thought to bring a shawl along. I did, however, listen to my mother's advice to put some patents on over my black satin slippers. If I hadn't, my heels would certainly be sinking into the wet, muddy ground with each step. I cross my arms together and rub my hands up and down them, trying to warm away the goose flesh. I shiver and bounce my legs a little, then for one sweet, blissful moment a warm wind blows past me, warming my nose and cheeks.

The soldiers unload the casket and carry it to the grave, and we watch as they set it on ropes and lower it down. I would have given anything to have been able to say a proper goodbye to my father. We heard of the cave in and that they were unable to recover his body, because the stones were so locked up, but that was all. Nothing more. It still feels so uncertain at times, like he's just gone away on a trip somewhere, but deep down I know he is never coming back.

We don't stay to watch the casket being buried. Putting all that earth back in the hole will take some time. Mother is on the move only after a few shovelfuls. I don't want to stay any moment longer than necessary, so I follow her as she makes her way to the king, who is already halfway to his grand, golden carriage. Mother calls out to him while we are still many steps away.

"Must you be so hasty, Gervais?" He turns sharply, and I can tell from his expression he's not surprised, nor happy. We catch up to him quickly.

"I've got a kingdom to run, Margaret. A kingdom to save."

"You named my husband's successor at his funeral. We hadn't even put him in the ground yet!"

What? I hadn't heard that. I must have missed it completely. Oh, why did I let my thoughts wander?

"Well, now you know who it is. You can go marry him."

"That's not fair." Mother's voice is low and cold.

King Gervais takes a step forward, looming over her. His words are low and quick. "He was my friend, Margaret, and you barely let his body grow cold before you—"

"I had a family to take care of."

"But why did it have to be Bastien?"

I'm having difficulty keeping up. Isn't he the one who would have kicked us out of the palace if she hadn't married Bastien, as he is doing right now? I thought he was the one who suggested Mother marry him in the first place. Why would this hurt him so?

"You are the one who found him and Brielle." She says Brielle's name with importance, pulling her existence into their argument. What does Brielle have to do with any of this? "I do what I need to survive. We all do."

I can see Mother's lip quiver, and I am terribly afraid that the strong woman—that solid rock—is about to break and crumble.

If Kade were here, he'd fix everything. He wouldn't let our parents talk to each other this way. He'd sit us all down to figure things out.

King Gervais pulls away from her, letting out a cloudy puff of air. "You have a home in the mountains, Margaret. It's not as if I'm putting your girls on the streets."

She looks like she wants to say something. She looks like she wants to say a good many things, but all I hear before we turn to leave is, "We'll be out within the week."

* * *

The moment we reach the palace, Mother orders us to start gathering our things, and yells similar commands to the servants who came to help us out of the carriage. She might have said we would move out of the palace in a few days, but she is acting as if she wants to be gone by sunset.

We spend the day wrapping and packing our many dresses while the servants take the filled trunks and set them in piles in the salon. By evening my room is barren, clear of everything except the essentials. I wonder who its next occupant will be? Is Bastien's replacement young or more mature? Is he bringing youthful lords and ladies or a load of small children? I sincerely hope whoever stays here appreciates the lovely view of the mountains through the window.

Even though our whole suite is a bustle of activity and trunks and boxes, it's hard to believe we are actually leaving. It doesn't feel real. I've known no other home than the palace. We've visited our château more than a few times through the years, but those were always short holidays as a family. There was never any thought that it might someday be our permanent home once more.

A few servants are preparing my harp to pack into a large wooden crate. Even though I am not as accomplished at it as I could be, it hurts a little to see it boxed up. I beg the servants to be gentle with it, running my hand over the smooth wood before it is covered completely. My eye catches a lump of warm colored wood at the crown of the harp. My tuner!

"Wait just a moment!" I call, then quickly reach out to pull it off the neck of the harp. It should be in my personal trunks, to avoid getting damaged or lost. I thank the servants, then rush to the parlor to put the tuner with my things. Mother is there, standing in the middle of the room in her black gown, directing the confusing mass of servants rushing this way and that. I spy the pile of trunks that will go out last, the ones that will travel with us, personally. Mine are stacked directly in the middle of Lacey's and Brielle's. I move to open the topmost trunk, but . . . wait.

My trunks are beside Brielle's?

"Mother, what are Brielle's things doing with ours? Might they get mixed up when the servants are loading the carts? What if some of them accidentally get sent to the château?"

Mother looks at me strangely. "All of Brielle's things *are* going to the château with us."

"But, why? Surely, she's not going with us." I can hear the distaste in my voice, and I am ashamed of it, but it's hardly something I can control.

"Of course, she is." Mother points toward a pile of bags for a servant to add a bundle to. "There is nowhere else for her to go. She has no one."

Yes, she does, I want to say, but we've already tried to have that conversation before. She doesn't belong with us. She has a mother of her own. I shouldn't have to share mine. Now she'll be living with us forever, and we'll never truly be a family again. How can I be happy when she must rise above me in everything? Understanding how Kade's gadgets work. Riding a horse instead of riding in a carriage. And of course, being the most beautiful, radiant girl anyone has ever seen in their entire life. So why would anyone—a prince, a duke, even a stable boy—want me when they could fall in love with her?

I open the trunk, throw the tuner in, and slam the lid back down.

"Great! We might be rid of her father, but of course, we'll never be rid of her!"

I turn to flee but stop directly as I see Brielle standing in the doorway. Her face is ashen. She takes a step back, almost stumbling on my words. That was cruel, I know. I am cruel. I want to stop hurting and to stop hurting others, but I just can't. I want to be supportive and helpful to Mother, to Lacey, Kade— even Brielle, but everything has just been so upside down since Papa died, and I can't make sense of any of it. It hurts too much.

"Charlotte," Mother says. "You will apologize this instant."

A loud sob escapes my lips, and I run from the parlor, nearly knocking Brielle over as I pass. I go to my room, perhaps for the last time, and throw myself onto the bed, crying myself to sleep.

Chapter 20

I wake up, cold.

Mother must have known I needed rest and let me sleep my temper off, for when I look outside, everything is dark. I struggle out of my clothes, put on my nightgown, and hastily brush my hair. Luckily, my warmest robe is lying at the foot of my bed instead of being crammed into a trunk, and I gratefully wrap it around my shoulders to keep out the chill.

I know I won't be able to fall back asleep. I suppose that is the harm in going to sleep so early in the evening. There is no clock on the mantel for me to check, and it would be wonderful to know how many hours I might need to fill before the sun rises. I believe Mother has left a mantel clock in the parlor, and I might possibly find a book or two that hasn't been packed yet.

My fingers are stiff from the cold, and it takes a few

moments to light a candle. I shield the flame with one hand as I make my way to the parlor. The hallway is crowded with crates and piles. Weaving my way through them, I hope my footsteps won't wake anyone else.

The parlor is even worse, packed full of all our belongings. A few of the stacks even reach past my head. Perhaps, Mother actually did pack the clock away. She's stowed everything else!

It's colder in here than it was in my bedroom. There are small tendrils of frost on the windows, and I move around a pile of trunks to get a closer look. The frost is so beautiful—almost like white pine branches swooping across the glass. I reach to touch the cold, then watch as the ice melts around my fingers.

A quiet, sleepy sigh comes from across the room. I look around and my eyes fall on a soft, fuzzy lump by the fireplace. I don't need to investigate up close to guess that it's Brielle, wrapped up in a heap of blankets on the hearth.

She sleeps so soundly; she must be exhausted. I think back to the first days after losing my own father, how I wanted to sleep all the time. When I was sleeping, I could forget he was gone. I could dream about happy times and feel no pain.

What will Brielle do? Surely with a mother of her own she will not want to stay with us. Perhaps they were able to finalize some plans this evening at the fireplace. I set the candle down on a crate and rub my eyes with the tips of my fingers. What has become of me? Thinking of my stepsister setting up a rendezvous with her mother through a magical fireplace portal in a kingdom that hasn't known magic for fourteen years! Things truly have changed.

I reach for the candle, but the flame blows out by my movement. It will be impossible to find a match in this mess, but I look around, despite my misgivings.

Flames suddenly erupt in the fireplace, sending out a gush of warm air across the cold room. I jump back, bumping into a pile of crates, but luckily, nothing falls over. The noise wakes Brielle, and I duck down behind the crates before she can see me. Hunched over my folded legs, I peek around the pile.

Brielle sits up, peering into the giant flames. The blankets have fallen to the floor, making a cozy nest around her.

"Mother, is that you?" She gives a small laugh, then whispers to herself, "Of course it is. Who else would it be?"

A face appears, dancing in the grate. It is the same face I saw before in the fireplace a few nights ago. The woman's hair flows wildly about her face in the fire, moving with each lick of the flames.

I duck behind the crates again, afraid the firewoman might see me. The room is slowly growing colder where the warmth from the fire isn't touching. When I peek back around the crates, my face almost burns from the warmth, but the rest of my body is freezing.

"Have you come to get me?" Brielle asks.

The woman's face is full of sadness and pain. I recognize that pain, and I remember that my losing a stepfather means this woman just lost her husband...or lover...or whichever he was. She looks much like my mother looked after Papa died.

"You know I can't, darling. The Wall is still too powerful. It's taking much of my strength only to talk with you here. It's difficult for me to enter the kingdom of Floraison, and it will be until the Wall is completely broken."

Brielle almost crumples at the words, but then she is up again, excited.

"Margaret is taking me to their château in the mountains. It is just outside the Wall. Surely you can come and get me there?"

The woman purses her lips and shakes her head.

"Remember your purpose, Brielle. You must stay strong."

"But Papa is gone." Her voice quivers.

"I know, darling." A single blazing tear travels down her cheek. "He is gone, but our errand is still the same, and your role is much more important than you realize."

My legs feel thick and numb from being crouched over as I am. I shift my legs a little to bring some life back to them and try to wiggle my toes, but they are so cold I can barely move them.

The fire flickers, almost burning out.

"Mother!" Brielle whispers urgently, but then the fire is back again, and the woman is back as well.

"Have you given it to him yet?"

Brielle shakes her head, and I shake mine as well. Given what? To whom?

"I think I might not need it, Mother. He's taken to me already." Taken to her? Who in the four kingdoms is she talking about? She spends most of her time in our parlor, embroidering. The only *he* she spends any time with is Kade. It couldn't be Kade, could it?

It couldn't be.

It had better not be.

"We cannot leave anything to chance. If we are to unite the kingdoms, you are our best hope. Floraison has been safe all these years, but you've seen what it is like outside the Wall. The people live in constant fear, and the Snow Queen rages and schemes, waiting for just the right moment to swoop down on us all. We must have unity between the kingdoms if we are to defend ourselves from her attack."

Clouds above! She must mean Kade.

She wants Brielle to marry Kade.

But Floraison and Lunain are already on better terms now. We don't have to arrange a political marriage to unite the kingdoms, and who is Brielle, anyway? She's no princess!

I can't hear their words now; they are speaking too softly. All too suddenly, the fire disappears, and we are plunged into darkness. I duck back behind the crate. Will Brielle come this way? I am in the only usable path through this mess of packages. If she lights a candle to leave the room, surely she will see me! I press myself hard against the wood behind me, making myself small.

I listen.

There is a rustling of blankets, some scooting on the floor, and then she lets out a small sigh. Certainly, she can't be comfortable here on the stone floor. My bones ache just thinking of sleeping on the hearth. Or perhaps I ache from the cold? I am tired, all of a sudden, despite sleeping all afternoon and evening. Oh, how I wish I could go back to my own bed and curl up in the blankets just as Brielle is doing now, but if I move, she will hear me.

I wait, hugging my legs to my chest to conserve what little warmth I have, until I know for certain she is asleep. I had a lot of practice listening to Lacey fall asleep each night when we shared a room as young girls. She never wanted the curtains open at night, because she was afraid of the goblins, but I was more afraid of the dark than of goblins and wished for the moonglow. Once the lights were extinguished each night, I would lay in bed with my eyes shut tight until Lacey was asleep, then I would tiptoe to the window to open the curtains. I never once saw a goblin peeking in at us.

After cautiously making my way to the hallway, I race to my bedroom and climb under the covers, hugging my arms around my body and rubbing my feet together to warm them. I want to think of all I heard Brielle and her mother say. I wonder at their plan and want to make plans myself to catch Brielle or get more information from her, but I am overcome by exhaustion and fall asleep the moment my limbs start to warm under the blankets.

Chapter 21

"Honestly, Charlotte, this is the third time I've come to wake you. It is time to get out of bed. Have you been sleeping this whole time?"

I rub my eyes and sit up. Mother paces back and forth in the room, picking up articles of clothing I shed and left on the floor during the night. I yawn.

"The carriages are waiting. The servants have been loading wagons since sunrise. Lacey is awake and ready. It's time you were up as well."

She dumps the clothes on my bed, then turns to leave. Surely, she can't expect me to wear the same gown as yesterday, but as I look around my barren room, I realize there is nothing else to wear as we leave the palace. Whatever happened to leaving within the week? The funeral was just yesterday!

"What about Brielle?" I ask.

Mother stops in the doorway.

"That silly girl was asleep by the fireplace in the parlor. She awoke once the servants came in to start loading everything. She's running around the palace somewhere, but I've sent someone to find her. We must be off soon." She emphasizes the word *soon* by clapping her hands. Yes, I understand. I need to hurry.

I wish I could have a warm bath drawn for me, but I suppose that will have to wait until we get to the château. There is a wash basin and pitcher of water on my dressing table, which I suspect Mother asked one of the servants put out the first time she tried to wake me. I pour the water, splash some onto my face, then dry off with a soft towel. Judging by the bustling noise from the hallway, there is no one to come do my hair for me, so I simply brush it out and pull it back a little with some pins. A small cluster of pearls clings to the end of each pin, which seem to float in my hair once in place. I am quite happy with it. But now I need to find Kade before Mother ushers me into a carriage. I cannot leave without saying goodbye.

I am shocked when I enter the hallway. Where once there were piles and stacks from floor to ceiling is now empty from wall to wall. I hurry to the parlor, and sure enough, all the crates, trunks, and bags are gone. The fireplace has even been swept clean. There is no evidence of Brielle even being there last night.

"Charlotte, please make haste!" Mother calls in the direction of my bedroom. I do not see her, and I don't believe she sees me, so she must be calling for me to hurry dressing. I sneak out the door before she knows I am up and stop the first servant I see: an aging man carrying a small bedside table I recognize as Lacey's. Should I be bringing my furniture, too?

"Can you direct me to the prince?" I ask, stepping in front of him to get his attention. He sets the table down and scratches his cheek, stretching his mouth at the same time. I tilt my head to the side, watching him.

"Can't be sure where he is exactly, miss. He took off with the golden one a while ago."

The golden one? What, in the name of Spring, is he talking about?

Then it hits me.

"Brielle," I whisper.

"Yes, that's it! I couldn't quite remember her name, beggin' your pardon, miss. Prince Kaderic and the lady went that way," he gestures toward the palace gardens, "a little while ago."

I grab my skirts, muttering, "She's no lady," before I leave.

Who does she think she is? Waltzing in here and stealing my best friend. Why did Mother have to wake her before me? Oh yes, because she was sleeping in the goblin-taken fireplace! That little cinder wench!

Mother calls, and I groan. We can't leave yet! I'll say anything to stall Mother's hurried departure.

"I'm looking for Brielle!"

Lacey comes to stand next to me, taking my arm.

"She's there, see? With Kaderic." Lacey's voice is low and raw. "Mother will see that she comes."

I do see. They're coming around the corner of the palace now, following a flower-lined path to the drive. Kade sees me watching for him, and nods in my direction with a smile. He is wearing his favorite green vest, the one with darker green vines and clovers embroidered on it, and a striped green frockcoat. Brielle is also wearing green, as if she dressed to match. I know it couldn't have been planned, but it upsets me all the same.

He'll come to say goodbye as soon as he is free of Brielle. I know he will.

"I need to say goodbye to Kade." I try to pull free from Lacey, but Mother calls again. She is already standing by the carriage, poised to climb in.

"Can I—" I start to ask, but she cuts me off.

"Quickly, ladies! We must be going! Lacey, Charlotte! You're in here with me. Brielle, you'll be in the second carriage."

Brielle gives a tiny nod of her head, and she and Kade head slowly toward the carriage behind ours. Blast her silly, fluttery steps!

If only I could—

"Now, Charlotte!"

I stomp to the carriage behind Lacey, but pause before climbing in. I turn to look at the palace, my only home. It will never be my home again. I think of Kade's workshop, of Father's tools I've forgotten to pack. All left behind. Kade will take good care of them, though, and perhaps I could come back for them soon. Just because I will never live here again, it doesn't mean I can't visit. I wipe a tear from my eye and look around one last time.

Kade and Brielle stand by the second carriage not too far away. She hands him something small, wrapped in a bit of fabric. A present! What could she own that Kade could possibly want? Is this what her mother spoke of in the fireplace? *Have you given it to him yet? What is it?* A lock of her hair or a portrait so he won't forget her beauty? He opens it, but I can't make out what is inside before he puts it in his coat pocket. He is saying something to her. What is he saying? Brielle curtsies, bowing her head, then he helps her into the carriage, shutting the door gently.

I can't help myself. There is no way I will let that image be my last memory of living in the palace. I run to Kade before Mother can say a word and throw my arms around him.

"I don't want to leave you," I sob. "You're my best

and only friend, and I don't know what I'll do without you!"

He hugs me back, and I cling to him, fiercely.

"Oh, Kade!"

"We'll see each other again soon," he says. "You know I can't live without you, either."

I pull back and look up to him. He smiles at me, almost laughing at my dramatics. I love the way his eyes crinkle when he smiles like that.

"Promise you'll come visit me, even though it's so dreadfully far away?"

"It's not that far," He pulls me in for one last hug and kisses the top of my head. "You couldn't keep me away."

I pull back again, reluctantly, then run back to the carriage, completely ready to endure anything my mother might say.

Chapter 22

It is late afternoon by the time we arrive. Traveling by carriage can be irksome and slow, especially when the caravan consists of two carriages and three overloaded carts.

Our carriage pulls into the drive of the château, and my heart soars with memories of all the wonderful holidays we have enjoyed here through the years. The grounds are not nearly as immaculate as those at the palace, but I love the untamed wildflowers just as much as the orderly rows at the palace gardens. The three-storied château stands proudly among the pine trees. It is a handsome manor that compliments the surrounding forest, instead of competing against it.

Papa purchased the château soon after I was born. It was far enough from the official borders of Lunain to keep me from being stolen by the Snow Queen, but close enough to focus on the Wall when he needed to, then come stay with us when he was able.

We had no time to warn the caretaker of our arrival, so we are greeted by a thick layer of dust sitting atop the sheet-covered furniture.

Mother touches the fireplace mantel, then inspects her finger, and shakes her head. If we had been given more time to prepare, she would have sent people ahead of us to clean and get everything ready for our arrival. As it is, there is much work to be done even to get it ready for us to sleep tonight.

Mother puts us to work right away. The servants carry everything in through the front door, and it is our job to direct them. It's difficult to tell which room to place something without knowing what is inside of it, so there are many times Lacey and I tell them to set their crate down for a moment so we can inspect its contents.

Because she's never been here before, Brielle has been given the job of pulling and folding the sheets from the furniture, then sweeping the floors once she's done.

"Be careful with that dust!" Lacey shouts as Brielle pulls a sheet close by. "It's getting in my eyes!"

Brielle apologizes, then goes to work in the other room.

A servant stops in front of me, waiting expectantly.

I motion for him to set his trunk down, then I open the lid. I recognize the slippers sitting on top as the ones Brielle wore on her first day at the palace.

"Mother!" I call. "Where are we putting Brielle's things?"

I think through all the rooms but have no idea where Brielle will be staying.

Because my parents knew we would be moving back to the palace permanently once the Shard War was won, they didn't need a very large, grand place. Three bedroom suites, plus the servants' quarters, a parlor, a library, Papa's study, and the kitchens and pantry, of course. There's a wine cellar and storage in the basement, and a gallery just to the left of me. I can't think of any room that isn't already in use.

Mother comes in from the forecourt and ponders for a moment.

"There's a small room on the top floor. She'll most likely need to clean it up a bit—move some of the extra furniture out—but the light comes in nicely through the windows, as far as I can remember. She'll enjoy that. Put all of her things in there, please."

I direct the servant up the staircase with vaulted ceilings and tell him to go three levels up. He gives me a look that shows his displeasure, but he wouldn't dare say anything aloud.

"Oh, come now. We're all doing our part. Truly, it's

not all that heavy, I'm sure."

"Yes, miss." He heads up the stairs, but not without a few grunts and groans.

A line of servants forms from the forecourt all the way to the second floor. It reminds me of the men pulling stone from the mountain and hauling their heavy barrels to the shaft house. I peek out the door to see the wagons are almost completely unloaded. It's amazing how quickly this has all happened. Not too many months ago, we lived at the palace, with father focused on the Wall and Mother considering prospective husbands for us. Even though I never took much interest in the latter, I knew there would be a future for me somewhere. But now I'm beginning to think a bit more like Mother. Outside the Wall, how will we put ourselves forward to claim any husband at all? What future can we possibly have out here?

I suppose there is still the ball Kade was telling me about. Its purpose might be to find him a bride, but it wouldn't hurt for us to use the opportunity to look for husbands as well. My mind catches an image of Kade and I can feel his arms around me again, hugging me goodbye. He said the ball meant he would have no choice in whom to take as his wife, but if he did have a say, is there any way he could . . .?

"Charlotte, there you are." Brielle has a huge lump of white sheets bundled in her arms, and she is covered with dust from head to toe. "Where does your mother want me to put these?"

I pause. I have no idea. I tell her so and start up the stairs to explore my bedroom suite and unpack, but then I remember something.

"What did you give Prince Kaderic before we left the palace this morning?"

Brielle shrugs under the mass of sheets and I feel a pang of guilt for the work she has done. Perhaps I should tell her to put the sheets in the basement.

"Nothing of consequence," she says. "Just a pair of spectacles for him to wear. It should help with how intently he looks at his inventions. He puts too much strain on his eyes."

Brielle walks away, and I notice that for the first time since I met her, she is walking like a real, normal person. No minced, fluttering steps. I suppose she only uses her "fashionable" style of walking at the palace.

Spectacles. I didn't think Brielle would have such a strong opinion on Kade's eyes. She's only been in the workshop with him a few times. But her mother asked if she had given Kade—or someone—a gift yet. Are the spectacles what Brielle's mother was talking about?

What does he have to remind him of me? Certainly, I can think of something better to give him than a silly pair of glasses.

* * *

It is going to take several days—possibly several weeks—to settle into our new home. Every time we've come to visit before, we brought half our servants from the palace, and life went on smoothly. Now our servants have been promised to the new Overseer and his family, so they have returned to the palace, leaving us behind with only our cook, a stable boy, and the groundskeeper that has always lived here. Our old servants didn't even stay long enough to help us unpack our trunks. They simply plopped them in our rooms, then went on their merry way.

I didn't mind unpacking my own things, but I gave up quickly after Mother asked Brielle and me to help Lacey. If I heard Lacey yell, "Be careful with that!" one more time, I knew I would scream, and that certainly wouldn't welcome sisterly affection. I decided to do what I sincerely felt was best for all of us: I dropped Lacey's dressing gown *gently* on her bed and left.

Moving my father's many, many books from the crates to the shelves in both the library and his study turns out to be a much bigger chore than any of us imagined. Mother and I are the only ones with enough perseverance to attempt it, and it takes us a few days to feel up to the challenge. I believe it is because we both know how much these books meant to him, and they represent one small way he is still with us. We treat each book with reverence, and I don't think we put a single book on the shelf without skimming through its pages first.

Many of the books are ones Papa collected through the years, written by colleagues of his or by men from other kingdoms, but a few are geological journals he kept himself from both before and after the War. Some of these are ones I've never seen. He must have stored them somewhere other than the workshop, back at the palace. But I recognize quite a few of the others, which are especially dear to me, because they were my favorite to look through as a child with Papa by my side, teaching me as I read. Sometimes Kade would join us, which is how he and I got started working together to create the energy tiles for his inventions. First, we would study the books or ask my father questions, then we would take that knowledge to combine the magical stones in different ways to see what the result would be.

I pick up one of Papa's field journals and hug it to my chest, breathing in the woody paper smell. I flip through the thick pages, reading bits and pieces of my father's notes and marveling at his detailed drawings of all the different kinds of rocks, both magical and non-magical. In the margins of some of the pages are little scribbled notes in shaky, sloppy handwriting, and I recognize them as information Kade and I wrote down long ago, when we first started learning.

"Difficult to break, but makes a marvelous powder," was written in one of the columns. That must have been me. I don't recall Kade ever using the word *marvelous* when he wasn't put upon to impress courtiers at royal functions. I search a bit longer and find a notation he wrote.

"Be careful. Gets crumbly."

Oh, what am I going to do without him? And what can I possibly give him that might best the spectacles Brielle gave?

I reach to put the journal on a high shelf to keep it safe but stop to look at it again. The journal! Of course! What better way for Kade to remember all the wonderful times we've shared together? My heart twists as I contemplate giving away one of Papa's journals, but Kade will take care of it, and he is even more special to me than all the books in the world. Setting the journal aside, I think of how happy it will make him and turn my attention back to emptying the crates and filling the shelves.

Mother sighs and puts her hands on her waist, stretching backward.

"I am not used to this physical labor." She shakes her head. "You are lucky to still be so young and healthy."

"You are not very old," I say, putting another book

on the shelf. She sits on a chair next to Father's desk.

"Twice widowed, the mother of two girls almost grown. I might not be ancient yet, but I've definitely seen my share of life. I'm so tired, Charlotte."

"Then you go lie down and take a nap while I finish here. We're almost done, anyway."

Mother stands slowly, then stretches again.

"Thank you, Lottie. I'll send Brielle in to help you."

"No!" I reach my hands out in desperation. I don't want her touching Papa's books. I don't even want to think about it. She learned enough to know how Kade's contraptions work and, basically, kicked me out of the workshop in doing so. I don't want her to learn about the stones, too. Then I would have nothing left to call my own.

Mother looks a little confused but doesn't argue with me.

"I'll have her move out the crates when you're finished, then. And sweep the floor."

I nod. That will be good. All the books will be put away by then. I start a separate pile of books to put in my bedroom, away from the possibility of prying eyes.

Chapter 23

I am waiting on breakfast the next morning when there is a knock at the front door. I listen for a moment to see if I recognize the voice of our caller, but I don't hear the door open. I don't even hear anyone walking toward the front of the house to answer it. I drum my fingers on the tablecloth. Pierre has usually answered a call and shown the visitor in by now. Where is everyone?

Oh, yes. Pierre would show visitors into our family suite *at the palace*. All of our servants have gone back to the palace. It's going to take quite a bit of time to get used to this.

Whoever is standing on our front porch knocks again, and I suppose I can go answer the door myself. Lacey is at the top of the stairs in her night dress and wrap as I pass.

"Who is it?" She whispers, harshly. "Who could be calling this early?"

Why does she expect me to know? I shake my head. I have no idea.

Grasping the metal handle, I struggle to squeeze the latch with my thumb.

"Hurry up!" Lacey hisses from her perch on the staircase.

Finally, I hear a *click!* and the door pulls open. I almost fall backward from having pulled so hard, and my arms wave in the air to catch my balance.

Kade stands on our doorstep in the early morning light. He is dressed in a simple velvet suit with a wide-skirted coat. He is not wearing a cravat underneath the high collar of the suit, and I can tell he is freshly shaven. He must have gotten up quite early and ridden here like a madman to arrive so quickly.

His eyes match the brown of his suit, but they are almost hidden behind the thick glass of his spectacles. The ones Brielle gave to him. Why would he be wearing them now? She said they were to help in is workshop.

Never mind that. He's come to see me! He said he couldn't keep himself away from me, and here he is My heart pounds in my chest, and I can't stop smiling.

"Oh, how wonderful! Come in, please. This is such a great surprise."

Lacey shrieks from up above, and I turn to see a

dash of white streaking away. I giggle and look back to Kade, wanting to share the moment with him. He's come inside, but he's looking up the staircase, craning his neck to see farther.

"Was that Brielle?"

"No, just Lacey." I take his arm and guide him to the breakfast room. "I've never heard her scream so at the sight of you. You must be absolutely horrifying this morning!"

He chuckles, but he's still looking behind us.

"Is she up, then?"

"Who? Lacey? You just saw her."

We sit beside each other at the large oak table.

"No. Brielle. I know it's early, but I was hoping she'd be awake."

Oh.

"She'll be in soon for breakfast. You must join us, of course."

Why is he so intent on seeing Brielle? Surely, it's not to thank her for those ridiculous spectacles. He doesn't look quite like himself in them. Not quite right. They're not such a great present, after all.

I clap my hands together and jump up from the table. Kade's present!

"I have something for you. I found it while I was unpacking," I call over my shoulder as I hurry to Papa's study. My skirts rustle as I run, and I concentrate on the noise to slow myself down. My mind is moving from question to question almost as fast as my feet are dashing down the hall.

Does his showing up so quickly hint he might have stronger feelings for me than seeing me as just his friend? Does my racing heart mean that he has become dearer to me? Does his father know he is here?

I head straight for the desk and grab the field journal. Holding it close, I rush back to the breakfast room.

"You probably don't even remember it," I begin, even before I'm through the doorway. "You wouldn't believe how surprised I was to open it and find—"

Kade is gone. His chair sits crookedly away from the table, pulled out like mine, as if he got up in a hurry. But where did he go? Lacey might have come down and asked for help with something. No, there's no way Lacey could have dressed so quickly.

"Kade? Where are you?" My voice is a little shaky. The excitement that filled my body just moments before is sinking to my toes, melting into the marble floor.

I search the foyer, the parlor, and the library, almost running into Lacey after finding them all empty.

"Was that Kaderic at the door?"

I nod.

"I couldn't quite tell. He looks a little . . . different."

She thinks on that a moment, then shrugs her shoulders. "Where is he now? Is he staying for breakfast? Did he bring a message for Mama? From the king or something?"

The nervous feeling that started a few moments ago is beginning to pull itself into a ball in my stomach, turning and building with each of her questions until I want to explode.

"How do you expect me to know these things? He hasn't been here but a few moments and has barely spoken a word. Blast it all, Lacey, I cannot read his mind!"

Lacey gives me the squinty eye and curls her upper lip.

"Why are you attacking me? I haven't done anything! It's not even ten in the morning and already you're yelling at me. I'm barely out of bed, completely innocent of all wrong doing."

I leave her ranting outside the library to continue my search.

"And now you're ignoring me!" she yells. "Of all the snippety, selfish snobbery I've ever encountered—and from my own sister!"

"Oh, hush, and go eat your breakfast!" I wave her away, behind me.

Where could he have run off to?

I rush past the breakfast room, peeking my head in

one last time to see if he's returned, then dash through the vestibule at the garden entrance. My kidskin slippers barely make a sound on the paved walkway. There is still a slight chill in the morning air that cools my skin as I run. I should have simply looked out the window. He doesn't seem to be out here, anyway.

Slowing down, I round the corner, and there before me is Kade standing under the whitebeam tree with his arms around Brielle, hands on her tiny waist, and their faces so close they're almost—no, they *are* touching. Kade moves a hand to the back of her neck, gently pulling her closer.

My skin tingles, sending tiny pricks of pain up and down my body.

She is kissing him! And he is kissing her! How could they? How could *he*?

My feet are frozen to the ground. I want to run away. I want to run to them and shout all sorts of horrific things Mother would never approve of. I want to sink deep into the dirt beneath me, living with the goblins if I must, to get away from this sight. But my feet just won't move.

All I am capable of doing, it seems, is letting out a tiny little, "Why?"

They both look to me, startled. My face flames red hot, and I cover it quickly with both hands, turning and running as fast as I can back into the house.

Chapter 24

I don't want to see anyone ever again. I realize I cannot spend my entire life in my bedroom, but how can I overcome this mortification? How will I ever be able to look at Kade without the image of him and Brielle appearing in my mind? It's as if I can't see anything else anymore. I look at the ceiling, and I see them. I look at the merry pictures on the walls, and I see them. I shut my eyes as tightly as I can, pushing my face into my pillow, and I still see them wrapped in that intimate, loving embrace.

I thought he said he loved me!

No, he said he didn't want to be away from me for very long. That's entirely different, and he gave me a sweet little kiss on the head like I'm a child or a sister or a friend. Just a friend. How could I be so silly to think I could have been more to him? Whom did he walk the gardens with before we left the palace? Brielle. Whom did he escort to the carriage? Brielle. And to whom did he race so early this morning to visit? Certainly, not me.

I stay in my room the rest of the morning, skipping breakfast. I would stay in my room all day if I could, but Lacey comes to find me, eventually. She barges into my room without knocking and goes straight to my dresser, picking up brushes and combs, one by one, studying them absentmindedly.

"It's almost time for dinner. Mother's requesting you join us."

"I really don't want to," I reply from my bed. I haven't burrowed under my covers yet, but now she is here, it's quite tempting.

"You've got us all baffled, Charlotte. You were so excited when Kade arrived this morning, yet you've spent all this time in your room. We've had a grand time, and you've completely missed it."

I roll over onto my back and look back up at the ceiling. It's still there, that horrible picture in my mind. I should ask how they've spent their morning, what fun, wonderful things they've done, but I don't think my heart can take the news. Best to leave it alone.

"I would really prefer to stay up here until Kade is gone. He is leaving, eventually, isn't he?" I grab my pillow and pull it over my face. Still there.

"As soon as dinner is over, I suppose. He said he had business to attend to this evening, otherwise he would stay the whole day."

"I'll bet Brielle would like him to stay forever," I grumble into the pillow.

I regret it instantly. I expect Lacey to pounce on the idea, but she must not have heard me, because all she says is, "Dinner is soon, and Mother expects you downstairs immediately. No excuses."

Fine. Alright. I'll go downstairs, but they can't force me to be sociable.

I move as silently as I can down the stairs and straight to the library, shutting the door softly behind me. I press my ear to the door, listening to hear if anyone saw me come down. I'm not ready for Mother to call me to the dining room, yet. All I can hear is quiet conversational tones, and I breathe a sigh of relief.

"Charlotte?"

I jump at the sound of his voice. I thought I was alone.

What is Kade doing in here? My face burns. I don't want to turn around, but I can't stand here, facing the door, forever. Pasting a smile on my face, I turn, slowly.

He is reclined on the settee, a book in his hands. He sits up quickly, accidentally dropping the book. He fumbles for it, but it hits the ground, anyway. The sound makes both of us flinch.

"I wasn't expecting anyone to be in here, Your Highness. Please forgive me for interrupting your solitude." Face still hot, I give a delicate curtsy and reach for the door knob behind me.

Kade flinches.

"Oh, come now. Why the formality? What's wrong?"

Does he really expect me to answer that question?

"Absolutely nothing," I say. "I'm simply recovering from the shock I received when I saw you kissing my stepsister in the garden." My words are harsh at the end, and they come out cold, as if they are an insult.

Kade picks up the book and tosses it on the settee cushion.

"You're upset I kissed your sister." It is not a question. More like a judgment.

"Stepsister," I correct him, moving away from the door and searching for a safe place to stand. I don't want to be close to him, but I can't stop myself from moving forward.

"Why would that upset you?"

My mouth opens, but not a word comes out.

"So, I kissed a pretty girl. You think that means I'm going to marry her? I've kissed a few other girls, and I haven't sent out any wedding announcements yet."

"Kade!"

I'm in shock at such an admission. This is not the

Kade I know.

"Do you think it even matters? Do you think I'll get a say in who I marry, Char? Father will make that decision for me. He's planning the whole thing now."

"Planning what? Your wedding?"

"No. The ball! The stupid ball. He's gone crazy. It's all he talks about now. Honestly, I can't wait until the whole thing is over and we can move on with our lives. I should be able to find a little bit of love on my own before I'm told who to give my heart to, don't you think?"

I step closer, anger boiling up inside me.

"So, you'll—what? Come to visit Brielle every day until the ball? Bring her back to the palace? Are you going to try to convince your father to choose her? What's your plan, Kade? You're making a fool of yourself!"

"Making a fool of . . . what are you talking about?"

"You barely know her. *I* barely know her, and she's supposed to be my family. She doesn't hold any title, even before her father died. She's a nobody from a different kingdom. A kingdom we don't even have good relations with as it is."

"Since when did you care about status and titles? She's a nobody, then. Who would you have me be with? Someone like Lacey? Like you?"

My eyes sting.

He doesn't stop.

"Who are you to judge? You've no royal blood. You're the daughter of a widow who had to make a hasty marriage to maintain her position at the palace. The sister of a girl who pushes herself on others to leech off *their* titles. Don't tell me she doesn't, Char. She's been throwing herself at me ever since your father died and she started to receive fewer invitations to her precious parties. And you—you are so lost in your own grief and self-pity you can't even see how others might be hurting. If anyone can understand what Brielle is going through right now, I would think it would be you. But instead, you've turned your back on her just like everyone else. I am all that she has, and she is the only person I know who doesn't take my status into account. Who actually—"

"I don't." The words are out of my mouth before I can stop them. "She's not the only one. I mean, it doesn't matter to me—the fact that you're a prince. I love you, because you're you." I shut my eyes tightly, for just a second. It hurts to look at him. Now that I've said it, I know it's true. Truer than anything I've ever said in my entire life. "I love you, Kade, and I would love you even if you were the poorest, lowest man alive."

Oh—shafts below!—I've got to stop.

Kade stretches his arms wide, raises his eyebrows,

then lets his arms drop to his sides. His spectacles slide farther down the bridge of his nose, making his eyes appear large and fierce. He turns his back on me, walking around to the back of the settee.

Please, say something. Anything.

He pushes the spectacles up his forehead a bit and presses his fingers to his eyes, rubbing and stretching his temples.

Then he lets his glasses fall back into place.

For one long moment, he looks at me, and it feels as though my insides are being ground to bits. "I used to love you, too, Char, but I have to face reality. You aren't fit to be queen. Brielle is far better suited for royalty than you'll ever be."

Before I can respond, he stomps to the door and pulls it open. He doesn't look back, not even once, and I can hear him in the hallway, cheerfully greeting Lacey. She asks him about his glasses, wonders why he's never worn them before.

"They were a gift," I hear him say. "One that I never knew I needed, but I can't imagine ever taking them off. Everything is so much clearer now. I know exactly what I want from life."

What?

Lacey acknowledges how distinguished he looks and asks why he is leaving just before dinner. A knot twists in my stomach. His reply blurs in my head. It doesn't matter. He did not come to see me, but he is leaving because I am here. In this house. In his way of getting Brielle. I stand still through their awkward goodbyes, listening for the front door to, finally, close behind him.

Chapter 25

I don't even bother to wipe the tears from my face. My legs are shaking. I wrap my arms tightly around my body, as if my whole being would fall apart if I let go just one bit. I don't know how long I stand here like this, my mind completely numb, my heart cold.

How could he say such things about my mother? About Lacey? He accused us of being social climbers. He accused me of being unfeeling. He accused me of never loving him, when in fact he has been all that has mattered for so long. I just didn't see it. I didn't know.

Well, fine!

I pick up the book he had been reading and slam it onto a nearby shelf. *Desconoise's Dictates on Relative Consociation.* I'm glad I didn't give one of Papa's books to Kade. He doesn't deserve it.

Throwing the library door open wide, I head

straight to the kitchen to wash my face. The cool water wakes up my skin, rejuvenating my entire being. Hopefully, the cold will calm my puffy eyes, but there is no mirror to check, so I simply wipe them dry and smile, falsely, at the new, fresh feeling. I shake my head, willing every bit of sadness away from my body and replacing it with forced determination.

I lost my father, and I survived. I lost my home, and I am still breathing. Kade was my best friend. He could have been more than that, but now he is gone. I can survive this, too. I have my entire life ahead of me, and I promise myself it will be wonderful, even without Kade.

Cook bustles back and forth, between the kitchen and the dining room, preparing for dinner. She focuses on carrying the food-filled platters to the dining room, but every time she comes back to the kitchen empty-handed, she looks at me, puzzled.

"Life is simply wonderful, is it not?" I ask, keeping my eyes wide in hopes of stalling the tears.

I believe I have confused her even more, especially when I grab the latest platter from her and carry it to the dining room, myself.

"Oh, Charlotte," Mother says as I enter. "There you are. I trust you're feeling well."

"Absolutely," I beam, planting the platter right in the middle of the table. A chunk of sadness still clings to my heart, and I try to squash it and kill it, but it will not let go. Never mind. "I have never felt better in my entire life."

Mother gives me almost the same look that Cook did, except she raises one perfectly groomed eyebrow along with it. I just smile at her and shrug a shoulder. I can do this. I can lie to myself and everyone else. I will just have to force myself to be happy.

Lacey and Brielle are already sitting at the table with Mother. My stomach does a little twist at the sight of Brielle, but I ignore it. She can have him. I don't care.

"I'm so glad you're feeling better," Brielle says. "Prince Kaderic was worried you were falling ill."

I smile again and take my place.

"Of course, he was." If he even cared how I feel.

Now that we are all seated together, we close our eyes for a moment of silent contemplation, to thank the season queens for a bountiful harvest and for all the food on our table.

"This looks just delicious," Mother exclaims, which gives us all permission to stop thanking the queens and open our eyes.

"What a joyful surprise to have the prince come visit this morning," she continues. "We are lucky, ladies. Not every household is fortunate to be so close with the royal family. It seems as though we are not forgotten, even though we've been," she stops,

thinking for a moment, "even though we live out here."
There is a hesitation—a frankness—to Mother's voice
that makes me wonder if she truly is glad Kade came to
visit, but I can't think of any reason it would upset her
at all.

Lacey nearly jumps out of her seat in excitement at
the mention of Kade's visit.

"Kaderic said he's hosting a ball, the grandest we've
ever seen. Did you hear that, Mother? And very soon,
I believe. He said a messenger would be sent with an
invitation in the next day or so. The king is inviting the
whole kingdom, and I think some people from outside
as well." Outside, like us.

I place the tip of my fork into my mouth and
delicately pull a square of peach from it. And smile.

"And did you hear why the king is going to such
expense?" Lacey asks.

Brielle blushes. I try to hold my smile, then take a
sip of wine to cover my failure at doing so.

When nobody speaks up, Lacey answers her own
question.

"It's to find Kaderic a bride! I've always thought
they would select someone political for him, but
apparently, they're letting him choose from just about
everyone." She leans in close to us, whispering, "I think
he came today to invite me, personally. He pulled me
aside after breakfast and told me about it. Do you think

that means . . .? I mean, I knew he always liked me, especially, but I never guessed he would choose me over any other girl in the kingdom. I suppose they should just cancel the ball and throw an engagement party, instead!"

Knowing the truth, I hurt for Lacey. I believe I hurt for her almost as much as I hurt for myself. But I wonder if she suspects something between Kade and Brielle, or at least suspects he doesn't think as highly of her as she lets on, because there is a bit of falseness to her voice as well. My goodness! Are we all pretending? Is Brielle the only one of us truly happy today?

"That's very exciting," I say, trying to fill my voice with all the happiness I'm trying to feel. "I know how much he means to you."

Lacey agrees with me that, yes, he means very much to her and tells us all about how handsome he is and a great many other things I don't want to pay attention to.

Brielle purses her lips and sets her serviette on the table, pushing her chair back. Mother gently places a hand on her arm before she can get away.

"Cook is feeling a bit unwell today, Brielle. Will you be a dear for her and clear the table?"

Brielle nods her head once, gives a brief, "Of course," and picks up her plate and glass. I watch her as she carries the dishes out of the dining room. What is she thinking right now? Is she reliving that kiss in her head? Is she thinking of Kade and looking forward to seeing him at the ball?

She has a small, pleasant smile on her face, even though she is carrying plates smeared with sauce. She must be thinking about him, because I can't think of anything, at the moment, that would make anyone so happy.

Chapter 26

I can't stop thinking about it, no matter how hard I try. Brielle and Kade. Kade and Brielle. It shouldn't have come as a surprise. I noticed the way he looked at her, the way he invited her on a private horseback ride, the way he sought her out before we left the palace.

But did he truly seek her out, or might it have been the other way around? I think back to the last time I saw Brielle conversing with the woman in the fireplace. I remember they were talking about Kade . . . At least, I assume it was Kade. Whom else could it possibly have been? Brielle said Kade already liked her, that there was no reason to give him a gift, and the gift ended up being the spectacles. And now, all too suddenly, Kade is head over hammer in love with her. Could it be possible the glasses are magical?

If someone were to tell me about magic glasses a

few weeks ago, I would have thought they were telling stories from before the Shard War. But now that the Wall has been destroyed enough to let magic into the kingdom, and I have seen a woman's face flickering in the flames of a fire, it seems highly believable for there to be spectacles that can make someone fall in love. Why else would Kade fall in love with Brielle?

My mind ticks off nearly one hundred reasons Kade would fall in love with Brielle all on his own, but I push them aside. The possibility of magic spectacles has brought hope to my heart, and I will not let go of that hope.

I need a plan.

I need to find some way of making someone— anyone! —believe Brielle is, indeed, talking with her own mother in our fireplaces and that she has bewitched my friend—the Crown Prince, even—to make him fall in love with her. Surely, that will be enough to send her packing back to the country where she belongs.

I don't know if her mother's image will visit her out here, but it seems likely, especially since the château is situated outside the Wall, where magic is completely uninhibited. I can watch each night to see if Brielle goes to any of the fireplaces, and if her mother appears, I'll run to fetch my own mother, who will then see I've been telling the truth the whole time. Hurrah! It is a marvelous plan.

A marvelous plan indeed, except Brielle's mother doesn't come the first night, nor the next two. The messenger delivering our invitation to the ball has come and gone and the house has become a flurry of dresses and shoes being repaired and washed and pressed. I almost forget about my plan in all the madness, and I cling to the small hope that Kade might notice me at the ball. That he'll forget about Brielle and remember how much I've always cared for him. How perfect we would be together. At least, how perfect I believe we would be together.

Lacey and I try to help as best we can, but we've never taken care of our own dresses before. Brielle seems to catch on to using the linen smoother the best, so we leave our delicately ornamented dresses in her hands.

With the king in such a hurry, we've had very little time to prepare. The ball is tomorrow, and it's nearly impossible to hide both my giddy excitement and my fearful apprehension. Will Kade feel the same way about me as he did outside the palace as we were saying farewell, or will he feel the same way he felt in the library? Will he treat me as a friend or an enemy? If I can get those spectacles away from him, perhaps he might see me as something more than a friend.

My dress hangs on the dressing curtain, clean and

beautiful. It is pale lavender with golden vines and flowers embroidered all about it. The overskirt is full and elegant with a wide ruffle along the bottom that will show through the opening of the mantua robe. The robe follows my waist perfectly, joining in the front to a stomacher covered with so many of the flowing golden flowers, that it seems to almost be made completely of golden thread. The sleeves are fitted to the elbow, then expand in double tiered ruffles that brush my wrists when I walk.

My slippers are dyed to match, with tiny, delicate lace sewn around the ankle, and I can't help but put them on as I get changed for bed. They are new enough to have no stains or obvious creases, but worn enough that, hopefully, they will not give me blisters when I dance.

I bend forward and lift my nightgown, poking out a foot in front of me. Imagining myself all dressed up in the palace ballroom, I take a step forward and turn. Kade is there, in my mind, and he is no longer angry with me. He looks at me without those wretched glasses, and I can see the love I feel for him reflected at me in his eyes. What would it feel like to have Kade's arms around me in more than just a friendly embrace?

I hum a dainty tune, dancing around the room. Two steps left, another spin, and suddenly my ankle turns sidewise and I can hear a *crack!* underneath my foot. I tumble to the floor, knocking my elbow on the side of the bed frame on the way down.

Shafts below!

I lift my foot and pull the slipper from it, carefully moving my ankle in gentle circles to make sure the fall didn't cause any harm. Thank the fairies, all seems well. Even so, I groan. My slipper didn't fare as well as my ankle. The heel has broken completely off. My eyes scan the floor for the broken piece. It must be here somewhere . . . there!

After picking it up, I try three times to push it back together, knowing full well my attempts will not work.

Blastity blast, blast!

I see no way we can repair it in time for the ball tomorrow. Even if we still lived at the palace, closer to more than a dozen cobblers, they are most likely overflowing with orders and repairs, what with everyone in the kingdom invited to the ball.

What am I going to do?

I rush to the wardrobe, hobbling crookedly with one slipper on and one slipper off. The shoe basket is a jumbled mess, and it's difficult to even find a matching pair. I find blue, green, and even silver; but you can't mix silver with gold. How vulgar! My brown boots are easy enough to find, but I would rather throw myself in a goblin hole before attending a ball wearing them. Finally, I find a deep purple pair at the bottom of the pile and hold them up to my dress. They are a bit creased at the toes, and one has a small tear on the side, just under the arch. My dress is long enough that no one will even see them for more than a second.

I lay them next to the dressing screen, under the mantua robe. Yes, the colors work well enough together. It's not a perfect fix, but it will have to do. I slide the good lavender slipper from my other foot and set it and the broken one into the shoe basket, so I am not reminded of them in the morning.

But maybe I could fix the broken slipper. The heels were put on with glue in the first place, why can't I attach it again?

Grabbing my wrap and pulling it around my shoulders as I head downstairs, I think of Kade and wonder what he will be wearing. I also fret about how I will convince him to take off his glasses, if he is wearing them at all. Perhaps someone else with good sense will tell him they are not practical to wear to a ball.

That smell of books envelopes me. I have always loved that smell, but now entering the library forces me to remember Kade's raised voice and harsh words. I don't think I will ever come in here again without thinking of our argument. Failing to find paste of any kind, I start to leave, but stop when I see a book sitting on the settee.

Desconoise's Dictates on Relative Consociation. The book Kade was reading earlier today.

Without thinking, I pick it up and hold it close. Will I ever get him back? I carry the book out to the foyer, not yet ready to put it down. Before I make it to the stairs, I see a flicker of light coming from the kitchen, and my heart begins to race.

Cook never has a fire lit this late in the evening. This must be what I've been waiting for! Brielle's mother has come to the château at last! Tucking the book under my arm, I walk quietly toward the kitchen to investigate, the light growing brighter with each step. With the placement of the kitchen fireplace and stove, it is hard to get a decent view without being seen myself, and I must remain hidden so as not to alert Brielle.

I peek around the doorway a little farther, and yes, there—I see her. She is looking so intently into the flames that she doesn't notice me. She must be waiting for her mother's image to arrive. Well, I can wait, too.

I make a quick dash to the other side of the doorway where I can sit in the corner. Feeling a chill from the marble floor, and envious Brielle can wait comfortably in front of a roaring fire, I pull my wrap tighter about me and tuck my feet under the skirt of my nightgown.

I can be patient.

Even in the cold.

It's no problem.

I start at the sound of voices. Clouds above! I must have fallen asleep.

I peek around the doorway again.

The voice from the fire must be Brielle's mother, but this time she sounds more angry and cold, whereas before it was more cautious and urgent. What's happened to make her so upset? Their plan is working. The Crown Prince of Floraison has suddenly fallen deeply in love with Brielle. What could possibly be the matter?

"It just doesn't feel right. If he loves me, I want it to be real," Brielle is saying.

Fingers squeezing my wrap tightly, I burn with anger. You should have thought about that before you gave him the spectacles.

"Real love won't get you a crown," the voice says "Real love won't reestablish your people or bring harmony to the kingdoms. It doesn't matter if he loves you, anyway. He won't be around long enough."

My heart stops beating. He won't be—what? Around long enough?

"But Father—" Brielle cries, but she's immediately cut off by the woman in the fire.

"You've shed enough tears on this hearth. It's time to move on. Do you think your father would want you to squander your power? No. He would want you to achieve greatness and establish harmony between the four kingdoms once again."

There is silence, for a moment. Then a cough and a sniff from Brielle.

"I want him to be proud of me. I want you to be proud of me. But the discordance between the kingdoms was not my doing, nor do I think it is my place to fix. I cannot control the Snow Queen, and how can anything be right again until the Goblin Queen has been changed back to our beloved Moon Queen? Please, let me come live with you. That's all I want."

The light brightens at the mention of the winter queen, and it takes a moment for Brielle to finish her question. Is her mother as afraid of the Snow Queen as the rest of us? Who is this woman, that has power to speak over great distance through fire, but fears the season queens?

Brielle continues.

"I don't understand how marrying Prince Kaderic fixes anything."

"It doesn't, in and of itself. Just trust me. Trust my plans." There is a *chink!* on the hearth. I lean further around the door frame to see Brielle retrieving a tiny object from the floor.

"It's beautiful." Brielle slips a ring onto her finger, then holds up her hand to admire it. "Thank you, Mother. I've never seen this stone before. What is it?"

"Fire opal. It is very rare, and very powerful."

Brielle is kneeling at the fireplace, her back toward me. I stay crouched close to floor, as far back as possible. I can tell Brielle is looking at the ring in the light of the flames, but I cannot see it, myself.

"What is it meant to do?"

"This ring will bind the prince to you. He will do whatever you tell him to. Without a thought of his own, he will agree with anything you say."

"No."

"Yes!" The face moves forward in the flames, and Brielle's mother almost hisses the word. "It is the only way. Hold the prince's hand during the wedding ceremony, with the stone turned toward his palm." Brielle holds her hand higher and twists the ring so it is backward on her finger, shaking her head, slightly. The woman starts to sing, and I recognize the words. It's the Hymn of the Roses. One of my favorites.

The rose in the valley is blooming and sweet
And fairies descend there, the children to greet.
The Rain Queen returns to warm our cold hearts
And the sun rushes in as Spring finally starts.

Her voice floats above the crackling of the fire, eerie and cold.

"As the prince sings those words, the ring will suck his soul away from him. Once he has pledged himself to you, seal the spell with a kiss, and he will be bound to you forever."

No! She can't!

Brielle is silent for a moment. "But they don't sing the rose hymn as part of the wedding ceremony," she says.

"You will make them. It is fitting, after all. The Rain Queen has, indeed, returned."

Brielle stares into the fire, rubbing the ring and spinning it around her finger. "What of the king? I cannot control him, and I don't believe he ever listens to the prince."

The woman's face glows brighter and her fiery eyes flicker with hate.

"I'll take care of the king later."

My skin prickles, and it feels, for a moment, as if I cannot breathe.

What do I do? Why didn't I get my mother? I need to get Mother!

I push myself up from the floor, but before I can come fully to my feet, there is a loud *womp!* on the stone.

The book! I must have set it on my lap while I was sleeping.

The fire dies out in one *shush* of air. Brielle whips around and glares at me. Her eyes look raw, and her cheeks are still wet with tears.

"What are you doing down here?" she asks.

"I—I—" I don't know what to say. "I came down

to get a book," I stoop over to pick it up, holding it for her to see. "Then I saw a light, and I wondered why the fire would be lit so late at night." I step into the kitchen and set the book on the table. My mind is trying to keep up with my mouth, trying to think of something she will believe. "Is it cold upstairs? Is that why you sleep down here, by the fire? You've been so kind to help us with our dresses today. Thank you for—"

"What did you hear? What do you know?"

"I promise you. I was just coming down for a book."

Brielle stands, looming over me. I can tell she doesn't believe a word I've said. She twists the ring around her finger, glancing at it for a moment. Then she looks back to me with venom in her eyes.

"You are no threat to me. I know you want him, but he is mine. He will always be mine."

No. He will not.

I glare at her. "I'll tell my mother."

She laughs.

"She won't believe you. No one will believe you."

She's right. I tried telling Mother before, and she didn't believe me. Not even for a second. Brielle steps away from me, moving toward the door in the darkness.

"This is bigger than you or me, Charlotte. Bigger than you could imagine. I have just a small part in it, and there is nothing you can do to stop it."

"I can stop you," I say, but she is already gone.

Chapter 27

I could barely sleep all night. I lay awake, my mind full of worry and dread. Every time I managed to drift off, my dreams were filled with a mindless, choking Kade, with Brielle smiling smugly beside him, and I would snap awake again.

Why didn't I stop her? Why didn't I rip the ring from her finger? What can I do to keep her from Kade?

I will not let him be her marionette. This is the day that he, or more accurately, his father, will choose a bride, but if Brielle is not at the ball, she will not be available for them to choose. The difficulty lies in trying to figure out how to keep her here at the château while we go to the ball without her. I've tried asking her to do extra chores today, like milking the cow and feeding the chickens, and it's worked marvelously well to keep her busy. I suggested them at breakfast, and she couldn't say no, because Mother agreed it would do wonders for us to have a little bit of fresh cream before leaving for the ball, to keep our strength up through the night.

I smiled a little—truly, I smiled a lot—when she came in from the barn smudged with dirt and smelling of animals, but I couldn't think of anything else for her to do. She's spent the afternoon washing and perfuming and powdering just like Lacey and I, and I fear she's going to make it to the ball and look just lovely, despite my efforts.

With no servants to help us dress, Lacey and I are forced to help each other, and it's taken longer than we're accustomed to. The sun is already setting, and we should have left quite a while ago. Mother is in the entry, most likely pacing, and calling for us girls to hurry. I check my hair in the mirror one last time, smoothing the twists and braids Lacey put in.

I do a quick plié, a turn, then rise up with an *elevé*, watching my skirts swish and sway around me. Perfect. I glide gracefully to my bed, sit carefully as to not rumple my skirts, and tuck my feet into the dark purple slippers. They are a bit tight, but I manage to pull them on.

My heart feels torn in two. It beats with excitement for the only ball I've ever looked forward to, but also sinks with dread every time I think of Brielle's plan. If

I can manage to keep her away from Kade, everything will be alright, but I must think of something incredibly fast, because Mother is calling again.

I nearly fly down the stairs, my feet moving quickly on tiptoe in the too-tight slippers. Mother and Brielle are waiting at the bottom. Brielle is wearing a scarlet-colored gown, a beautiful, bold choice. She looks incredibly calm for someone planning to steal a heart, and I glare at her on my way down.

"Now where is Lacey?" Mother asks, then calls, "Lacey! We are *leaving now!*"

We all look up the stairs, waiting for her to come down, but instead we hear her voice in the kitchen.

"Whose is this?" she asks. "I found it next to the fireplace."

Brielle and I both look down at her hand. Her fingers are bare. She rushes toward the kitchen calling, "Is it a ring? I believe it is mine." I follow her.

"Ladies, I am heading to the carriage. If any of you want to go to the ball, you must come now!" Mother heads out the front door as Brielle and I run toward Lacey's voice.

We reach the kitchen almost at the same time, and there we see Lacey standing by the fireplace holding a red-stoned ring between two fingers. She is wearing a dress the color of the sky with tiny red jewels sewn into the bodice and sleeves. I have never seen her so beautiful.

"Yes." Brielle looks flushed. "It is mine. I don't know how I could have lost it. It is very dear to me." She hurries toward Lacey and the cold, empty fireplace, holding out her hand.

"But it's so pretty," Lacey coos. "Will you let me borrow it, please? Just for tonight. It matches the jewels on my dress perfectly." She looks at Brielle with dangerous eyes. I am quite familiar with that look, and even though I do not like Brielle, I am scared for her.

"I do apologize, but I was hoping to wear it tonight. It matches my dress as well." Brielle holds out her arms to show off her daringly red dress. "See?"

Her hands dart out in front of her, grabbing the ring and Lacey's fingers. Lacey howls like I've never heard before. They struggle for a moment, then stand face to face, locked together. I move around beside them, not knowing what to do.

"What was it doing here in the first place?" Lacey asks. "Have you been sleeping in the fireplace again, like at the palace? You are a little cinder wench, aren't you?"

"Give me my ring." Brielle's jaw is tight, her eyes narrowed.

Lacey changes tactics but keeps an iron grip on the ring.

"I saw you with the prince from the window. Do

you honestly think you could win him over with flattering words and a sweet pair of lips? I've known Prince Kaderic my whole life."

"Then why hasn't he kissed you?" Brielle asks through gritted teeth.

Lacey wrenches her hand free from Brielle's grasp and throws the ring in the fireplace.

"I don't want your ugly ring. It's probably worthless, anyway."

The fire opal ring lands deep in the cold ashes against the back bricks. Brielle grabs the tongs from the hearth as Lacey marches out of the kitchen. It feels as if ages pass while I watch her reach the tongs toward the ashes. I can see her there, standing in her beautiful dress, sparkling like a ruby against the drab, gray soot.

But I also remember her mother's face from the night before, and right before me lies the ring that could take Kade—the Kade I know and love—away from me, forever. My stomach twists, and all my muscles tense with one quick, instant decision.

Brielle will not be going to the ball with us.

I take one step forward and shove against Brielle's back as hard as I can, sending her flying into the fireplace. A cloud of soot comes billowing forward, but I manage to jump out of the way before it can spoil my dress.

Brielle is not so lucky. She is covered in ash from

head to foot. If I didn't know better, I would never guess her to be a great beauty or a possible contender for the prince's love. She looks like a goblin stepping out of the shadows, and no one would ever invite a goblin to a ball.

I look directly at Brielle's glaring green eyes, which contrast gloriously with the gray mess all about her.

"Stay away from my prince."

And with that, I walk as calmly as I can toward the front door, hoping she doesn't hurl a handful of soot at me or chase after me to pull me into the ash as well.

Get out the door. Get out the front door and into the carriage before she can do anything about it. There is no way Mother will wait for her to clean up and change. I've done it. Kade will be safe, and I might have a chance at winning him back. But even if he doesn't choose me tonight, I can live happily, knowing that whomever he marries will not be a scheming stepsister, who plans to control his mind for the rest of his life.

Chapter 28

The ball is even more magnificent than any of us imagined it to be. Reflections of candlelight from the low-hanging chandeliers dance along the polished floors. It looks almost like paintings I've seen of the ocean on a calm night, reflecting the twinkling stars in the sky. There are jugglers wandering the room, tossing brightly colored balls or ribbons high in the air, just as Kade promised.

Music floats through the air, landing delicately on our ears and filling us with excitement. On the back wall, there are tables piled so high with food I don't think I could reach the top even if I stood on my tiptoes.

The room is crowded already, and we join the line waiting to be introduced to the king. At least we are early enough for that. Whoever misses the formal introductions will not be added to the list of attendees, and I'm guessing, cannot be considered as a possibility to be Kade's bride.

I try to force my eyes to look anywhere but at Kade, standing beside his mother and father. I do not succeed. He smiles at everyone as they are introduced to the royal family, no matter how splendid or poor their dress. He stands tall and strong, perhaps even a little taller than his father, bowing as each name is announced.

He wears a trim frockcoat of a deep blue, with what appears to be golden-orange flowers embroidered on the edges all along the front and around the collar. I have never seen him so handsome. I only wish he would take off his spectacles, so he could truly see me and how much I love him.

At last it is our turn. Mother hands a card to the steward, and he announces our names as we all curtsy to the presence of the royal family. The queen steps forward, taking both of Mother's hands in hers.

"I am so happy to see you here," she pauses, "after all that has happened. I trust you are doing well."

Mother's eyebrows raise for just a moment, but then she replaces her surprise with a smile. "Very well, thank you, Your Majesty."

"And your daughters . . . Look how they've grown. It feels ages since we've seen you." Mother bows her head, nodding quietly. "Margaret, your daughters look so lovely tonight. Let's have them perform the first opening dance, shall we?" She turns toward the king, fluttering a fan to get her husband's attention. "Gervais, what do you think? Is that all right?"

My whole body turns to stone. Other than Kade inviting me to dance at the ball for Mother's wedding, I've never given any thought to the possibility of being asked. Certainly, not by Queen Sorrel, herself.

King Gervais gives a grunt and quick nod of his head. He is too busy looking about the room, searching for someone, it seems.

"I'm sure they would love to," Mother says. "And what a wonderful opportunity. Thank you. Do you have partners in mind for them?"

"Let them find partners," King Gervais waves his hand in our direction. "Quickly, so we may get on with it. We should have started ages ago."

I am at a loss. Usually, from what I've seen during other balls, the king and queen assign partners for the opening dances, but he's just given Lacey and I the task of finding our own. How humiliating! Mother has told us time and time again that it is most unbecoming for ladies to beg for dancing partners. It is better to be among the flowers on the wall than to push yourself on a gentleman. For once, I agree with her. I wish I could be standing against the wall, instead of given the task to dance before the king.

Lacey walks straight for Kade standing on the dais. Is she mad? I wish her luck in my heart, but I'm not surprised when she walks away, disappointment showing in her face. All eyes are on us, and everyone in the room just witnessed the prince snubbing my sister.

But I cannot dwell on that. I must find my own partner! I look around, not recognizing anyone close by. My stomach turns, and my hands moisten. I take a step toward the crowd. Luckily, a most handsome gentleman comes to my rescue, stepping forward to meet me. He must have seen the alarm in my eyes, and I am most grateful to him. I have never seen him before and hope his dancing skills are as great as his generosity. Most likely, he is a new courtier wanting to impress the king, and I pray to the queens that this is true, because this dance *needs* to be impressive.

I glance to where I last saw Lacey and then all around me. She has disappeared! I was hoping she would either dance first or that we would join as couples for a contredance, but it looks as though I am on my own.

I wish I could wipe the wet from my hands, but I know everyone will see, and it might leave sweaty streaks on my pale skirt. I should ask for my partner's name, but I am too nervous to speak. Instead, I give him a shaky smile.

He leads me onto the dance floor and everyone backs up to make space for us. I only need to get through this one song, then I can disappear into the background and, hopefully, convince Kade to talk with me and forgive me. And take off those wretched glasses.

My partner and I face the royal family, standing together with our hands clasped. As soon as I see him bow, I give a curtsy, then we turn and give reverences to each other. My legs are shaking, but I try to lower myself as smoothly as possible. Once we are standing again, the orchestra starts to play a minuet, as tradition requires for the first few dances. I pretend I am in the garden, with only trees and flowers to watch for my mistakes.

I *demi coupé* in a circle, rising and falling with the beat, mirroring my partner. He is light on his feet and seems sure of his steps. My slippers pinch my feet. We step together in our imaginary circle to join hands, *plié*, then let go again. I circle around him, trying to ignore the many faces surrounding us. The room is quite crowded now.

All eyes are on me, it seems, except those that matter: Kade's. He doesn't seem to care that I'm the opening dance of the ball. The Kade I know—my Kade—would have been excited for me. My Kade would have volunteered to dance with me or Lacey, even before his mother was finished inviting us. This Kade is watching the dance, but he is not watching me. It is like I am any other girl in the kingdom, not his close, most favorite friend.

It's those spectacles. I know it. Even though I've only seen him for a short time since moving from the palace, and much of that time was spent seeing him kiss Brielle, I know his vision has been clouded ever since he set them on his face.

Take them off! Please! If he would only remove them, even for just a moment, he would see Brielle as just a pretty girl, and I would be important to him again. If he could see me clearly, then he would forgive me for not realizing sooner that I . . .

But he won't. As long as he is wearing those blasted glasses he will see only Brielle and feel love only for her.

I join hands with my partner again, and we face the royal family, walking toward them in little skips and hops. Tears sting my eyes. I have lost him. He will never be my Kade again.

We stop moving forward, and I move around my partner, again, in a circle. As I come around to face the front of the hall, I catch Kade's eyes, and my heart starts to pound. Can he see me? Can he see how sorry I am?

It feels as though we are connected, like there is an invisible thread tied to each of our hearts. I don't want to move. I don't want to break contact, but I can't break step. I need to walk in another circle with my partner again, but even before I start turning, Kade looks away toward the opposite end of the ballroom.

The dance doesn't matter anymore. Ignoring my partner, I look behind me to see what has caught Kade's attention. As if I conjured her up with thoughts of the spectacles, Brielle is there, standing at the top of the stairs on the other end of the ballroom. I am too shocked to wonder how she came to be here. I can only stop and stare. My partner and nearly everyone else in the ballroom are equally surprised that I've stopped dancing, and they all turn to look in the direction of my gaze. At Brielle.

She slowly descends the stairs, taking those tiny steps of hers, and I can tell without even looking behind me, that Kade's and her eyes are locked as ours had been, seeing no one but each other.

How, in all the seasons, did she get here?

Her dress is no longer the brilliant red that was destroyed in the fireplace soot, but a vibrant rose color with full blooming flowers trailing along her neckline and up one shoulder. Her wide skirts are covered with tiny silk rosettes in swooping, graceful lines. I have never seen a dress so remarkable in all my life, but what captures my attention are the slippers that peek out from beneath her hem with each step she takes down the stairway. They glow with a soft pink light, almost like the yellowish light that emanates from moonstones, but I've never seen a moonstone shine with that color before.

By now we are all motionless, transfixed by her glowing beauty. The orchestra has stopped playing and all are silent as she moves closer, descending to the ballroom floor. A drip of wax falls from the chandelier onto my sleeve, but I can't bother to wipe it away right now.

Kade brushes past us, moving briskly across the room. He meets up with her too quickly on the dance floor and holds out a hand to her, which she takes. I can see the ring on her finger as she raises her hand, and I imagine Kade turned into a mindless puppet for the rest of his life. But what can I do? She was right. No one will believe me.

The orchestra starts to play again, and I stand here, next to my partner whose name I do not know, dumbfounded. I should be embarrassed to have my song interrupted, but no one is watching me anymore. I am completely forgotten. Now, even my benevolent dance partner is disappearing into the nearby crowd.

I walk to the edge of the floor to join the crowd, watching Kade and Brielle bow and curtsy to each other. I've never given any thought to it before, but now I wonder: is it disrespectful for the dancers to remit paying homage to the presence of the king if one of the dancers is the king's son? I don't believe they mean to be disrespectful; they are simply wrapped up in the presence of each other. I'm certain they would have bowed to the king if they had only realized that he is in the same room as them—that any of us are here with them.

The orchestra begins to play, and I recognize the song. I watch as Kade and Brielle bring their hands together. He turns her gently around him without letting go of her hands. I know which dance this is. Completely, and absolutely, out of order from any other ball I've ever been dragged to, they are dancing the allemande. But the allemande should not take place for at least three or more songs! It should be someone else, not my Kade, dancing the allemande with Brielle.

I think back to the minuet that was playing just moments ago, where my partner and I were always more than an arm's length away from each other. Clasping hands was the most our bodies touched. In the allemande, the dancers hold each other much more intimately, and every time I see Brielle's arms move around Kade, I imagine the ring ensnaring his heart and his soul.

No. It will not happen.

The crowd gasps in awe every time Brielle's skirts flare out in a turn or a hop. Her slippers glow like the sunset, and I find myself wondering, again, what they are made from.

"What sort of magic is this?" the king asks, behind me. "I've never seen the likes of those slippers."

"Neither have I," an older gentleman says. "Do you think she is the one?"

"I want her brought to me as soon as the song is over."

Who does he think she is? Who is he hoping to find? The new spring fairy? Certainly, he doesn't expect she will make herself known at a royal ball, and certainly he doesn't think Brielle is the Rain Queen! I mean, she couldn't be. Could she?

I've always imagined that if the new spring fairy were to show up, she would burst forth from a giant flower or descend from the heavens or anything other than showing up on my doorstep as my wretched stepsister in fancy slippers!

It seems as though the king's wish will take some time to be granted. Kade and Brielle don't stop dancing after the first song is over, nor the second or third. I've stayed in my spot next to the royal dais, so I can be near when Brielle is brought to the king. The spell of reverent surprise we all felt at Brielle's arrival has worn off, and a few couples have joined the two of them on the dance floor. It is harder to see them now, and I'm forced to walk along the edge in order to keep them in sight. But the dancers all jump and turn, then skip in a circle, and I cannot see them anymore. I bend low to the ground, looking for her shining shoes, but I cannot see those either.

Where have they gone? The image of them kissing in the garden blares across my mind, and I think of the words the woman spoke from the fireplace. He will no longer have a single thought of his own. Oh, Kade! I rush across the dance floor, weaving around the dancers, my feet pinched and sore. I cringe with each step but push on until I reach the other side. They are not in the ballroom. I must look outside.

A man at the front of the crowd grabs my hands, enthusiastically, and he tries to pull me back toward the dance.

"Please!" I shout, finding myself surrounded by dancers again. "I've got to find the prince!" Either he can't hear me, or he is ignoring me. "I have to go!"

I've escaped from goblins. Men are nothing compared to them, and I will do all that I can to get away, just as before. I stomp on his foot, most likely surprising him more than hurting him, then run away as he takes a step back.

The balcony doors are just ahead of me. I am almost there, just a few steps away, when I hear my name shrilly called.

"Not now, Lacey," I cry.

She grabs my arm, sinking her steel-like fingers deep into my flesh. I can escape from goblins, and I can escape from men, but there is no way I can escape from my own sister.

"Can you believe her?" she asks. "How did she get here? Whose dress is she wearing, and where did she get those shoes?" I don't have any answers to give her. "When we get home, I'll tell Mother to forbid her to ever leave her room. I'll put her to work in the barn. I'll do anything it takes to keep her away from my prince!"

She doesn't even know. She thinks Brielle is merely after Kade to gain a husband. She isn't aware of Brielle's plan, but if I tell her, will she believe me?

I have no time to find out. I see a bright pink figure dashing through the gardens below. Brielle!

Wrenching my arm from Lacey's grasp, and ripping the ruffle halfway from my sleeve in the process, I run through the ballroom toward the entrance. Everyone is so busy and merry in their dancing, they hardly notice me dashing past them.

Chapter 29

What is she doing? Why would she run away from Kade?

I make it to the entrance hall in time to see her, running up the side stairs from the garden, clutching her skirt in her hands. The grandfather clock in the hall chimes the change of the hour.

I run through the open doors, panting, just as Brielle reaches the top of the steps.

"What's happening?" I ask, but she ignores me, turning immediately, running down the front path toward the most magnificent carriage I've ever seen. It shines and sparkles as if there are a million diamonds laid atop glowing moonstone. A million diamonds. After all I've seen the past few weeks, I believe it just might be true.

"What's happened to Kade?" I shout down the

stairs. "Where is he?"

She stumbles and turns for a moment, looking up at me with what appears to be just a tiny bit of guilt in her eyes. But then the clock chimes again, and she flees down the remainder of the path, leaving one glowing slipper behind.

"What has she done to Kade?" I run down the side stairs, toward the garden. He is there, safe and whole, running toward me. No, not me. Running to Brielle. He shouts for her to wait, asks her where she's going, but by the time he pushes past me and reaches the top, there is only her splendid, sparkling carriage rolling away from the palace.

I shrink back to the corner of the portico, hiding in the shadows. He doesn't want to see me. It is best I stay hidden. I struggle to get my breath under control, trying to fill my lungs as best as possible in the constraints of my dress. My feet burn and ache where my slippers have pinched them through the night.

Kade slowly descends the stairs and picks up the lonely slipper. The glow is quickly fading until it looks like any other normal, everyday slipper in his hands. He turns it over a few times, inspecting it with a baffled look on his face.

"It's only sunstone," he mutters, walking back up the stairs.

Sunstone? Sunstone doesn't glow as it did when it

was on her foot. I've never seen nor read about sunstone that glows. Impossible!

When he reaches the top step, Kade looks directly at me. My heart stops, and I wonder what he will say. I imagine him lecturing me on whatever cruelties I've committed toward Brielle that she most likely told him about all night, or the fact that I was obviously trying to spy on them, otherwise how would I have known Brielle was running away? I imagine all the horribly true things he might say to me, but all I hear from him is a simple, "Come."

His lack of words startles me even more than any lecture could have. It takes a moment for me to recover enough to follow him, but follow him I do. Straight through the entrance hall, then directly up the middle of the dance floor in the grand ballroom. He walks straight to his father, with me right behind, trying not to limp on my sore feet. The crowd parts for us, and everyone watches as Kade holds the slipper up to his father. I stop behind him, not knowing what to do. I curtsy to the king, because it is all I can think of, then hold myself perfectly still.

Why has Kade brought me here? Why didn't he leave me be in the shadows? What purpose could I possibly have, standing here in front of the entire kingdom while his father inspects a stone slipper?

"I believe you're in luck, Father." He accepts the

slipper back as soon as the king is done with it. "I have found the girl I love and want to marry." My heart shrinks as he says the words. "And I believe she might be the same girl you are looking for, as well."

He turns away from the king to address the crowd. I step away from him, wishing I could simply disappear.

"My father has been searching for the new Rain Queen for many years." He shouts to be heard across the room. "Our kingdom will be frozen in the season of spring until she returns. And Lunain stuck in autumn, Solair in summer, and Neimonte in winter. All seasons halted when the Rain Queen died. This ball was held in hopes of finding the Rain Queen, most likely born during the Shard War. I am happy to announce that we have, indeed, found her."

He steps up on the dais next to his father, and I can hear the king question, "Kaderic, what are you doing?"

"This slipper," Kade holds it up for all to see, "glowed with the softest, sweetest light when it was worn by the Rain Queen tonight, but now that she has disappeared and left it behind, it is dim. Almost as dim as my heart in her absence."

Well, that's a bit much.

Kade continues. "This slipper is proof she is the Rain Queen, that she is able to bring magic back to our land while the Wall is intact. No other fairy queen could do that, because this is where she belongs."

Kade stops and motions for me to come near him. He also commands a servant to bring a chair to his side. I don't want to be near him. I don't even want to be in the same room with him anymore. He has broken my heart with his lovesick stupidity, and right at this moment, I don't care what Brielle has planned for him. I am angry that he's brought me in front of everyone, after ignoring me all evening.

"What do you want of me?"

He doesn't acknowledge my question. It is as if I am not allowed to have feelings or emotions around him anymore, as if he doesn't even know I have them. He takes my hand and guides me to sit. His hand feels cold around mine, and I shiver as I sink to the chair.

Without asking, Kade kneels before me and lifts one of my feet in his hands. Horrified, I grasp the arms of the chair. "What are you doing?"

He takes off one of my old purple slippers, and I pray no stink ascends to his nose. But even worse, my foot is swollen, and tiny spots of blood seep through my stocking where blisters are forming. Can everyone see it? Are they close enough to see? It doesn't matter, because I know Kade has. He replaces my slipper with the one Brielle left behind, and now that I see it up close and feel its warmth on my own foot, I agree it is made of sunstone. The softest, smoothest sunstone I have ever touched. It is a deep, rich pink that matched the shade of Brielle's dress perfectly.

The room fills with an anticipatory silence, and it seems as though everyone finally breathes once the slipper is on my foot.

The slipper fits well enough, but it doesn't glow on my foot as it did on Brielle's. It is still as dull as it had been in Kade's hands.

Kade lifts my foot a little higher for all to see. My cheeks flame, and I yank my foot away from his hand, peel the slipper from it, and escape the dais.

Kade continues as I cling to the edge of the room. "I believe this slipper will only shine when being worn by our very own season queen, the woman I want to marry. My father wanted to find the Rain Queen, and I have found her. I love her, and I vow to marry her."

The tears that have been threatening all evening flow freely now. I scurry to the front steps, away from the crowd and the slipper laying on the dais. Away from Kade and his unforgiving eyes. I tuck myself into the shadows of the portico again, and there I will wait until this horrible ball is over, and we can go home.

Chapter 30

Lacey and I are quite surprised when Brielle comes down from her bedroom in the morning. I don't know what we expected. That she would have returned to the palace when she heard that Kade wanted to marry her. That she would have kept going to wherever she was heading, after her escape from the ball, until she was simply *gone*. That she would disappear just as suddenly and as magically as she had appeared at the ball last night.

Lacey's jaw drops nearly to the table when Brielle walks into the breakfast room.

"Is your mother up?" Brielle asks.

I am so baffled, that instead of accosting her about the previous evening, I answer without thinking. "She's gone to town."

But Lacey recovers more quickly, waving a hand in

my face to quiet me.

"What do you think you're doing?" she asks Brielle. "We've known Prince Kaderic our entire lives. We've lived in the palace for just as long. We know the rules of society, the responsibilities of royalty. You have no idea what it will take to be queen. Kaderic needs someone who can support him without bringing her silly Lunarian traditions to court. You've barely been in Floraison for a month. He can't possibly love you. You're stealing him away from me, and I won't have it."

I ignore the fact that Lacey never had Kade to begin with. Neither of us did.

"Have you never heard of love at first sight?" Brielle asks. "All the stories we tell in our kingdom are full of men and women being so perfect for each other that they fall in love instantly upon meeting." Brielle sits at the table, across from Lacey, and daintily picks up a fruit-filled pastry for herself.

"Or maybe love at first sight is merely a magic spell," I say. Lacey looks at me with confusion in her eyes and a snarl on her lips, but Brielle knows exactly what I'm speaking of.

"Magic doesn't exist in Floraison." She tears her pastry in half and takes a bite from the soft, fruity center. "That's what the Wall is for, remember?"

The Wall. Well, apparently, the Wall isn't protecting

us from magic as well as it did when my father was alive. If it was, Brielle would have never been able to use magic in the fireplace so many times. Father worked so hard to keep dangerous magic out of our kingdom, and now that he's gone, it's found its way in through my very own stepsister, and I haven't been able to stop it. I haven't done a thing, but what can I do that could stop Brielle? She's already won Kade's heart, or *stolen it,* as Lacey so accurately said. She's been chosen to be Kade's wife. The next queen. The Rain Queen, even. As if that's even possible.

I think of the diamond-studded coach Brielle climbed into last night, and the rose-covered dress she wore to the ball, and the spectacles she gave Kade that must certainly be magical. And, of course, the glowing sunstone slippers. Could she possibly—truly—be the new Rain Queen?

But I remember her standing in the kitchen, the fire glow on her face, examining the ring that will capture Kade and leave him a puppet in her hands. Season queen or not, I can't let her do that to him.

"Do you even love him?" I ask.

I want to intimidate her, to make her feel guilty for her plans, but really, I want to know. If the Kade she wants to be married to will only be an empty shell that looks like Kade, how could she possibly love him for who he truly is?

Brielle picks at the remaining bits of bread on her plate.

"Prince Kaderic is a wonderful, handsome man." She speaks slowly, still tearing bits of crust and letting them fall to her plate. "A lady doesn't speak of her romantic adventures, which is something you should have learned if you paid any attention to your mother. But if you must know—if you want to pry—yes. Why would I have danced with him all evening if I didn't love him?" She makes a point to emphasize the dancing part, most likely to rub in the fact that neither Lacey, nor I—nor anyone else! —danced with Kade last night. "Why would I want to marry him if I didn't love him?"

I narrow my eyes in my best impression of Lacey's squinty glare.

"I know exactly why you want to marry him, and it has nothing to do with love."

Brielle pushes her chair from the table and stands, gathering her skirt in her hands. She gives a pretty smile.

"I have no idea what you're talking about."

*   *   *

Lacey and I spend the remainder of the morning nervously checking the windows in the parlor, waiting for someone from the palace to collect Brielle and her things. I pretend to read one of my father's books, but

I can't focus on more than three words at a time before I sit up, again, as tall as I can, to see if anyone is coming.

I pray it won't be Kade. I cannot face him after the humiliation I suffered last night.

A horse whinnies outside, and both Lacey and I jump from our seats.

"It's Mother!" Lacey exclaims from the window, and I follow her out the front door.

"Where did you go? Where have you been? What's going on?"

We plague her with questions before the caretaker can assist her from the carriage. She ignores our questions and silently progress up the steps, shaking her head. I shield my eyes from the bright sun with my hand, after turning to follow Mother back into the house.

"What's happened?" Lacey almost trips on her skirts as she rushes up the stairs.

"Where is Brielle?" Mother asks the moment she is inside, but before we can answer her, she calls up the stairs, "Brielle! Brielle! Come down here this instant!"

"Mother, tell us!" Lacey looks as though she might faint.

"Hush!" is all she's given.

I've never seen Mother behave so abruptly with Lacey, at least not since we were children. She reprimands me all the time, but usually she and Lacey are in complete agreement.

She doesn't look at either of us. She keeps her eyes focused on the stairs, waiting for Brielle to come down.

Lacey stands beside Mother, hands perched on her waist. I back away toward the library until I feel the wall against my back.

At last, Brielle appears at the top of the steps.

"I want you to tell me what is going on," Mother declares. "How did you get to the ball last night?"

I imagine Brielle has been expecting this question. She doesn't even pause to think.

"My fairy godmother helped me."

Mother takes a step back to allow Brielle to pass her to the main floor.

"I want answers, girl, not some made up load of gibberish."

"But I'm telling the truth, step-mother. A woman came—my fairy godmother—and she . . . she changed my dirty gown," with this she looks at me, scowling, "and turned mice into horses and a pumpkin into a carriage and—"

"Fairy godmother!" Mother says. "This is absolute nonsense. Who's ever heard of a fairy godmother?"

"We have mice?" Lacey gasps.

"And the slippers?" Mother takes a step toward Brielle. "Where did they come from?"

"From her."

"Your fairy godmother."

"Yes."

I am nearly as baffled as my mother is, but I have a guess as to who this fairy godmother might be.

"What are they made of? How do they glow?" Mother asks.

"I-I'm not as knowledgeable with the stones as you are. She said they're made of the purest sunstone ever known, and that is why they glow."

All heads turn toward me. I am the only one besides Brielle who has seen the slippers up close and have touched them. I am the only one with enough knowledge about the stones to know whether or not Brielle might be telling the truth.

I shrug my shoulders. "They're made of sunstone. She's right about that, but it didn't glow on my foot, so there must be more to it."

Brielle recoils, a look of disgust on her face. "You tried it on?"

I have never seen her make a face that was not beautiful and pleasant to look upon, but the look she gives me now comes as close to being ugly as I believe she will ever be.

This is unfair. It's not my fault. None of this is my fault.

"Prince Kaderic made me."

She glares at me.

"Where are the slippers now?" Mother asks, turning the conversation back in her control.

Brielle looks back and forth, nervously.

"Everything disappeared at the last stroke of midnight."

Is that why she ran away from the ball so early? If she would have stayed, her dress would have changed back to a sooty mess, and she certainly couldn't ride home on a pumpkin pulled by a group of mice. Oh, this madness is getting out of control!

"Then why does Prince Kaderic still have the slipper you left behind?" Lacey asks.

Brielle's eyes widen. "He does?"

"Of course, he does," Mother says. "And now he's promising to marry the girl who can make the slipper glow."

Brielle seems to find strength in this, and she takes a small step forward.

"That's me."

"We know it's you, and the prince knows it's you, but the king is not fully convinced. He is forcing Prince Kaderic to try the slipper on every maiden who attended the ball, and whoever can make the slipper shine will be brought back to the palace." She closes her eyes, squeezing them tight, and presses a delicate hand to her forehead. I've never seen my mother so agitated before—so nervous and scared. "Brielle, listen to me. A fairy godmother did not visit you last night. I don't know what other kind of story you need to think up, but you will tell King Gervais that you are not the Rain Queen. Do you hear me?"

* * *

Nothing Mother says or does can make Brielle change her story. A fairy godmother, of course, and mice turned to horses and a magnificent sparkling carriage made from a pumpkin. It is a fantastic story, and I am the only one who believes her.

I don't admit it, of course. I don't want to be paired with Brielle against my mother and sister. We would never win, and I don't like her, anyway.

At last, Mother sends Brielle to her bedroom and forbids her to come down. Ever.

We are all exhausted after the interrogation, and both Mother and Lacey excuse themselves to their bedrooms. I consider doing the same, but with everyone upstairs, I have the entire main floor to myself, and I might as well take advantage of it. A small idea began to form when Brielle started talking about the sunstone slippers and how they glowed, and now seems to be the perfect opportunity to explore it.

As soon as I am alone, I head straight to the bookcase in my father's study and run my fingers across the books. I've read so many of these, but none of them seem to match my purpose.

Principles of Aventurine.

The Structure and Distribution of Sedimentary Stones.

Determinative Minerology.

King Gervais wants to try the slipper on every maiden in the kingdom. I think back to his frantic questions in the mining tunnels that first time I was lost. He's desperate to find the Rain Queen. What if Brielle isn't the only girl who can make the slippers glow? Even if I am not the new Rain Queen—because how could I be?—I can still stall Brielle's conquest of the throne. But how am I supposed to learn how to make the slipper glow with no instructions? Is there no book in existence that teaches how to make sunstone glow?

I look around the room, then rush to the corner table and heft a stack of books to Papa's desk. Picking them up, one by one, and reading the titles doesn't get me any closer to my goal.

Maybe there is no way to make the slipper glow without the fairy queens' magic. I imagine how marvelous it would be if I had my own fairy godmother. I could certainly use some magical assistance to help me out of this terrible predicament, but I am not so lucky.

I pull open the top drawer of the desk and rifle through the papers inside, scanning them for the words *sunstone, magic, glow,* or *shine.* Then I check the next drawer, and the next.

Finally, I slump to the floor and throw my hands over my head, pulling at the soft tufts on the rug. The hair pins on the back of my head dig into my scalp, so I rub my head a bit and turn to lay on my side, adjusting my skirts so they don't tangle around my legs.

There, under the desk, is a thin book that might have been set there ages ago by my father. Perhaps he was setting books on the floor after he went through them and had forgotten to put this one away. Perhaps we would have found it sooner if we had more servants to help us clean as we moved in. I reach for it and hold it close with one hand while I pull myself up to the chair with the other.

Solair Stones: Magical Properties

My heart beats faster and my fingers tingle as I flip through the pages. This might be it!

There is a whole section on all the different types of magical stones, even the rarer ones that are found farther away from Floraison. Samples of those are not easy to come by, which is why my father, Kade, and I have mostly worked with sunstone and moonstone through the years.

I turn to the section about sunstone, and of course, it has many applications on the power it possesses to give warmth, and I even find a large scribbled diagram on one of the blank pages that has some possible patterns of combining sunstone and moonstone together. This must be one of the books Papa was using before he started building the Wall!

After scanning the pages multiple times with no success, I skim through the rest of the book. Ice quartz, angelite, rainstone, etoilite, moonstone, and there at the very end, a section entitled, "Magical Combinations."

This is also filled with sketches and notes made by my father, and I wish I had more time to slow down and read them all, but Kade might be here at any moment, and I can't take that chance. I move my finger down each page, reading the titles of each section carefully.

There!

A recipe to make sunstone glow. I don't know if it will work. It seems to be more of a mix of stones in which sunstone is included that can be put inside a glass jar, or something similar, to make a lantern. Even so, I must give it a try.

I read through the instructions again, then hurry to a cupboard near the window to gather my supplies. I'll need to make a few changes, because there is no way I can try on the slipper with a bunch of crumbly rocks in it. I just hope Papa has everything I need.

Sure enough, there is a mortar and pestle in the cupboard, and even a mat to set it on so as not to scratch the desk. That must have been Mother's doing. I grab it all and set them out on the desk, then take the book with me, back to the cupboard. There are four different stones I need, leaving out the sunstone, and two of them are quite rare. I have to stand on my tiptoes, balancing the book with one arm, while searching for the bottles and bowls containing the correct stones.

Bless you, Papa! They are all here!

I leave the book in the cupboard, gather the containers in my arms, then set them beside the mortar and pestle on the desk. Opening them one by one, I take out a few small stones from each and place them in the stone bowl, but no! There is merely a tiny bit of lavequartz left. Just two small pebbles. I hope it is enough.

Taking the pestle in hand, I crush the stones together, grinding them into a powder. My arms shake from the exertion and excitement. I haven't been able to try anything new with the stones for a long while. Except the tile I started with the ice quartz, but I wasn't able to see that to a finish. I wish I could share this small adventure with someone, but I must keep it secret from the entire household.

I wish Kade were here. The old Kade. My friend.

Kade would have loved discovering this with me, before Brielle came. I imagine us together, reading the instructions, mixing and applying the powder, rejoicing when we discover it actually works. I hope it will work! That Kade is gone, though, and I'm beginning to believe that I am the only one who can bring him back.

Determination courses through my body, giving me strength and courage. Now that all the different stones are mixed together in a fine, dusty powder, I need some sunstone to test it. I go back to the cupboard but can't find a single jar labeled *sunstone*. Oh, this is ridiculous!

I burst through the library doors and out through the back of the house to the garden. My stomach lurches, just for a moment, when I see the whitebeam tree, but I can't think on that now. My eyes scan the edges of the garden, and I rush to grab the first sunstone I see, then run back in the house.

"My goodness, Charlotte! What are you doing?" Cook asks as I dash past her.

"Nothing!" I shout, then shut and lock the doors to the study behind me.

My heart is beating so fast, and I need to catch my breath, but I can't wait. I place the sunstone in the bowl with the powder, and immediately it begins to glow.

Hurrah! Wonderful!

I've done it, but I must test it for certain. I pull the stone from the bowl and wipe all remnants of the powder from it, until it stops glowing. Next, I set it on the desk—on the mat, of course—and rub some of the powder on my hand, coating it as well as possible.

Please work.

I shut my eyes and feel for the sunstone. It is warm to my touch, as sunstone always is. I'm scared to open my eyes, because if this fails, I don't know what else I can try. I have no fairy godmother.

The warmth spreads from the stone through my hand to fill my entire body. Or maybe that's just my nerves.

I can do this. I've done this.

It. Will. Work.

Slowly, I open my eyes, and before my lids are fully raised, a soft, beautiful glow fills my vision. I can make sunstone glow. *My skin* can make sunstone glow. The room is now filled with the triumphant light. Praise the fairies! I can make sunstone glow! I place the sunstone in the top drawer of the desk, then pick up the small bowl of powder and rush it upstairs where I can tuck it safely away in my bedroom.

I am ready.

Chapter 31

The next few days drag on and on. We startle at every noise from the drive, but it is never him. Lacey holds true to her promise made at the ball and gives Brielle chore after chore, monitoring her until each task is completed. I wonder why a girl who believes she will be our future queen allows Lacey to boss her around so, but maybe Brielle is simply biding her time, enduring until Prince Kaderic comes to save her. Oh, she is going to be so surprised!

I check on my powder multiple times each day. No one knows where it is. No one even knows it exists, but I'm terrified something will happen to it. I even coat my hand in it once again, on the second night, to make sure it still works. I pray that the slipper Brielle described as being pure sunstone, holds enough of the same properties as the sunstone I took from the garden. There is no way of knowing if it will glow on my powdered foot until I try, but by then it will be too late.

Brielle is in the yard, I believe attending to the chicken coops, if I heard Lacey correctly. I head to the garden and find Lacey relaxed in a chair, a closed book on her lap. Her head is tilted back, and her eyes are closed. A smile plays on her face.

"What, exactly, is your plan, sister?" I ask, taking the chair beside hers. "You can't make her do chores forever. What are you going to do when Kade comes for her?"

Her eyes snap open, and she looks at me, blankly, for a moment.

My whole insides feel as if they are bubbling, and I don't know if it's because I am nervous or excited or terrified out of my mind. I feel powerful with my secret, but I am so scared of what might go wrong. I want to tell Lacey of my plan, to lord it over her and finally be the sister with the upper hand, but I can't tell anyone. Besides, if I told Lacey, she would simply take control of the powder and the plan, and I would be left helpless.

I laugh.

"You have no idea, do you?" Lacey hefts the book from her lap to pound it on the top of my head.

"Ow! I was only asking."

"It's rude to disturb a lady's rest, Charlotte."

She tosses the book to the ground in front of her. I rub my head, massaging the pain away.

"Oh?" I say, "I suppose you took lessons on politely slamming books on people, because there's no way that could ever be considered rude."

I play my fingers through my hair a bit to smooth the strands disturbed by my rubbing, tucking them into the knot at the nape of my neck. It's not perfect, I know, but never mind that.

"You deserved it," Lacey says.

"I did not!"

"Goodness, Charlotte, can't you see how much pressure I'm facing right now? Everyone expects me to win back Kaderic, but how can I when he's enamored with that girl?" She stands and throws her arms in the air. "I don't know what to do. *I don't know what to do!* I'm trying my hardest, and you're not helping at all." Goodness, is she crying? "And then you come over and ask if I have a plan." She says it like I've done a horrific thing. "You're such a lazy, selfish—"

"Ladies!"

Lacey and I both whip around. Mother stands in the vestibule, Kade right beside her, hiding a little in the shadows.

"The prince has come." She is calm, but I can see the warning in her eyes. "He requests you try on the mysterious slipper."

Lacey looks at the slipper in Kade's hand and gives a sweet, pouting smile. Whatever tears were filling her eyes only moments ago have completely disappeared.

"Kaderic, what took you so long? Oh, you look exhausted! Here, let me help you back into the house."

Before any of us can move, she is on his free arm, leaning her head on his shoulder as she turns him around. He shakes her off and walks back into the house.

I feel numb. He's here! What do I do? I've thought this moment through a thousand times, but now that it's here . . .

"Come, Charlotte." Mother follows Lacey and Kade into the house. "You might as well get Brielle, too."

Brielle! Yes. All my plans and ideas come back to me, running through my mind like goblins in a tunnel race. I've got to get Brielle out of the way. I don't know if she's finished cleaning the chicken coop yet, but she won't be busy for much longer. I can't just leave her there. There's got to be something else I can ask her to do.

I make my way around the house to the coops. Brielle is bent over, halfway in the shelter, her skirted legs dangling out. She backs up, holding a basket of mucky straw in her arms. I cover my nose with my handkerchief. There is straw in her hair, and dirt and heaven knows what else on her face and arms.

"Did I hear correctly? That the prince is here?"

I consider lying. How easy it would be to say, "Of course he isn't here. Get back to cleaning those coops." But I can't bring myself to do it.

"He is. And since you're the one that's already mucked up from the chickens, we have a job for you to do." I try to summon any amount of authority I might have, trying my best to speak like Lacey. Brielle listens to her. "We need you to see to his horse. It's already in the stable, I'm sure, but it needs water and . . ." I swallow, ". . . fresh oats?"

Brielle sets down the basket and wipes her hands on her skirt. "What? Are you frightened? Did your mother ask *you* to do it?"

"No, of course not. She knows I'm afr—" No need to humiliate myself further. "The prince asked for your assistance, specifically. He said you have a special connection with big, dumb animals."

Now I am lying, and I hate it, but what else am I to do?

"Give up, Charlotte. You don't know what is at stake. Just give up." She walks past me and toward the house. "I'm going to go wash up. I have a prince to win."

"Never," I whisper, biting the inside of my cheek,

and formulating a new plan.

A breeze tickles my cheek, and I scratch it away. I make my way to the house as fast as I can. I have to beat Brielle to the parlor.

Once I reach my bedroom, I fling open my wardrobe and throw myself to the floor, reaching to the back for the bowl of powder. I throw my slipper and stocking to the floor and scoop the powder into my hands. Sitting on the bed, I rub the powder on my foot, making sure to cover it evenly.

But wait! Which foot is the slipper meant for? I think back to the ball and try to remember which foot Kade put the sunstone slipper on, but all I can recall are feelings of shame and betrayal. I kick my other slipper off, yank off the stocking, and rub the remainder of the powder on my skin. It's not enough! I reach for the bowl again, but there is only a tiny bit of powder left in it.

I scoop out all that I can, scraping the sides of the bowl with my fingers. It will have to do. After replacing my slippers, I wash my hands in the basin and dry them, taking a few deep breaths before going downstairs.

Mother sees me first, and I can tell she wants to ask where I've been, but instead, she says, through tight lips, "Wonderful! Charlotte's here. Now we can begin."

"Where is Brielle?" Kade asks.

Why must he always ask about Brielle?

"Never mind Brielle for now," Mother says, before Kaderic can ask any more questions. "Let's start with my daughters, and then you can be on your way."

Lacey goes first. Lacey always goes first. I don't mind now, though. It would be a bit of a disappointment for her to fail so miserably after seeing me succeed. She sits daintily on the chair by the fireplace, then lifts her silk-covered foot from beneath her skirt. Suddenly, my bare skin seems so obvious. What will Mother think of me presenting my naked foot to the prince?

Kade steps to Lacey, kneels before her, and holds the sunstone slipper out to her. He places it gently on her foot, and we all exhale together. The slipper stays a dull, polished pink. She groans. I don't know why she thought it would work in the first place.

Mother says my name, and I step to the chair.

"There's no need for Charlotte to try." Kade stands, stepping away from me and the chair.

What?

"She already tried the slipper on at the ball. We know it doesn't work on her."

"Please," I beg, "Let me have another chance."

Kade looks at me, coldly.

"You've had plenty of chances."

I let out a hoarse sob. I didn't think he could hurt me any more than he already has, but true to form, I was wrong.

"What's happened to you?" I cry. "I used to be your closest friend, but now you hate me. What have I done to offend you so? Take off those spectacles. Look at me. Take them off and look at me!"

"I see much better with them on, thank you," he says, as calmly as he would thank a servant for a bowl of soup.

"Then let me just try on the blasted slipper."

I yank the shoe from his hand as both my mother and Lacey gasp with surprise. I drop onto the chair and slip my foot from my own shoe, praying the powder hasn't rubbed off from wearing it.

The stone is thinner and more delicate than I remember it being. It's a miracle I didn't crush it when I pulled it from Kade's hands. *Please glow. Please glow.* I pause, caught with doubt.

In just one moment I'll know. Everyone will know.

I slide the slipper onto my foot, and immediately a sparkling, pink light shines from the stone.

"It glows," Mother whispers, incredulously.

"It glows!" Lacey shrieks.

Kade takes a couple steps toward me. "Charlotte, what did you do?"

Must I have done something? Yes, of course I *did* do something, but why is his first thought so utterly sure I can't be the new spring queen? That I have, indeed, *done something?*

"Why can't it be me? Would that be so bad?"

Kade shakes his head, rubbing his eyes beneath his spectacles.

I remove the shining slipper. Luckily, it stops glowing once it's off my foot. I slip my foot into my own shoe and stand, offering the sunstone slipper back to Kade.

"This proves Brielle is not the spring queen." I tell him, quietly.

We are both touching the slipper now, holding it between us.

"But I love her just the same."

"You think you do."

"I do."

I let go.

Brielle comes bouncing into the room, clean and beautiful and glowing almost as much as the slipper was a few short moments ago. She runs to Kade and throws her arms around him, pushing me out of the way with her body.

"My prince," she murmurs into his neck, squeezing him close. "Let's get away from here."

She takes his hand, looking at all of us, and pulls him to the door. I suppose there is no need for Brielle to try the slipper on. She doesn't need to prove herself to Kade.

Mother holds up a hand. "You have to take Charlotte with you. The king will want to know."

Brielle looks back at me, confused. Mother continues.

"The slipper was as bright as the sun on her foot. I'll have a carriage made ready. She might also be the new spring queen."

Chapter 32

The carriage ride to the palace is more miserable than listening to Lacey count strokes when brushing her hair each night. I sit alone on the bench, Kade and Brielle across from me. I can't stop looking at their hands knotted together between them. Brielle alternates between looking at me with one eyebrow low in confusion and staring out the window at the passing trees. I knew she would be surprised.

She is certainly not the only one lost in confusion. Before I left the château, Mother took me aside and whispered, "I need you both to come back to me, Lottie. Do you hear?" But before I could ask what she meant or how I was to accomplish such a task, I was hurried along by Kade and Brielle.

Now that I'm traveling to the palace as a possible candidate to be both the new Rain Queen and Kade's wife, what do I do next? And why does Mother want both me and Brielle to come back to the château? Doesn't anyone realize what Brielle is planning? I've still got to get her out of the way, but how do I convince Kade she's planning ill for him? If I can get him to take off his spectacles, would that be enough for him to forget his apparent love for her? Even if he wasn't under her spell, would he believe me when I tell him about the woman in the fireplace and the fire opal ring?

My insides are tight and tangled by the time we reach the palace. My hands and feet feel hot and sweaty. I force myself to breathe in and out, slowly and quietly, so I can think and figure this out. If I can get Kade away from Brielle, away from everyone, for just a moment . . . but how? She hasn't let go of his hand since he helped her into the carriage. I doubt she'll ever leave his side.

Kade helps Brielle from the carriage, then instructs the waiting servants to bring in our things. I step down behind them, sending a small puff of dust into the air around my foot. The sky is heavy with dark clouds. I hurry to catch up.

"I'll give you both some time to freshen up, then I'll take you to the king," Kade says. "He'll want to see you try on the slipper."

I stop.

Of course. Why wouldn't the king want to see us try on the slipper? After all, he is the one we must prove ourselves to—not Kade. I wiggle my toes, wondering if there is enough powder still on my skin. Most likely, not.

A servant appears beside me, informing me that he is to see me to a private room. I watch as Kade and Brielle go through the palace doors. No doubt Brielle won't be escorted by a mere servant. I follow the girl, even though I know exactly which rooms we'll be brought to.

Two men drop my trunk to the floor after we enter, then bow to me before leaving me all alone. There are plush furnishings all around me—velvety smooth chairs, a cushioned settee in the corner, and even a window seat piled with pillows—but I don't feel comfortable here. I don't want to feel comfortable here. I'm standing in one of the most opulent guest rooms in the only real home I've ever known. I've never been a guest in the palace, and I refuse to be one now.

I sit atop my large trunk and remove my slipper, inspecting my foot. I cannot see any trace of the powder on my skin. If only I had a bit of sunstone to test with. There are a few moonstone figurines on the mantel, a basket of exotic shells by the door, and a paper weight on the desk. I rush to it. Yes, it's sunstone, carved into the shape of a bear. I touch it to my foot. Just as I thought, it doesn't even shimmer with the tiniest bit of light.

What am I to do? I think through the list of stones used in the powder. Certainly, I can find them here. I hope I have enough time to mix some up. I replace my slipper on my foot, then walk quickly through the palace to Kade's workshop. Luckily, I pass no one on my way, and I breathe a sigh of relief as I shut the door behind me.

Dashing about like a mad woman, I nearly tear the cupboards apart looking for the ingredients. The workshop is stocked much better than my father's neglected study, and I am able to find all four stones. I hit them with the pestle, crushing them into smaller and smaller pieces. I'm running out of time! What will I do if they go to the king without me? I'll have lost my chance, forever.

Push, push. Grind, grind. I've got to get this done and on my foot!

"Charlotte, what are you doing in here?" I've been pounding so furiously, I didn't hear the door.

I spin around, clutching the dusty pestle to me chest.

"I've never had to ask permission before." My heart is racing, and I can't keep the anger from my voice. "This place used to be mine just as much as yours."

Kade moves closer, holding the sunstone slipper. Most likely, he hasn't let it out of his sight since the ball. He's taken off his waistcoat and cravat, and he looks much more like the Kade that I've always known. He sets the slipper on the workbench, then picks up a small hammer, fingers the claw for a second, then sets it down again.

"No, I mean—what are you doing? It's almost time to go see my father."

I look to the powder, almost complete.

"I—I was thinking I would work on that tile I started, to keep busy. I'm a little nervous."

He takes off his spectacles and lifts a bit of his shirt to rub the lenses, setting them on the table when he's done.

"But I finished it. Didn't you see?" He reaches for a cube I hadn't noticed. It's smaller than other cubes he's made, and I move closer to get a good look. He holds it with the tile I had started facing toward me. The violet swirls cover the tile, surrounded by tiny dots of ice quartz, just as I had imagined. It's the most beautiful tile design we've ever created.

"I had to cut the tile down a size," Kade says. "I accidentally chipped it when I was trying to add another swirl on the side." He points to the side where the swirls hit the edge of tile. "The other tiles I did myself, but you can probably tell, right? Should have left the carving to you."

I take the cube from his hand, reverently, and examine all the sides. There is a definite difference between my tile and all the rest, but he's used the same mixture of sunstone and ice quartz on them all, even though they have different designs. He's put in some moonstone and aventurine as well, the most abundant stones from the four kingdoms. I turn the cube about in my hand, not taking much time to inspect the designs.

"What's the power like?" I ask. "What can it do?"

He shrugs as I hand the cube back to him.

"I don't know. I haven't tried it yet."

"Well, try it! Hook it up to . . . to . . ." I look around the room, looking for the best contraption to connect it to. My eyes scan back to Kade, and I can't help but laugh. He's grabbed a moonstone about the same size as the cube and juggles them from hand to hand. The glowing moonstone and the flashes of light reflected from the cube nearly mesmerize me, but I don't lose my sense, completely.

"If you drop that . . ." I warn.

"I won't drop it."

Kade lifts one of his legs out in front of him, bent a bit at the knee.

"No," I say, but he does.

Reaching one arm under his leg, he keeps juggling

the stone and the cube. I can see he is at least being a little cautious, because he's not tossing them into the air nearly as high as at first. He almost misses the stone during the catch and hops forward toward me, pulling his arm back out from under his leg. The cube arches to the side, and I gasp, imagining it crashing to the floor. But his hand shoots out, grabbing it from the air, then he holds both objects out in his hands and gives a dramatic bow.

I clap slowly, smiling.

"Well done," I say. "You nearly sent me into a fit."

"Because you were so impressed?" He stands straight up again, grinning, and I have to catch my breath.

I'm laughing too hard to answer.

"So, tell me. What, really, are you working on?" He motions to the mortar and pestle where my half-made powder sits. Then he moves the stone into the same hand as the cube, sets them both on the table, and picks up his glasses. I grab his arm, stopping it in front of us. Can I tell him? Will he believe me?

"Kade, there is something incredibly important I have to tell you. Brielle is—well, I don't know what she is or isn't. She might be the new spring queen. She might not. But that doesn't even matter, because she's—" I don't really know what to say. Where do I start? How much do I tell? "She's been talking to a woman in the fireplace. I know it sounds insane, but you must believe that it's true. At first, I thought it was her mother and she just wanted to go home, but it's so much worse. She wants to take over the kingdom. The woman gave Brielle a ring that's going to—she's going to turn you into a mindless puppet, Kade and I—"

I run to my table and grab the stone bowl, rushing it to his workbench. I set it down and reach for some powder, but when I look up I can't say any more. He's put his spectacles on again, and he looks confused and angry. Mostly angry. I let the powder run through my fingers and let out a long breath.

"You're jealous," he says.

"No. Yes. Oh, but it's not like that, Kade. They're going to kill your father, I think, and once you've become king—"

"That's ridiculous. Brielle wouldn't hurt anyone."

"Truly," I say. "She has a fairy godmother, and they want to take over the kingdom, and she's the one who made it possible for Brielle to go to the ball. That's why her shoes—" I reach for the slipper, and it shines bright in my hand.

Oh, no.

Kade's seen it, too. He misses nothing in those glasses. Without saying a word, he shoves his hand in the bowl, coating it with powder, then takes the slipper from me. It doesn't stop glowing for even a second.

Next, he wipes off both the slipper and his hand, and it immediately turns dull.

"Charlotte."

"No."

"You will leave immediately."

"Please, Kade," I cry. "You have to believe me."

"I don't have to do anything. Now leave. Go collect your things. You're going home."

I cry out, sobbing.

"Leave!" he yells, and I run out the door.

It's a good thing I know my way around the palace, because I can hardly see a thing through my tears. My feet carry me to the door, but apparently they can go no farther, because I collapse against it, struggling to breathe.

He's never yelled at me before, even when we were little. We didn't quarrel like most children do.

I push away at least two servants who try to comfort me. Have they been sent to see that I am on my way home? Or are they just lending a bit of sympathy to a broken, distraught girl? Either way, I don't want their help. I am not ready to go.

Finally, I grab the door knob to pull myself to my feet, then straighten my dress and wipe at my face. I will not leave the palace in tears. Two men pass me through the doorway to get my trunk. I suppose it's a good thing I didn't waste any time unpacking. It takes only a moment for them to lift my trunk and bring it to the hallway, and just like that, it is time for me to go.

Not yet.

"Wait," I call after the two men. "Might you tell me which room," I swallow before saying her name, "my stepsister is in? I would like to wish her farewell." These men don't need to know that what I'd really like to do is give her a piece of my mind.

They point down the hallway and tell me which door to go to. I walk to it and stare. This is the room we were never allowed to go in when we were young, even when it was empty. It's reserved for only guests of the highest importance. I shouldn't be surprised.

I hold my hand up to knock, but then pull at the knob, instead. The door easily swings open, and I follow it in.

Brielle sits on the bed in a lovely pink dress reminiscent of the one she wore to the ball. Her golden curls are artfully arranged around her head and dangling over one shoulder. A glass bottle of oil is sitting beside her on the bed, and she has one foot pulled up on her other leg. Her hands are shiny with the oil, held frozen over her foot from being interrupted.

I stare at the foot, mouth open. I've forgotten what I was going to say. All I can do is stare at her lovely, dainty foot that makes those blasted slippers glow. She has some strange discoloration on the top, near her toes. A birthmark, perhaps? Or possibly it has something to do with the way her godmother—I mean, *fairy* godmother—makes the slippers shine. My mind swirls with questions, with possibilities I can't think all the way through.

Brielle grabs the stocking from beside her and pulls it quickly over her foot.

"Help!" she calls, looking toward the open door.

At once a servant appears and pulls on my arm. He is strong, and I am too confused to fight.

"Let's get going, Miss," he says, and I let him pull me outside to Mother's waiting carriage.

Chapter 33

The carriage stops just inside the eastern kingdom border. I've been watching the Wall get closer and closer, and now we've come to the last village before passing through it. It won't be long until we've reached the château. The sun has been lowering in the sky behind us, and the sky has darkened to a murky blue, preparing to show the stars.

The driver, our caretaker, taps on the top of the door to get my attention.

"I'd like to let the horses rest for a spell before crossing the border into the forest, miss. This is the second time they've made this journey today."

I know. It's also my second time.

"Of course," I say. "Is there somewhere I might go to stretch my legs while I wait?"

I open the door and step to the ground. This is my

second time emerging from the carriage without assistance as well.

"There's a market down that way, nice and close to the road. I'll keep an eye on you."

"Thank you," I say, nodding my head.

The market is nothing more than a few canopies set up here and there with sellers and their wares underneath. I expect to find basic necessities, like food or fabric for clothing, but most of the tables hold trinkets and novelties. There must be a good many travelers stopping here on their way out of Floraison.

The first stall holds clay pots and vases. Some are quite basic and inexpensive, but in the back, on a tall shelf, sit flower painted teapots that look so delicate that I hold my breath so as not to break them. My fingers itch to stroke the smooth surface.

"They are beautiful, are they not?"

A woman has appeared beside me. She seems a full head shorter than I, although she might be close to my height if she wasn't hunched over so. Her hair is gray and frizzled with patches of white here and there. She looks clean enough, and even though she is missing a few teeth, her smile is warm and welcoming.

"Oh, indeed," I say. "Did you make them?"

"No, no, my dear." She gestures to the tables and shelves all around us. "I make the cooking pots. They're quite useful, and very sturdy. My mother taught me, and we are still using one she made when I was just a child. Now these, I cannot claim these beauties." She lifts one of the teapots from the shelf, and I hold my breath again. "My son is the talented one. He always makes a teapot or two when he visits, but that is not very often. Has a family to take care of, and a farm of his own. He has beautiful babies, too. My grandchildren. They are my true treasures."

I smile and watch her replace the teapot beside its friends on the shelf.

"He also makes figurines. Come, I'll show you."

She goes to a basket sitting on the ground and pulls out a little clay doll. I fear, for a moment, that she might topple over, and I reach out to steady her. She feels more solid than I imagined. I apologize, but she just shakes her head and hands me the doll.

"It's a goblin," I say, inspecting the green figurine. It has a large head and pointy ears and is even wearing scraps of fabric for clothes. It is obviously made from lumps of clay, but the details, like the eyes and the wicked grin have been etched and painted with full detail.

"He used to make them for his children, as gifts, but they've grown too old for playthings, so he brings them to me. The goblins don't sell very well. We don't see many goblins in these parts. I don't think I've ever seen one for real in my life, but some have, and we hear stories of the monsters from all sorts." She reaches into the basket again, and my hand shoots out, instinctively, to help steady her. Taking advantage, she sets a doll in it, then grabs a few more to fill her arms. "The children dolls sell the best." She holds up a boy and a girl. "My daughter-in-law sews the clothing for them. Every now and then someone will buy the prince doll, but we don't have very many of those."

I look down at the doll in my hand. It is tall and thin and wearing a gold waistcoat and breeches. There is a mop of brown yarn on the head, and the eyes are painted a deep shade of brown.

"It looks just like him."

She shrugs. "I wouldn't know. Are you close to him?"

"No," I shake my head. Not anymore.

"He has the tall and skinny part right," she says. "I can tell that much. I've only seen the prince as he goes by on that huge horse of his. He rode by just this morning, in fact, looking for that girl from the ball. He didn't stop here, though. There's not many girls of age, and none of them went to the ball."

"That's too bad." I fiddle with the yarn hair.

"I'm glad he's found her, though. They say he's head over hammer in love with her." She drops the children dolls back in the basket, then reaches for the goblin and prince I am holding.

"Oh, no. I think I'd like to buy these, if I may."

"Yes, yes. That will be fourteen coins, please." I reach into my purse, holding both dolls in one hand as I count the money.

"Even a prince deserves to be happy," she continues. "And they say she's the new Rain Queen, though I hardly believe that, but if he wants to marry her tomorrow, that's fine with me. As if he'd ask for my opinion."

I freeze.

"Tomorrow?" I ask. My hand clutches the prince doll, and I don't care at the moment if his head snaps off the little clay body.

"Yes. A man came through just a while ago. Said he'd come from near the palace. Prince Kaderic found the girl and they're to be married in the morning. Now, you'll have to excuse me. I've got another customer."

How could this woman have heard so fast? I left the palace just a short while ago, and there were no plans for the wedding then. Apparently, news travels faster than horse drawn carriages, or maybe it's been in the works all along, and they just had to get me out of the way.

Tomorrow. Tomorrow morning.

That girl doesn't waste any time.

"I'm actually here to retrieve Lady Charlotte." Our caretaker apologizes to the woman, then I follow him back to the carriage and cry the rest of the way home.

* * *

I don't want to talk with Lacey or my mother when I reach the château.

"I failed!" I yell as I run up the stairs, and I let the rest of their questions follow me to my bedroom, ignored. I throw the prince doll against the wall and slam the door behind me.

The sun set more than a while ago. I can't see across the room to see if the doll survived the crash and fall. There's no need to check. I don't care. I truly don't care, anymore.

"Go ahead and be a puppet for the rest of your life," I mutter to the darkness. If Mother or Lacey had followed me up the stairs, they would fear I've lost my mind, but I think they're allowing me to rage in peace. "You've got less of your wits than that doll, and it's only going to get worse! Of course, you'll have a beautiful wife to look upon, and isn't that all that matters? You would have probably chosen her even if she hadn't given you those spectacles."

I pace back and forth in front of my bed, waving my arms wildly as I yell. It honestly helps me feel better, but even I am frightened for my sanity. I pick up the prince doll from the floor where it crashed into the wall. The head has come off completely, along with one of the arms, and I pick those up as well, mourning what has become of the doll and fearing what will become of Kade.

What more could I have done? I tried to tell him, but he wouldn't believe me. No one will believe me.

I set the doll's body, along with its dismembered head and arm, on my dresser, then sit on the bed, still holding the goblin. It looks so nonthreatening in my hands, the tiny thing. Just as nonthreatening as the goblins used to be when they were mere shadows following my father and me home from the mines. Now that I've seen their yellow eyes and sharp teeth and have felt their strong grip, I have reason to be afraid. I fear them now almost as much as Brielle does. I think back to when she first came to the palace, how she hesitated to walk down the narrow hallways and always poked her head through a doorway before entering a room.

Yes! Brielle is terrified of goblins! Maybe I can use her fear to my advantage. If I can bring the goblins to her, she might be too frightened to go through with her plans. My mind works quickly, devising a plan, and I grin to myself.

I know now how to make her leave Lunain and Kade forever.

Chapter 34

For the third time today, I prepare to make the journey between our château and the palace. I won't need a trunk filled with my finest dresses this time. Nor do I need a special powder. The only things I really need are all the strength I can muster and a whole lot of luck.

I turn the handle on the door as slowly and as quietly as I can, then open the door only wide enough to let me through. Of course, no one is in the hallway, and I make it silently and successfully to the back-garden door. Just a few steps through the garden and around the house, and I can see the stables.

Dark clouds have shifted to cover the moon, and I slow down as I cross the yard. This entire area is unfamiliar to me. Even when I used to explore as a child, I always chose to climb up the mountain through the trees. I had no interest in spending time with the cows, horses, and sheep.

The first drop of rain hits my cheek just before I pass through the stable door. I should go back for my cloak, but returning to the house would increase my chances of being caught. There is no way Mother would allow me to go through with this crazy plan. I'll have to go without it.

It is so hard to see in the stable without any light coming in from the doorway, but there are moonstones strapped to the stall rails, which helps a little. I stop before stepping any farther in. This tiny building is full of creatures much taller than I, with hard hooves and strong legs. My heart is already pounding, and I can feel it speeding even more now that I can smell the beasts.

A horse snorts just in front of me, and I jump, clamping a hand over my mouth to keep from calling out. Calm, calm. I must stay calm.

I think of all the times I've ridden in carriages, safely carried here and there, but those horses were strapped to the carriage. There wasn't even a possibility of being trampled to death!

Breathe.

My father rode horses all the time. Kade rides them all the time.

I take a small step forward. I need to hurry, or Kade will be married before I can even leave this stable.

The first horses I come to are the ones that carried me to and from the palace today. I cannot ask one of them to make the journey again. Keeping my distance, I pass their stalls, holding my hands out in front of me as if to push the horses back.

"Stay," I say, stepping sideways down the corridor.

Apparently, those are the only two horses we own. The other stalls are empty, except for the back corner, where Kade's horse pokes its large head over the door. It must have been left behind, with Kade riding back to the palace with Brielle and me. It stamps its feet as I approach, and I swallow hard.

"Stay calm. Quiet." I don't know if I am talking more to the horse or myself.

I approach slowly, arms raised, until I am looking directly at its heavily lashed, dark eyes.

"It's okay. I need your help." Its warm breath moistens my face, and I close my eyes, tight, against the assault. "I'm coming in now. I'm opening the door. Please don't rush out. Yes, stay there. Good boy. Are you a boy? Never mind. Oh, I'm talking to a horse. All is well. I can do this."

Standing beside the beast, I reach up and stretch my arms across its back. There is no way I can jump up on this thing, but at least it hasn't run off without me. I look around for a saddle or that rope that goes around its head, but I wouldn't know how to put them on even if I could see any. The rain is hammering the roof now. This is not going to be a pleasant ride.

I try to jump and swing a leg over, pulling on the horses back. Please don't startle! How am I to get up there? Maybe I can climb the side of the stall. There is a ledge at the bottom of the boards I use for footing, but now that I am clinging to the top of the divider, I see no way to get my body over to the horse. Sitting back on top of it will only fling me over its body and onto my head.

Turning sideways and clutching the wood, I reach a leg out, lifting it as high over the horse as I can, then I rest it on top.

The horse snorts, shaking its head.

"No, I'm not going to hurt you. Please, don't hurt me."

I stretch my hand to the back of its neck, feeling the course hair at my fingers.

Oh, this is ridiculous. Just get on the horse!

I throw my body at it, and land with a thump, holding tight around its middle with my arms and my legs.

"Bless your patience," I breathe. "Now, please, go."

Its soft neck is warm against my cheek, and my nerves begin to settle as it walks leisurely through the stables and into the rain. It keeps going, around to the front of the house, and down the drive, but its steps are so slow. It will take all night to get to the palace. I am already soaked from the rain, and the horse is getting too slick to hold onto.

I sit up, as if I am in a saddle, and grab hold of the horse's mane.

"Go!" I yell, squeezing my legs together. The horse sprints into action, and I nearly topple over the side. I don't know if I'm supposed to still be squeezing its sides or not, but I fear I will slip right off if I loosen my hold even a little. I have no idea how to direct the beast, so I pray it will follow the roads, which should take us to the palace easily enough.

It is not long until we pass through the Wall's gate, and I can see the small market where I bought the dolls. Fabric walls have been added to the canopies to protect their goods through the night. Kade's horse carries us past, quickly, and keeps thundering down the road.

My rain-soaked hair falls in streaks over my face, but I don't dare let go to brush the strands from my eyes. We run on, much faster than the carriage rides earlier today. I think through my plan, over and over again, realizing it's not much of a plan at all. So much can go wrong. So much is still left undecided. I have a spark of an idea that I hope will guide me through each step. It will be a miracle if the night doesn't end with me murdered by goblins or wasting away in prison, even if I succeed in saving Kade from Brielle.

The rain has slowed to a drizzle and the sky begins to lighten as we near the palace. The horse has slowed as well, trotting through the muddy streets. I cling to its neck, trying not to slip from its back in my exhaustion. I am glad the horse knows its way home. We go straight to the palace stables, stopping at a trough on the side of the building, filled with hay.

It takes a moment for my muscles to relax, releasing the grip I've had on his middle. Leaning forward to hug its neck, I let go of its mane and slide one leg over his back. I drop to the ground, but my tired legs buckle beneath me, and I find myself on my hands and knees in the mud. Slowly, I push up with my legs, and I am able to stand—and even walk, if I focus hard enough. I just need to get my legs moving again, then they'll be fine.

Once again, I am cursing myself for not having paid more attention to the stables. First at the château, now at the palace. The nearest palace entrance is . . . yes, I think it will do. A service door would be best, anyway. If there have been any guests invited to this rushed wedding, they will be coming through the main entrance.

A woman carrying an armload of flowers passes me in the hallway, but I keep my head high and my shoulders back and nod to her as if I, and my sodden dress, belonged here. Kade's workshop is empty, which makes perfect sense. Who would be tinkering around in an old dusty workshop a few hours before his wedding? Kade would. At least, the old Kade would. Current Kade is most likely still asleep, dreaming of his beautiful, conniving bride.

The new cube is still on the table, next to the small ball of moonstone. At least it looks like the new cube. The designs are the same. My tile is right there, but the swirls are no longer violet as they were when I ground the stones together. They are now a striking blue, close to the ice quartz we started with. Could the ice quartz have absorbed the sunstone, perhaps? Never mind. It doesn't matter now. I grab it and stuff it in my skirt pocket, but what I need is some aventurine, and the supplies were a bit low when I tried to make the powder yesterday. I remember leaving the supplies on the table, though, and I believe there should be just enough left. I hope the goblins that chased me through the tunnels aren't the only ones who yearn for aventurine. I need to attract as many goblins as possible for this to frighten Brielle enough to abandon her plan.

The shelves and cupboards are packed with Kade's creations, and it feels like forever passes before I find what I'm looking for. I grab the spider and some stretchy twine from my side of the room, then strap the aventurine to the round, wooden body. My muddy shoes and dripping dress have left a trail of dirty water about the room. I wish there was some dry clothes I could change into, but of course, there is nothing available in the workshop. I do, however, find a towel I can soak away some of the water from my skirt.

I race through the hallways, clutching the spider in my hands. I wish I knew what time it is. How much longer until the wedding? I don't think I can get to Brielle's room in time and even if I could, how would I search it for a goblin hole without her seeing me? Impossible!

There is a back door to the Cathedral that only the Hand of the Queen uses. At least, she is the only one who is supposed to use it. When Kade and I were younger, we weren't very good at following that rule, and discovered that the door led to both the front of the cathedral and a small staircase to the upper balcony. With the wedding being so rushed, I doubt there will be many guests. The balcony should remain empty.

Pausing at the top of the staircase to catch my breath, I look out over the pews. Servants bustle about below me, scrubbing the floor, placing flowers, and stringing ribbons. They are too busy to notice me, but I crouch behind the pews all the same. It's been so long since I've been up here. We haven't explored the castle looking for goblin holes in years.

I scan the floor along the back wall as I crawl, feeling for breaks in the stones with my free hand. At last, a stone jiggles as my fingers press against it. It's difficult to get a firm grasp on the stone, and I have to dig into the crevice around it before successfully pulling it from the floor. A small gust of stale air hits my face. Wonderful! I've found a goblin hole.

Sitting back, I reach into my pocket and pull out the power cube. With it being smaller than the other cubes Kade usually uses, will it fit into the belly of the spider? I'm also quite unsure about how this new cube will perform once it's in the spider, if it works at all. So many unknowns, but it is too late to go back for another.

There are so many flowers filling the Cathedral below it smells as if I am in the palace garden. I wish I could be there now, wandering the paths or reading a book, and knowing that Kade was safe at the palace. That he wasn't marrying Brielle.

The pews are starting to fill with guests. I recognize a few of them from all the balls we used to attend, but I am too far away to make out the features of the people I am unfamiliar with. The wedding must be soon!

I turn the spider over in my hands, inspecting the underside. There is the square chiseled into the wood to hold the cube, but just as I feared, it is too large to hold this new, smaller cube. As long as one side of the cube is touching the wood, the energy should be able to flow through it enough to power the spider. I think.

I kick off my slipper and pull at my stocking, bunching it up into a ball. I place the cube into the groove, stuffing the silky material around it. My fingers brush against the side of the cube, and I can't help but look at the designs on the tiles. The side facing me is a tile Kade did on his own. The stones are all embedded together into a tiny etched word I hadn't noticed when Kade was juggling the cube in the workshop. *Charlotte.* It stretches from corner to corner, filling the tile diagonally. The R and one of the T's are a little too big, and the letters are not straightly lined in the least, but seeing it makes my throat thick and fills my eyes with tears.

He must, at least, still care about me a little.

The spider is filled with a sort of buzzing current now that the cube is plugged in. I believe all I have to do is talk to it. That's all Kade did, but then again, we also had to chase it down the mountain into the river. It works now.

I hope it works now.

"Spider," I whisper. I don't want anyone below to hear me. "Go down this hole as far as you can, until you reach some goblins, then turn around and run back this way." I have absolutely no idea if it can understand me, and even if it can, how does it know what a goblin is and how to turn around and come back again? Oh, blast it all! "Spider, run!"

I throw the spider down the hole, hearing it *clank* and *clump* against the sides, hoping no one else can hear. I listen until I can't hear it anymore, and there is nothing left for me to do but sit and wait.

Chapter 35

It feels as if ages have passed. I've watched countless people enter the cathedral and take their seats, all resplendent in their finest dress. How did they invite so many people in so little time? It seems like the whole kingdom is below me, and my hiding spot doesn't feel quite safe, anymore.

I dip my head into the goblin hole, listening for sounds of the spider coming back, or better yet, thundering goblins climbing up the hole. Nothing. All I can hear is the constant hum of voices whispering to each other on the main floor. Hurry, goblins! How am I supposed to frighten Brielle away without you?

The voices below hum a bit louder, then a hush falls. The king and queen have entered the cathedral. I must have missed them walking in, but now they are seated in the front row. Queen Sorrel looks beautiful.

Sweet and happy, like she always is. King Gervais looks happy as well. Happy and a little bit smug. His plan for the ball worked perfectly. Not only did he manage to find a bride for his son, he also found the new Rain Queen. That's two successes in whatever war he feels he's waging. I suppose I can't blame him for feeling proud of himself.

"Spider! Come back!" I whisper urgently down the hole. I don't believe it will ever come back.

Kade stands on the dais before the crescent altar, and even though I can't see his face clearly enough, I can imagine how handsome he looks. A flash of light reflects from his face for just a small moment as he looks around the room. Of course, he's still wearing the spectacles given to him by his beloved Brielle. If I succeed in saving him from that girl, I will never let him wear glasses again—magical or not.

He looks up to the balcony, and I duck behind the pew, my heart instantly beating rapidly. Did he see me? Even if he did, would he know who I am from this distance? Perhaps he thinks I'm a servant girl wanting to catch a glimpse of the royal wedding.

I peek over the pew again and I'm surprised to find Brielle standing next to Kade in front of the priestess at the crescent shaped dais. That was quick! Where did she come from?

Brielle is wearing a dress even more splendid than

the one she wore to the ball, if that is even possible. It is the color of ice. Blueish white, reflecting translucent rainbows in the light. Her skirts are wide and covered with white flowers and ruffles.

The high priestess of the seasons, the Hand of the Queen, stands before Kade and Brielle, and picks up the Rose Scepter.

No! Don't start yet!

"It is always a cause for celebration when two souls are joined to become one," her voice rings out over the audience, "but today there is even greater reason to rejoice, for we are celebrating not only the wedding of our prince, but the return of our Rain Queen!" At this there is an outpouring of cheers and applause.

The Hand of the Queen replaces the Rose Scepter and picks up the glorious sun. Too fast! This is all happening too fast! She talks about the summer. She talks about the possibility of children and admonishes Kade and Brielle to enjoy the time when their children are young and learning and growing. She tells them to love their children and to love each other, and all too soon she sets the Summer Scepter back on the altar and reaches for the Harvest Scepter.

A speck of red catches the light and flashes on Brielle's hand. The fire opal that will soon pull Kade's soul from him and trap his mind forever! Oh, where is that stupid spider? Why aren't there goblins climbing up the hole and storming the cathedral, scaring Brielle away? Why isn't this working?

I plunge my head into the hole, grasping the stones on the edge with both my hands. I can't hear anything. Not the hum of the spider or the soft pounding of its pointed legs against the dirt. Not the goblins' gravelly voices or the clod-like thumping of their blocky feet. A tiny draft of air brushes my face, but there is no indication of movement in the tunnel.

They're not coming.

I lift myself out of the hole, peek at the wedding below, then reach for my slipper and shove it on my foot. My pinky toe catches on the edge, and I have to pull the slipper off and try again. I stare at my foot, my mind caught on one single thought. I think back to Brielle's guest room at the palace . . . her foot on her knee . . . that discoloration on her skin. Its clearer in my head now. A crescent moon, surrounded by stars—the same mark I saw on top of the goblin's feet in the tunnel. Could she, in fact, be a goblin? Or at least sympathetic to goblin causes? In league with the Goblin Queen? That's ridiculous! She was only a baby, as I was, during the Shard War. She couldn't have possibly taken part in the attacks by Lunain to try to take over our kingdom, but the mark was there. I saw it. Goblin or not, those marks on her feet are absolute proof that she can't be the new Rain Queen. If only everybody knew . . .

A chorus of voices fills the Cathedral.

The sun, it has gone, and darkness descends.

The winter has come for the Snow Queen to tend.

I don't waste any more time trying to put my slipper back on. The Hymn of the Roses is being sung by the entire congregation below. I look down and see Brielle holding Kade's hand, slowly sucking the life out of him. Any moment now Kade will be married—trapped forever—and there will be nothing I can do about it.

We sleep thru the winter, for rest and repose.

We dream thru the winter of the soft, velvet rose.

The land slumbers in blankets of white, oh so cold.

And the Snow Queen reveals crystal beauty untold.

Leaving the hole uncovered, I run back down the side staircase, feeling the warm sunstone steps beneath my bare foot.

Then, as the last drop of ice melts away

The flowers, the roses, come to brighten our day.

The door is heavy, and I pull at it with all my strength.

The rose in the valley is blooming and sweet

And fairies descend there, the children to greet.

The Rain Queen returns—

"Wait!" I wave my hands in the air. "Stop, please!" I run toward the alter, screaming for everyone to be quiet.

The Hand of the Queen turns to look at me, confusion and shock on her face. Kade and Brielle look as well. Everyone is looking at me now, I'm sure. I hope they don't remember me as the poor girl with the blistered feet, who was forced to try on the sunstone slipper in front of everyone. But now I am the mud-covered girl with the wet, scraggly hair who has interrupted the prince's wedding. I don't know which is worse.

This. Definitely this.

Kade looks ill. I hope I'm not too late. Forcing myself to ignore the crowd, I speak directly to him.

"I've been trying to tell you. You cannot marry her. She's not the Rain Queen. She's a goblin! Look at her feet. She has the mark!"

Brielle's face turns bright pink. Kade looks from me to Brielle and back again, a confused look on his face.

"What is the meaning of this?" King Gervais leaps from his seat.

"Kaderic, you can't possibly believe she's telling the truth," Brielle pleads. "What do marks have to do with goblins? I'm no goblin. She's just jealous. She's been jealous and cruel to me from the moment I came."

I step closer to them. "Then show him your foot."

A dark shape moves along the balcony, climbing across the pews. Then another, and another. The entire balcony fills with the shadowy goblin figures. They leer silently from the darkness, intensely interested in this moment. They stare at Brielle with curiosity, but as far as I can tell, she hasn't noticed them.

Brielle blanches, scowling at me. She looks to the king and to Kade, wondering if they will force her to remove her shoe. Then she sees them. I know she sees them, because her eyes widen in fear, and she starts to shake.

I smile.

Kade places his hands on her shoulders, protectively. His eyes meet mine, icy and cold. "If she does this," he says. "If she removes her shoe, will you finally leave us be?"

I nod and swallow, hard. "Yes."

And I mean it. I've done my best. I've tried everything. If this fails, there is nothing more I can do. Kade will be lost to me, forever.

Brielle looks around her, panic showing in her eyes.

"You won't make me do this." She looks directly at Kade. "Send her away."

King Gervais advances toward the dais. "This is nonsense. Get her out of here!"

"No!" I glare at the king. He is so surprised I've spoken against him, that he stops, still as a stone. "I love him too much to let her hurt him."

Kade squints his eyes, blinking a couple of times, then turns his attention back to Brielle.

"She's given her word. If you show us your foot, we will be rid of her forever."

Rid of me. He's never wanted to be rid of me before. His words pierce my soul, cutting deep.

Brielle stares at me, and I stare right back, anger filling the space between us. She does not have complete control of him. I haven't won yet, but neither has she. If this wedding is to continue—if she is to complete the spell—she must comply with Kade's wishes.

She takes a small step away from Kade, then reaches for his hand as she bends over to grasp her foot. Her slipper appears to be made from moonstone—not quite clear with streaks of blue and white. A soft glow surrounds her, spreading to the floor. She slides the slipper from her foot and pulls her stocking off. The entire assembly gasps in unison. Just as before, when I saw her yesterday, there is the mark on her daintily-shaped foot.

"It—It doesn't mean anything." She straightens up. "Just some silly scar from when—"

"Traitor!" a voice calls from the balcony. A harsh, gravelly voice. A goblin voice.

At first it appears no one knows what to do, or even realizes who it was that yelled the word. But then the first shout of, "Goblin!" rings out from the audience, and suddenly no one can hold still. Shouts and screams fill the air. People run in all directions, even climbing over the pews to escape the Cathedral.

King Gervais appears at my side, grabbing my arm before I barely know he is there.

"What have you done?" he shouts.

"It's not my fault," I cry as he pulls me toward the back door. His fingers dig into my arm and I lose my footing as he yanks me away. I fall hard to the floor, hitting my head on the stones. The gilded ceiling above me spins and blurs with green shadows.

It worked. The goblins are here.

But now I have no idea what to do about it.

Chapter 36

I try to get up and away from the king, and he tries to lift me from the floor, but we are both pushed back to the ground by a heavy, green body. I scream, and the goblin weighing me down yells right back, sending a stream of putrid spittle to my cheek. It jumps away the next moment, and I am pushed back across the floor, away from the king.

Kade's mechanical spider scuttles past me. Both the king and I stare as it goes by, and soon the space between us is filled with bodies running toward the exit. He cannot catch me.

I look around before scrambling to my feet. There are goblins jumping from the balconies, climbing over the pews, grabbing people left and right, then hurling them away. The sun shines merrily through the stained-glass window, and I'm baffled by the number of goblins running about in bright daylight.

I'm nearly pushed over again, but I grab hold of a nearby pew to right myself more steadily. There are too many people and goblins between me and Kade. Too many opportunities for him to be injured or taken away from me. He holds the summer scepter, using its pointed sun rays as a weapon. He is doing his best to protect himself and Brielle, but there are too many goblins. What on the fairies' green earth have I done?

As if moving through tumbling water, I walk slowly across the room, arms extended to fight anyone standing in my way. I stumble so many times, pushed this way and that by the frenzied crowd. My mind flashes back to the goblins I met in the tunnels, and I remember the tenderness of their feet. Stomping forward, pushing my way through, I end up bringing my feet down on goblin and human feet alike. It doesn't matter, so long as it gets me closer to Kade.

The goblins howl in pain each time I strike, and now that they have reason to fear, the way starts to clear in front of me.

"Kade!" I yell as I near him. "Watch out!"

I shriek as a short, thick goblin jumps on his shoulder. Whether he heard my warning or not, I don't know, but he is able to shake the goblin from him without falling down himself, striking it with the scepter. I run closer, shouting his name again, and he whips around with an angry glare that is only intensified by the thick glasses on his face.

Brielle cowers behind him, and he shields her with his body and his free hand.

I don't know what to do. I've tried everything, and he is still protecting her as she would never protect him. He fights the goblins who seem stone-bent on getting to her, striking them down with the scepter to save his bride. Will nothing I try ever work?

We stare at each other, and it seems as if, for just a moment, the world has left us alone. No goblin tries to grab at Brielle. No human tries to pull the prince to safety. It is only him and me and those cursed spectacles. It's time for them to go.

I jump forward, reaching up toward Kade's face. He swings the scepter in front of him, and it swooshes between us.

My fingers clasp the thin, straight metal by his temple just as he swings the scepter back across his body. Pain explodes across my chest, just below my collar bone, and I rip the spectacles from his head as I fall to the floor.

The world around me disappears. My ears ring from the sounds of my own screams, and my whole body burns in agony. I grab the spectacles with my good hand and beat them against the floor beneath me. The metal bends and the glass of one of the lenses cracks a tiny bit, but I will not be satisfied until they are crushed to dust. I hit them against the stones, over and over again, my mind overcome from the pain in my chest. They break apart in my hand, and I grab the pieces, slamming them against the floor until my fingers are raw and bleeding.

My head pounds. It's so hard to breathe. There is too much going on, too many noises, too much pain. I let my head fall to the floor, curling my legs to my chest to protect myself from the chaos surrounding me. It seems as though most of the wedding guests have sought refuge beneath the pews, and we are all cowering on the floor as the goblins rage above us.

At last, Kade is knocked aside, and the goblins grab Brielle. Three of them—one with an arm around her middle and two others each holding a leg—vault over the pews in unison, landing against the side wall. The two goblins let go of Brielle as the other throws her over his shoulder and scrambles across the wall to the balcony.

I know where the hole is. I know where they are taking her, but I can't find the strength or enough air to tell anyone.

But isn't this what I wanted? Brielle is gone! Gone forever to live with the goblins, and aren't they just as much her people as we humans are? But I heard the fear in her voice the day she came to the palace, and

I've felt the goblins' stony grip, seen their razor-sharp teeth. There is no guarantee she will be safe, and even though I don't trust her or even like her one bit, no one deserves to be torn apart by goblins.

I try to sit up, but the pain is too great. My head spins with the movement, and I drop to the floor again.

"Help her," I breathe, watching her shimmering white dress disappear behind the balcony pews. I struggle to keep my eyes open. I must see. What is happening?

Fatigue claims me, taking away the pain and covering me with darkness.

* * *

"Charlotte. Please, Charlotte, wake up."

He is pleading with me. I can hear the desperation in his voice. How long has he sat by my side, wishing me to wake?

I listen for the sounds of screaming, or of goblins howling with glee. There is silence. I feel for the stones beneath me, but I am surrounded by warmth and softness. I open my eyes and look for Brielle, but I don't find her. She is gone, and it's all my fault.

My mouth feels as if it's been stuffed with cotton, and my eyes are heavy. A numb sort of throbbing pulses near my shoulder. I try to inspect the wound, but I can't see clearly. Everything feels cloudy and confusing.

"Where is she?"

My voice is so garbled and slow, I'm sure he doesn't understand.

"You're fine. You're safe." Kade smooths the hair at my brow. "Oh, Char, I'm so sorry."

I stiffen at his touch, and my hand inspects my sore, bandaged chest. Fear sets my pulse to racing. I can feel my heart pounding beneath the gauze.

Why am I afraid? Why am I so angry?

It's not his fault. Brielle put him under a spell that made him hate me and fall in love with her. I know it's not his fault, and yet I can't forget the way he looked at me after I exposed his bride. Shock, disgust, even hatred. There was not even an ounce of love in his body when he stared me in the eye and cut me open. Spell or no spell, my Kade would have never raised a hand to strike me. This man sitting beside me—the man who weeps and begs for my forgiveness—is a stranger to me, and I don't want him to touch me ever again.

"Are you ill? Should I send for the doctor again?"

I breathe in deeply, gathering strength. It takes a moment for me to focus on my surroundings, but when I do I recognize where I am. Kade's bedroom. I haven't been in here since we were smaller, but it looks exactly the same. I look down in alarm, and just as I feared, there is blood everywhere. My dress, the blankets, and even the sheet I am laying on are stained with wet, sticky red. I must have only been out long enough for the doctor to bandage me up. Kade sees my alarm and touches me again. A hand on my arm.

"Please," I say, turning away from him.

"Char?" He looks so confused and hurt, but I can't forget.

I breathe in again. "I just—"

I don't know what to say. Kade jumps from the bed, and walks away from me, his hands on his head.

"This is not my fault." He turns back to me and holds his arms out for a moment. "I don't even understand what happened, exactly." I sit still, trying to figure out what to say, trying to think through this fog in my head. "Why are you upset with me? You were the one who ran in and interrupted my wedding!" He steps closer, a finger pointed in my direction.

"You didn't love her!" My voice is clearer now and the numb, sore feeling in my chest is being replaced by a dull, throbbing pain.

"But I did. I do." He rubs his eyes and straightens his blood covered jacket. "I still do, a little."

"You don't know what she was going to do to you."

"Then tell me."

"You wouldn't believe me. I tried to tell you," I think back to yesterday—my goodness, was it only yesterday?—in his workshop, "but you didn't believe me then, and you won't believe me now."

"How can I believe a word you speak about Brielle when all I've heard from you about her is filled with venom? Look, Charlotte, I was cruel to you in a way you most certainly didn't deserve. I don't know why I was so mad. I don't understand any of this. I remember what happened, but it all feels so foreign, so . . . confusing. I don't see how it's Brielle's fault. You didn't deserve to be treated that way, but she doesn't deserve your spite, either. Oh, queens! She was taken by the goblins."

A tear runs down my cheek. I close my eyes again, wishing I could go back to sleep. Wishing I could wake up to another life in which Brielle didn't exist. He still loves her. He still believes her innocent of all wrong. At least, perhaps, some of those at the wedding might see her now for what she truly is. A goblin, or at the very least, a beautiful girl who acts like a goblin. Sneaky, manipulating, and selfish.

I've tried before, but I have to say it again now that the spectacles have been destroyed.

"You've cut me, Kade." He looks to the bandage wrapped over my shoulder and a new wave of sorrow passes over his face. "No, it's more than that. All I've said is true. Brielle turned you into a lovesick puppy with those magic spectacles, and she and her mother were planning to do much worse once you were married. They were planning to kill your father and possibly you, but the worst part, Kade—the worst part was watching you change. Watching you hate me for no reason."

My voice catches, and I take a deep breath to steady myself, but it makes the cut on my chest feel as if it is being ripped apart all over again. My hand covers the wound, pushing against it, protecting it.

I tell him everything. I tell him of every time I saw Brielle speaking to her mother in the fireplace. I tell him about Brielle being confidant that he was already falling for her charms, even before she gave him the spectacles. I even tell him about his visit to our château, though he was obviously there, but I want him to know how it hurt me to see him so intent on visiting Brielle, and not me. I mention their kiss only briefly. No need to suffer through those details.

When I tell him about the ring and the way Brielle vowed to take control of his very soul, I can see his eyes change. There is an anger there that matches the intensity of the look he gave me as he slashed open my heart. But this time the look is real. Genuine.

He is no longer under her spell.

Chapter 37

My chest itches, and I scratch it through the bandage. It's been just over a week, and the skin is closing back together nicely enough. It is healing well, yes, but I can't wait for this blasted itching to stop. Scratching would only do more harm than good, Mother says, so I must be patient. I unwrap the bandage from around my body, unlooping it from my shoulder and neck. Looking in the mirror, my fingers trace the coarse purple lines. There are three of them, traveling from just below my collar bone, to the middle of my chest. They are nearly the same violet color as the swirls on the cube Kade and I made, and I wonder if they will fade with time as the stone swirls did, or forever remind me of that sweet gift in the midst of so much betrayal.

I haven't seen Kade since he delivered me to the château after the wedding. I don't remember much of the carriage ride. My head was still foggy from a second dose of the doctor's medication, and I was so tired. Mother was so shocked by the state I was in when we arrived, that she rushed me straight up to bed. I didn't get a chance to say goodbye before Kade left for the palace.

I pull my chemise back up on my shoulder, then slip a simple dress over my head, pulling it closed in the front. I'll never be able to hide the scars.

No one else is awake just yet. Mother has had me resting so much that it's hard to sleep all night. I tiptoe down to my father's study, just as I have for the past few mornings. I've been reading his field journals, learning new things now that I am older and able to understand more. Truly, it's the most peaceful way to spend a morning.

I finished going through one yesterday, so I pull a new journal from the shelf before sitting at Papa's desk. It is one I've never read before, one of the new ones Mother and I found as we were unpacking Papa's things.

I read for a while, poring over Papa's notes and making my own comments in the margins as I go. The château is wonderfully tranquil, and it feels as though Papa is beside me again, sharing his love for the stones and his love for me.

A new page reveals smaller handwriting, the lines

squished together across the page. There are no diagrams, pictures, or equations. It seems more like a personal diary than a field journal.

I normally don't use this book to record my personal thoughts and feelings, and I hesitate to put these words to the page. But I must write them, because I cannot speak them. We have all been through so much that I feel I will burst if I try to keep it all inside. Perhaps I'll burn them when I'm through, because I cannot share this information with anyone, not even Maggie. I can't put her and the girls into more danger than they already are by simply being related to me.

My friend is gone. Gervais would have let him stay, but not everyone is so quick to forgive or to forget the things that Bastien did while still under the Moon Queen's rule. Besides, staying in Floraison would have pained him for the rest of his life. Those cursed marks on his feet! He says they burn like ice each time he takes a step inside our borders. I don't know how he lasted so long, helping Gervais and me. And his poor, sweet daughter, too. Branded while still a wee thing to prove his loyalty to the queen. That pained him more than anything.

I only wish things could have been different. That our girls could grow up together and be friends as we are. Brielle must not be too far behind Charlotte. They could have been such good friends, and yet I am one of the only people who knows that she exists, for if anyone knew who she is, she would be in the gravest danger from the Snow Queen. I'm sure he'll take care of all that once they're back in Lunain. Claim to be a widower, I suppose, left alone with his young child. I wish him the best of luck and thank him for all he has done for our kingdom and to protect the magic of our lands.

What? Bastien—as in—our Bastien? Of course, it must be. Papa talks about Brielle. It's right there! Bastien was a friend of my father's during the Shard War? Impossible! He lived in Lunain. He's always lived in Lunain, except for when he married my mother. And King Gervais knew him, too!

. . . and thank him for all he has done for our kingdom.

If he was originally fighting for the Moon Queen and was loyal enough to her to receive the marks on his feet, he must have betrayed her in order to aid our kingdom. He was a traitor to the Moon Queen and her people. No wonder Brielle was so afraid of goblins! And who could she possibly be? The Snow Queen stole babies during the Shard War, searching for the new Rain Queen. Is that who my father believed her to be? Is she truly the Rain Queen, as King Gervais suspects her to be?

It's been over a week since the wedding. A full week since Brielle was captured by the goblins. They must have recognized her as Bastien's daughter—all because I forced her to show the mark on her foot! What might they have done to her by now? But surely, they wouldn't hurt her if she tells them she is the Rain Queen. Would they?

Was I wrong to bring the goblins to the cathedral? To interrupt the wedding? No. I couldn't have let her trap Kade like that. I would do it all over again, if I had to, but . . .

Was I right to sacrifice her to the goblins? Is she even still alive? So many questions I do not have the answers to, and there is no way to find out. What could I even do to help her, anyway?

Chapter 38

I see him in an instant, and my feet run toward him, into the stables, even before my mind can debate whether or not it is right. I throw my arms around him, leaning over the gate and pressing my cheek against his warm neck.

"Oh, my dearest, sweetest, bravest friend," I cry, wrapping my arms even tighter.

Kade's horse snorts, and I cry out and jump back, then reach a hand out again, tentatively. He smells it, tickling my palm with exploring lips.

"I don't know what you like to eat." I rub his forehead with my other hand. I've seen our caretaker let out the horses each day to roam and eat the grass, but I've never seen him give treats to our old mares while they're in the stables. "Apples. I know horses like apples, but I'm sorry to say we don't have any at the moment. We do have carrots, but I'd have to swindle them from Cook. Do horses eat carrots? I've never paid attention."

"Most do, but I've never been fond of them myself," a deep voice answers.

I look around, but no one is there. Then Kade raises to his full height next to his horse in the stall, grinning.

"You scared me!" I cry. "Mother said you were heading to the caretaker's cottage."

He raises his hands, along with a thick brush, in surrender. "I scared you? I'm not the one talking to a horse."

We look at each other for a moment, then I move my eyes to the ground. What has he been thinking this week while we've been apart? How does he feel about Brielle now? How does he feel about me?

"Your sweetest, bravest friend, eh? I thought you were afraid of horses."

"I was. I still am, a little," I say, and suddenly this feels like these words have been spoken before. Brielle. He said he still loved her after the wedding, at least a little. I push the thought out of my mind. "I needed to get to you, though, and this was the only way I could think of. He should be considered a hero, if you ask me." I stroke the horse's long, soft nose again. "What is his name? I could never remember."

Kade moves the brush down the horse's side. "*Her*

name is Maesy. I call her Mae. She was my favorite foal when I was younger, so Mother said I could keep her for my own. My father wasn't too happy, of course. Says she's not tough enough, not manly enough, but I think she's just fine." He pats the horse's side, affectionately.

"Do you have to do that often? The brushing?"

"When I have time. Usually the grooms do, at the palace." He pats her side. "But she's a good sort, and I don't mind. Aren't you, sweet Mae? The best of company. She never complains." He keeps brushing, moving lower onto her belly, creating clouds of dust with each stroke. Then he looks back up to me. "Oh! Do you mean—Charlotte, do you really know nothing about horses?"

I don't bother with an answer.

"Come here. I'll teach you how." He places the hand strapped to the brush protectively on Maesy's back and uses the other to open the stall's gate. I've been doing quite well on my side of the gate, and I'm not sure I want to be in such close quarters with the horse just yet. I look to Kade's eyes. I don't know how sure I am of him, either.

I move into the stall, shutting the gate behind me just in case Maesy startles, though I haven't seen her spook before. Kade takes my hand and moves me between him and the horse. I feel so small beside the two of them. Kade hands me the brush, fitting the strap over my fingers. He guides my hand from top to bottom along Maesy's side, still steadying her with his other hand, and even though my heart beats faster than Maesy's hooves can run, I am surprised to not feel trapped in his arms. Silence drops between us as his hand continues to guide mine in even strokes.

"You're safe," he says. "Nothing's going to hurt you."

"I know."

I follow his movements, willing the fear to leave my body. I wish I could quiet my heart as easily as I can slow down my breathing.

"I'm sorry, you know." Kade's voice is quiet, calm. I can feel him against my back. Strong and firm, and even though I've known him for so long, completely foreign. "I'm so sorry, Charlotte."

"I know." At least, I think I do. "I'm sorry, too."

"I can feel more of a difference every day. More like myself. I was so angry all the time, except . . ."

"Brielle."

It takes him a moment to say, "Yes. I hate to think of the things I did. I'm so glad you came before it was too late." He chuckles. "I never thought I would ever say this to anyone, but thank you for crashing my wedding."

"I made a real mess of things, didn't I?"

His hand stops guiding mine, resting on Maesy's back, and I am enveloped in his warmth.

"The best mess, ever."

I rest my head against Maesy's side, closing my eyes against her silky softness. He said he's sorry. He said he's glad. Those are the words I've been waiting to hear for the past week—that I was right to interrupt the wedding and condemn Brielle to a life under ground with the goblins—but I can't deny the guilt weighing down on my mind.

I turn around and look up, locking my gaze with Kade's. "But what's happened to her?" I hate to say it, but I know I must. "Kade, we have to rescue her."

He pulls the brush from my hand, distracting me, but doesn't let go of my fingers once they're free. I look up to him, confused. Did he hear me? Does he believe that I am sincere? He stares at me in a way he's never looked at me before. Or perhaps, in a way I never let myself notice. My stomach dances, as if it is filled with dandelion puffs being thrown about by a spring breeze.

Kade lifts my fingers to his lips and kisses the back of my hand, closing his eyes for just a moment. But then Maesy snorts and I jump, and he is brought back to reality.

"It's more complicated than that, Char. My father insists I marry her. He's still convinced she's the Rain Queen." I want to say *she is!* but he doesn't give me a chance to speak. "They're making plans to rescue her now, but there's more."

The dandelion puffs floating in my stomach feel like stones now that I've heard the dread in his voice. What could possibly be worse than Kade still marrying Brielle?

"Father is preparing to go to war against the Goblin Queen."

Acknowledgements

Charlotte's story was born while I was driving home from a writing conference with a couple of friends. Michelle, Sachiko, and I were discussing the idea that every basic story has already been told, and that it is our job, as writers, to take those stories and turn them on their heads. Do something different. Tweak a little detail to make it new. Even if it's something completely unexpected—like making sweet, innocent Cinderella be "the bad guy."

I couldn't let go of that idea. And I didn't want Cinderella to just be mean or snobby. I wanted her to be *real* bad, and I had to figure out why she would choose to be a villain. The time I spent brainstorming and worldbuilding with Sachiko during those first few weeks were amazing. We learned so much about Charlotte and Brielle and the world they lived in: a mash-up of the stories Cinderella, The Princess and the Goblin, and the Snow Queen. Once we had that all figured out, the story of this evil Cinderella fell perfectly into place.

This book would not exist without the support and advice from the best writing group in the whole world: Good Writtance. Big Edna, Bawb Dawg, Canadian Kim, My Neighbor Sachiko, Shakespear, and Sharks— I love you guys!

A big thanks to all my beta readers and editors:

Alyssa, the Johnson girls, Nancy, Danyelle and daughter, Ashley at Eschler editing, and Shaela at Blue Water Books. You all helped make this story so much better than it would have been if I had been working alone. Thank you!

Shaela, you especially have been a humongous part in making this book polished and publish-worthy. You're the best editor and writing mentor a girl could ever hope for!

And thank you to all my family and friends who have supported me and encouraged me in my writing adventures. You don't know how much hearing the question, "So how's your book coming?" means to me. So keep asking. I'm still learning and writing, and hopefully my next book will be even better.

About the Author

Photo © 2016 Jill Clayton

Jacqueline began writing fantasy adventures in elementary school, filling all the spiral notebooks she could get her hands on. She continued writing through her teen and college years but stopped soon after getting married and becoming a mother. After maintaining a family blog for many years, Jacqueline remembered her love for writing stories, and she began again—this time using all the files she could click her mouse on.

Jacqueline lives in Washington State with her husband, four kids, and two cats.

www.jacquelineclewis.com